ONE
GOOD DAUGHTER

ISBN 1-56315-241-X

Paperback Fiction
© Copyright 2001 James M. Tuthill
All Rights Reserved
First Printing — 2001
Library of Congress #00-109356

Request for information should be addressed to:

SterlingHouse Publisher Inc.
The Sterling Building
440 Friday Road
Pittsburgh, PA 15209
www.sterlinghousepublisher.com

Cover Design: Michelle S. Lenkner — SterlingHouse Publisher, Inc.
Book Design: Kathleen M. Gall

ONE
GOOD DAUGHTER

By

James Tucci

Pittsburgh, PA

∽ PROLOGUE ∽

WOODEN BENCHES, RESTING on the bare linoleum floors, lined the hallway. Sitting directly outside courtroom B on the third floor of the federal courthouse, the lawyer waited with her client while the grand jurors inside deliberated.

"Pia, remember, if it comes back against you, this is only the beginning. We can't get our hopes up when the jury only gets to hear one side of the story, especially when it's from that sleazy Jay Cavanaugh. If they indict, the next time we'll be in the courtroom, presenting all your witnesses and cross-examining everybody they put on." Leslie Gabrielson wanted her client to put a good face on for the press that milled in the corridor.

The client wasn't so sure about that analysis. All the hard evidence seemed to be lined up against her. The drugs had been found in the closet, in her apartment, by three FBI agents, who certainly had not planted the stuff there. According to the newspapers, her father John Vittone, was tied up with the Mafia and the drug running arm of his crime family. Everything she had in her life she owed to that same criminal family. How would this lawyer, even the best lawyer in the city, create a reasonable doubt when all of those facts were stacked against her? It was impossible to cross-examine two kilos of cocaine hidden amongst her belongings, and ask them to identify the folks that placed them there. Those carefully placed drugs spoke volumes, and all the lawyers in the world could not refute the fact that the drugs were in her apartment.

Pia Vassar sat straight back against the marble wall with her knees tightly pressed together and her hands clasped on her lap. She knew she was nervous because her hands and underwear were damp. She listened to the words coming from her lawyer, but she thought they were only a locker room pep talk, just something to say to keep her hopes up and break the maddening tension of waiting for the inevitable.

Pia didn't realize that, in fact, these were more than just words. Leslie Gabrielson was a veteran trial lawyer, and she was a winner, one of the best. Twenty three years of waiting in hallways for real jurors, not these phony grand jurors, taught her a lot. Sure, the facts were bad, but she was positive that her client was framed. If she were innocent, then the evidence was lying somewhere once she started looking and investigating to prove the girl's innocence. An assistant U.S. attorney, with no opposing defense attorney in the courtroom, would surely get her indicted from the jury, but Gabrielson would have her day when the real trial began. Even the most hardened and coached witnesses could be broken. Once the events were logically and methodically placed in front of them, they would fall and stumble on the stand. Little by little, question by question, and witness by witness, the true state of affairs would rise to the surface for everyone to see. It would take a lot of work and late nights in law libraries meeting with investigators, but it would all come together.

The part Gabrielson hated was seeing the look of defeat on her clients' faces when an indictment was announced. They all took it as a loss, no matter how well she prepared them for the moment. But these so-called defeats meant that she could now start her case and get to work, taking the depositions and making enough motions to drive the government crazy and beat the other lawyers down. At times it scared her, and she would have to turn in her bar card and quit if a truly innocent client was convicted, because she would be so emotionally distraught. On the positive side, she was always exhilarated by the challenge, and it made her mind race to figure out all the pieces in the puzzle. Moving the witnesses across the chess board and wiping the prosecution out in closing argument was the greatest thrill of all. If the jury acquitted on a Friday, she didn't come down until Monday morning.

The assistant U.S. marshals wore green blazers. Most of them were former New York City police officers collecting a nice pension and now an additional salary at the same time. Their careers were over, and it took a lot on some drowsy afternoons for them to stay awake in the courtroom.

Hank DeLong had been in the corrections department for the

city for more than 20 years, and now he had the easiest job of his life. A man with a full head of thick, wavy white hair and salt and pepper eyebrows, he got along with every lawyer in the building. When attorneys appeared in front of his judge for a 9:00 a.m. motion hearing, he invariably invited them into his private cubicle for a freshly brewed cup of coffee. Leslie didn't get along with many people in the justice system; she preferred to operate alone, but DeLong was her buddy. He read juries better then anybody she ever knew, and at recesses, she always sought out his take on which way the juries were leaning.

She knew from the look on his face when he came out of the courtroom with the verdict in his hand that it wasn't good. "Miss Gabrielson, the U.S. attorney has asked me to pass out the verdicts." He gave her his grimmest look; he sincerely felt badly for her. He knew she was one tough lady, but he also knew that she frequently took cases personally because Leslie gave everything she had for her clients and worked day and night on their behalf. He admired the way Leslie Gabrielson never gave up.

It wasn't nearly as hard for her when the bad news was given by somebody that liked her and vice versa. She took the two pages from him and scanned them in three seconds. Probable cause was found and indictments were handed down on all four counts.

She looked down at Pia, who never budged on her seat. "Just as we expected. Indicted on all four. Okay this is where the fun starts. We'll see who wins the next round when we put everything together and shove all this crap down their throats."

Blinking back tears in front of the *Post, Times* and *Daily News* reporters assembled in front of her would not help her in the eyes of any future New York juries. New Yorkers liked their Mafia princesses, if that's what she was, to be fighters and defiant to the end, battling the power of the government, the same people that made their lives miserable every day with city, state and county taxes, parking fines and potholed roads. New Yorkers actually rooted for the bad guys. No, she would act the same way her father would if faced with this situation. She stood up abruptly and turned to Leslie saying, "Okay, let's go. We need to get to work." The cameras flashed, and she could see the next day's headlines reading, "Mafia Don's Daughter Indicted for Drugs." There was nothing she could do about that. Her father was not the type of man who ever gave up, and neither was his daughter. New York would find that out.

Leslie brought along her trusted private investigator, Mike McKenna, and four of his best men. They formed a wedge and pushed their way through the cameramen into a stairway that led them to the ground floor and out to the sidewalk. Pia never flinched.

Chapter 1

SARDINIA, MAY, 1968

While she waited for the questioning to begin, Pia's mind drifted back to the days before her family had settled in New York and to her childhood. Since she was a little girl, windowless rooms always frightened her. When she was still living in Sardinia, Pia and a 6-year-old girlfriend crept into an empty warehouse early one evening, where bales of tobacco were stored before they were shipped off to some factory on the mainland of Italy. They had on shorts and sneakers and thought this would make a great place to explore. The door was spring loaded, and one second after they were both inside, it slammed shut behind them. In front of Pia was the darkest room she had ever been in; there was nothing but total blackness, no windows at all, not even small ones.

Her heart jolted, and it felt like it stopped. Her hands were blindly stabbing at the wall, looking for any opening. She and Marina felt their way back to the door, twisted the knob open and gulped huge breaths of fresh air into their lungs. The cool night air totally engulfed these two young girls, giving them immediate relief from the dark claustrophobic conditions inside. After that, she knew that she would never want to be confined somewhere that there were no windows.

A beautiful child was the way that everyone on the island of Sardinia described her. Even in kindergarten, her teacher said there was already evidence of the fabulous future that lay ahead for this bright, inquisitive, native daughter. Her hair was as dark as the darkest night over the Mediterranean and her slender face, with the olive complexion, framed her green, almond-shaped eyes. For hundreds of years, doctors and philosophers tried to fathom why so many of the girls on Sardinia were blessed with emerald eyes, but the reasons were still a mystery, known only to the ancient Gods, who in mythology, stood guard over this piece of soil between the two great seas that lie off the coast of mainland Italy.

During her childhood, Pia always thought that she was living a perfect and normal life. Her mother was born a peasant girl, whose family tended grape and olive orchids, interspersed with a few sheep and goats that, in a sure-footed manner, transversed the rocky terrain. Each morning, Pia dressed in the uniform of the local parochial elementary school, with a white blouse and plaid skirt and walked with her mother the six blocks through the cobbled streets of Caprera to the two-story schoolhouse that sat on top of the hill, looking out at the Tyrherrian, the great body of water that ran between the coast and the Island named for the small warm water fish that provided a living for half the men living there. The 30-year-old woman kissed her daughter on the cheek each day before departing, and the child then sat at her desk with 20 other classmates.

Her father seemed to be like every other father on the island. He woke up at 6:30 a.m. and was off to work an hour later, wishing his wife and progeny a beautiful day. All that she ever knew was that her father ran a business selling beer and wine to the local restaurants scattered around the northern half of Sardinia and that he came home at 6:00 p.m. ate dinner and went to bed. Her parents rarely went out, and when they did, they took her with them to family functions where, most of the time, her father's uncle played the part of the host and head of the family.

Uncle Giacomo was a very funny and happy man, bearing a big stomach and a bald head with a little hair curled up in the back. He always wore a white shirt, opened at the collar, and dress black pants that drooped under his girth. Every lunch or dinner that he presided over was a festival. A three-piece band played, and invariably, some distant relative would have too much to drink and climb on the bandstand, grab the microphone and sing a few bars of some Italian love song. The crowd would howl in laughter, and the singer would almost fall to the floor, to be patted on the back and offered another glass of wine and a toast. Giacomo also was an amateur magician, entertaining the kids with his disappearing coin trick. A silver piece disappeared from his hand only to reappear a few seconds later in the ear of one of his young onlookers.

Occasionally, she would spy her great uncle ambling to the shores of the Straits of Bonifacia, that nine-mile stretch of dark blue, almost purple water, that separates Sardinia from her sister island nine miles to the north, the French principality of Corsica. What always struck her was that the only person that ever accompanied her grand uncle on these walks was her father, and the elder man always took hold of his nephew's arm and leaned on him, at the same time whispering into his ear in hushed tones. The rest of the family was always excluded from these trips down to the beach and the lapping waves of the water. A half hour later, they would reemerge, as if they had never been away, and rejoin the party. She knew that her uncle had put her father in his position at the warehouse and guessed that they were discussing ways to sell more of their products. Her father never, even in a rare moment, talked about his business and where he had been that day. The family kept to itself except to go to church and invite in her mother's girlfriends who dropped by for a cup of Cappuccino. John Vittone seemed to be a lonely man to the 6-year-old.

∼ CHAPTER II ∼

NEW YORK CITY, DECEMBER, 1998

GRAND JURY ROOM B SAT on the third floor of the Thomas A. Mann Federal Courthouse in lower Manhattan, on Foley Square. The walls were painted a pale green and fluorescent lights softly buzzed in the recessed ceiling overhead. In the middle of the room was a fold out Samsonite chair and a table. On the other side of the room were two rows of leather, upright chairs, double tiered. The floor was scuffed, and there were no windows to look out of. Seated in the folded chair, set apart from everyone else, was one of the most beautiful women that Jay Cavanaugh, the Assistant U.S. Attorney, had ever laid his eyes on. She was 5 foot 10 inches, with black hair down to her shoulders, green eyes, a well-shaped face and a perfect complexion.

On this bleak, gray afternoon, with traces of snow flurries in the air and the temperature hovering at 31 degrees, she was not cast in her usual role of a lawyer. Rather than asking questions and parading up and down in front of the jury as a plaintiff's attorney, she was the target of the U.S. Justice Department's most recent drug bust. Hounding her was Jay Cavanaugh, tossing questions at her about her father, his business associates and two kilos of cocaine that were found in the walk-in closet and refrigerator in her expensive, West Side, two story co-op. Her head started to throb with the increased intensity of the questions.

Only a month before, Pia Vassar was on a fast track, headed to the top of the world as the newest and youngest person ever to make full partner in her firm. Looking out from her corner office on the 40th floor of the skyscraper rising up next to the World Trade Center, she could see the Statue of Liberty to the south, and all the way out Long Island to the horizon to the east. Everything had changed in the short space of a few days. She still couldn't quite believe it all, but she had not been dreaming this.

It was on a Thursday night, a few weeks before, that the subway had stopped at Amsterdam and 48th Street. From there, she walked the five blocks to 53rd and then to the building that was in the middle of the block, but closer to Riverside Drive. It was 8:00 p.m., and she carried a valise with paper work that she still had to review before she went to sleep that night. She fished in her purse for the key, and just as she found it, three FBI agents were surrounding her, armed with a search warrant.

Somehow, she had managed to keep her composure. The lead agent assigned to rummage through her apartment was pleasant enough under the circumstances. He opened the sheet of legal-sized paper and let her look at it with him while he read it aloud. "To all the law enforcement agencies and peace officers under the authority and domain of the United States, you are commanded this 14th day of December, to enter the dwelling abode of one Pia Vassar, a.k.a., Pia Vittone, located at 1043 West 53 Street, New York, New York, and at that time and place, to make a complete and thorough search and investigation of the premises and to seize any illegal contraband or narcotics found in or about the area. Done and ordered in chambers in New York the day and year written above." Signed, Federal District Court Judge, Leonard Abrams.

She put her purse and case on the circular dining table as she sat down trying to look calm, but her thoughts were all mixed up. What were they looking for? She had no idea.

The police gave the living room and dining area a quick once over. They moved inside, almost like they knew where they were going, into her kitchen. "Miss Vassar, can you please come in here a minute." She rose and knew from the sound of the agent's voice that she was not going to be receiving good news. "Ma'am, before we touch anything, we wanted you to see that we haven't disturbed any-thing yet." In the middle of her refrigerator, sticking out of the side slightly, something was protruding, something that looked like the size of a bag of sugar from the store.

One of the agents pulled the two top boxes apart to reveal a cloth bag tightened around a rectangular shape. The bag was brought out into the kitchen and opened. Inside was a cellophane-covered package containing a pouch of pure, white powder. Agent Frederick Graham took a pen knife and carefully cut a 10th of an inch slit in the middle. He took his index finger and pressed it into the substance. He applied his finger to his mouth. "Miss Vassar, I'm sorry, but I'm going to arrest you on suspicion of possessing narcotics, and depending on how much this weighs, trafficking in narcotics as well."

The words gushed out of her mouth. "Officer, I don't have any idea how that got there. I know you don't believe me and everybody says that, but it's true. Somebody has gone to great lengths to hurt me."

"Miss Vassar, please, I know this is brutal, but if you are innocent, the courts will sort it out. You have got to put on your coat, and then we're going to cuff you. We'll make this as painless as possible."

"Where are you taking me?" she softly asked as her head fell downward. She walked back to the table and reached for her coat draped over one of the chairs.

"We'll have to process you through Riker's, that's the Federal booking center. Believe me, it's better than what the city has at the county jail. We're a lot nicer than NYPD." She put her coat on, and they placed the bracelets in front, across her waist, a rare courtesy, as most everyone had their hands locked behind them.

At the waiting vehicle, Graham opened the car door, lightly putting his hands on Pia's shoulder. "Miss Vassar, watch your head," he directed as he made sure that she ducked down. He slipped into the back seat with her, and they sat side by side as they rode together on Pia's darkest journey.

Just the name, Riker's, conjured up a dismal picture in the mind of the average New Yorker. Isolated in the East River, between the Bronx and Queens, it was truly a piece of barren earth surrounded by pollution-infested waters. Cement block buildings, painted battle ship gray, arose out of the ground. In December, a few patches of ice remained in the potholes, and the inmates wore knit ski caps and wind breakers emblazoned with the words "Federal Prisoner" across the back.

A boat pulled up to the ferry slip about every hour. This is the place, sort of a stepping stone on the way to hell, where the federal government held its prisoners who were awaiting trial and did not have the wherewithal to provide bail for themselves. Some had no choice. Their crimes were so heinous the court refused to set bond.

Pia Vassar stepped off the boat in her soft camel's hair coat and black high-heeled shoes.

Agent Graham led the way. The metal doors seemed so small in the middle of the outside wall of the jail that ran for close to 300 feet. A window with wires embedded in the glass, one foot square, gave scant view of the world inside. As the door opened, a visitor was left facing the sliding metal door up ahead, and a glass picture window to the left. Behind the glass was a corrections officer who controlled the opening and closing of the next barrier. As the portal closed behind Pia and her entourage, the door in front of her slid slowly and silently open. Now she was in a place where she had no say over anything, but was subject to the whims of her prison guards. The daily regimentation would drive her nuts within hours.

A booking desk was placed on a raised up slab of concrete. This jail was operated by the uniformed division of the U.S. Marshal's Office, which has a division separate from its plain clothes, tie and jacket officers, and it is these men who run the operation. A sergeant from the Marshal's Office stood behind the desk and barked out the questions, "Graham, what have you got?"

"A young lady, Sarge, a lawyer in fact, who needs to be printed and processed."

The older man peered down from his raised counter top. "She doesn't look much like the rest of the bunch in here. But you never know, I guess. What are the charges?"

"Possession and possible trafficking in cocaine. We've got to wait to get the lab results to see exactly what the charges will be."

Sergeant Walenski shook his head. Twenty-eight years on the job, and every now and then, somebody a little different came in. About 98 percent of everybody in the place looked and smelled the same. Most were repeat offenders. Obviously, this girl was out of the ordinary. "Coke," he mumbled. "It gets them all. The crooks and the high and mighty. Everybody is in here either for drugs or guns. Even a pretty girl like this." He shook his head. Pia looked at the front of the desk and at nothing else. She was a nobody in here. Not a great lawyer on Wall Street and not the daughter of a Mafia crime lord; she was just another prisoner.

"All right, Miss, step over here." One of the men from the bureau took her by the arm and walked her over to the table with a black rubber mat on it. Two fingerprint cards were laid on it together with an ink pad. She willed her mind empty and numbed herself. Walenski took each finger and pressed them into the ink and then lifted them onto the white cardboard pages. He rolled each finger from side to side. He did this 10 times and she never took her eyes off the table in front of her. Next to the table, like an assembly line, was a tripod and a camera. She took a seat in front of the camera and stared straight ahead for one shot, and turned to her right and then to her left for two more.

Graham bent down and looked at her as she sat there. "Do you want to call somebody?" Giving her father's name would curry no favor in here. She chose the only other person in her life who, over the years, she respected as being one of the brightest, most reasonable and compassionate persons she ever met. "Yes, I want to call my partner, Ronald Vining. I've got his home phone number in my purse." Graham told one of his underlings to retrieve her bag, and he put her in a room with a desk and a payphone.

"Do you need change?"

"Thanks, but I've got some in my wallet. I hope he's home."

"If he isn't, I'll let you call anybody you want. I've got bad news, though. Your bond is set at $250,000.00. It's a cash bond. That's a lot of money."

She turned completely around facing Graham. "Look, I know you found those drugs in my apartment and you've heard this all before, but I don't know how they got there. It's not your job to believe me, I understand that, but thanks for going easy on me."

"There's something about you that I don't understand. The Probable Cause Affidavit said the drugs were there, and sure enough, a kilo was in your refrigerator and another one was in your closet.

But you don't look like that kind of person. I don't get it right now, but I bet that someday, I figure this out. One way or another, guilty or innocent."

"I really hope that you do figure it out, because I'm on the innocent side."

"You know, so do I."

He left her so that she could make the call in private. Ronald Vining was the slickest lawyer in all of New York. His hair was combed back and his chiseled jaw and strong eyes reflected a strong personality for anyone stepping into his office. Vining's plan every day of the year was to get paid a lot of money and win each case. Foreign clients came to him because he had both the brains and the balls. No government was too big to tackle, and no lawsuit too hard or too complicated to win.

One ring was all it took to make him reach for the phone. He looked like everybody else when he was sleeping, but one level below, in his subconscious, he was always plotting the next step in the case he was working on at the time. He never owned an alarm clock in his life.

"Hello," he mumbled, half asleep.

"Ron, this is Pia."

"Pia, what bar are you calling from? That's what I love about you, it's never too late to talk about a case," he joked, sleepily.

"Ron, I'm not kidding. I'm in the biggest trouble in the world. I mean it. I'm in jail on Riker's Island. This is serious stuff, and I'm scared like you wouldn't believe."

"If you're on Riker's, I believe you're not kidding. Don't tell me anymore. I always read how those phones in jail are tapped. What do you want me to do?"

"I want you to call my father and come out here with him and bond me out. It's a $250,000.00 cash bond."

"That's a lot of cash. Who's got that kind of money lying around at night?"

"My father can arrange it. Just call him. Please."

"What's his name and number?"

"John Vittone. The phone number is 212-240-6480."

"Your father has a different name than you? Hey, wait a minute! John Vittone is your father? Wow!"

"It's a long story. You don't want to hear it now, but that's his private line, and that number can reach him anywhere in the world. Dial it and tell him to get the money. I really want to get out of here."

"Okay. Consider it done."

"Ron, believe me, I didn't do it. Do you believe me?"

"I don't know what it is that happened, but I'm with you all the way. I'll see you as soon as I can."

Forest Hills, Queens, is the United Nations of Long Island. Italians, Koreans, Jews, Irishmen and Germans all live next to one another. To an outsider, it is simply one of a 100 villages in the Borough of Queens, with pizza shops and appliance stores. However, to those who work on Park Avenue and rent space at $75.00 dollars a square foot, there is another side to the town.

Right in the center of the municipality is an enclave, open only to those with money and lots of it. This area is called The Gardens. Three-story houses with side wings and double-door entries stand above manicured lawns, signaling to the world on the outside the wealth contained inside. Houses start at $800,000.00 and work their way into the seven and eight million dollar range.

A cellular phone lay on top of the bed covers, now sounding its characteristic beeping. Vittone grabbed for it. Like Ronald Vining, the 63-year-old only appeared to be sleeping. Sleep was something that never really came easily to him. More often then not, he just dozed for an hour or so at a time.

"Yes," came the rasping, subdued voice.

"Mr. Vittone?"

"Yes."

"My name is Ronald Vining. I've worked at the same law firm with your daughter for 10 years, but we've never had the pleasure of meeting. I'm sorry to call you so late. Are you still there, Mr. Vittone?"

"I'm here."

"Mr. Vittone, I don't want to shock you, but Pia's in jail, a federal jail on Riker's Island. She needs bond money."

14

Vining could have said anything, that she was in the hospital, even that she was dead. But this meant trouble, something that was really close to him. He could feel it. John Vittone was not only totally unprepared for this announcement, but he always convinced himself that jail was not in the future for himself or any member of his family. He thought he could beat any rap and, in fact, that he would never be caught by the heat because he would get out of his business before that ever happened. That something could happen to his daughter and she would be arrested was almost impossible, like a bad dream. But he stayed calm, a calmness borne out of knowing that tragedy lurked everywhere in his life because of the path that he chose. As bad as this was, he was always ready for the unexpected and would act appropriately.

"How much?"

"The cash bond is set at $250,000. I know you can't get your hands on it tonight ..."

"I'll arrange it," the older man interrupted.

Vining was amazed. The man's tone never changed a bit; he didn't miss a beat.

"Mr. Vittone, I think it would be a good idea if we traveled together out there. I care a lot about Pia, too, and I might not be a criminal lawyer, but I can help."

"Where do you live?"

"203 East 84th Street."

"I'll be there with a car in 40 minutes." The phone went dead.

That was 11 days before. Now, standing over Pia in the center of the grand jury room, was Jay Cavanaugh, who for 10 years, had waged the battle to convict felons and put them behind bars. Never in private practice, never having to make a payroll on Friday, he had only represented the government his entire career. Now he had, before him, in the figure of Pia Vassar, a career case, his chance to rise above the faceless crowd of 30 year assistant attorneys and climb the political ladder. But, only if he got a big win with lots of good publicity.

In the grand jury proceedings, the witness, and at this moment, the accused, is not allowed to have a lawyer present. No one is there to make objections for the defense. The prosecution directs and choreographs the whole show. Only certain witnesses are called, and they're only asked certain questions. If the inquisitor does not like an answer he receives, he can close in on the witness, talk in a louder voice, fire off the questions one after another, and generally intimidate. There is nothing that the witness can do, except sit there and try to weather the storm.

Pia, against the advice of her legal counsel, waived the Fifth Amendment for this grand jury proceeding, and wanted to prove her innocence to these 22 people assembled before her. That was a mistake. While she denied knowing or meeting the family that her father worked for, or anything about the Pucchinis and their associates, or about the drugs in her apartment or how they got there, the weak nature of her answers, without any strong back up, made her look guilty, which is all it takes to hand down an indictment.

Cavanaugh turned his back on Pia and faced the jury and posed his questions. "Isn't it true, Ms. Vassar, that your real name is Vittone?"

"My real name is Vassar, Sir, I legally changed it when I was 22."

"Well, let me put it another way. When you were born, your name was Vittone, wasn't it?"

"Yes, Sir."

"And you are the daughter of one John Vittone, are you not?"

"Yes, I am."

"Isn't your father a high-ranking member of the Pucchini crime family?"

"No, Sir. He owns a very successful and large restaurant in Forest Hills."

"Oh, come on, Ms. Vassar, do you really believe that is how he makes his money?"

"Yes, Sir, I do."

"You grew up in a mansion in the Forest Hills Gardens, didn't you?"

"I don't think it was a mansion, but it was a nice house."

"And your father went to work every morning in Garden City, right?"

"He may have. I don't know where he went each and every morning."

"Well, you've been to his office in Garden City, haven't you?"

"A couple of times."

"Why would a man who owns a restaurant in Forest Hills take the Long Island Railroad out to Garden City each morning?"

"That's his office. He reviewed his investments there and frequently talked to his broker and maybe his partner on other ventures. I don't know really … I wasn't there. A restaurant isn't an office."

"At your home, he had a computer, didn't he?"

"Yes."

"Spent a lot of time there?"

"I suppose so. That way, he didn't have to go back to the business every night. He could monitor the payables and receivables. This is the computer age, Mr. Cavanaugh."

"For that matter, Ms. Vassar, your father rarely went to Ristorante Roma, true?"

"He went sometimes."

"About once a week, every 10 days, every two weeks?"

"I don't know. He had good managers."

"He was home every night, wasn't he?"

"I guess so."

"Did you ever see your father talking on cell phones?"

"Yes."

"Quite a lot, wouldn't you say?"

"He used them."

"Why always on the cell phone when the restaurant was a mile from your house?"

"I don't know. That's how he worked."

"You never worked in the Ristorante Roma, did you?" Cavanaugh intoned. He loved to drag out the Italian pronunciation. It made it sound all the more like these people were mixed up with the mob.

"No."

"Neither did your mother."

"No."

"Were you born in Sardinia, Italy?"

"Yes."

"When did you leave?"

"When I was 7 years old."

"And what did your father do there?"

"He had a wholesale liquor business."

"That was in a warehouse?"

"Yes."

"Do you remember anything about any other warehouses?" In a few short days, Cavanaugh had really done his homework. Some federal investigators left for Sardinia the day after Pia was arrested and checked into John Vittone's entire past. They knew a lot about him.

"Not really."

"How about ones where he ran crap games and casinos?"

"No, absolutely no."

"Do you remember your Uncle Giacomo?"

"Yes."

"Do you know what he did for a living?"

"He helped my father in the liquor business."

"Would it surprise you to know that an FBI investigator for the U.S. Justice Department will testify here later that he's a leader of organized crime on Sardinia?"

"Yes, it would."

"Your father traveled back to Sardinia every year, right?"

"Yes, he did."

"And you and your mother never went, correct?"

"No, we didn't."

"Was he trying to shield you from his criminal life?"

"No, Sir. I had to go to school, if you think about it." She was losing her patience, but she had been warned to stay cool and look like a sweet girl.

"You were arrested at 8:00 p.m. and taken to Riker's Island at midnight. At 4:00 a.m. your father handed over $250,000.00 in cash, didn't he, to bond you out?"

"Yes, my bond was made."

"Does your father always keep a quarter of a million dollars lying around the house?"

"I told you, he's very successful. The restaurant seats 300 people and does 600 dinners a night. He's a traditional Italian. He keeps his money to himself. He was born during the Depression. I have no idea where he keeps his money; it's his, not mine."

"You'd agree that bank deposits in America are insured, wouldn't you?"

"Yes."

"Ever hear of anybody losing money in a bank account in a federally insured bank?"

"I can't say that I have."

"You owe your father a lot, don't you Ms. Vassar?"

"Yes, I owe him my whole life."

"He sent you to Marymount and Columbia Law School and paid the tuition, didn't he?"

"Yes, he did."

"You had a Mercedes convertible?"

"Yes."

"And credit cards at Bloomingdale's, Lord and Taylor's, and Abercrombie's to name a few?"

"Yes."

"He even bought you the co-op that you currently live in; the same one where the drugs were found."

"He bought me a co-op." She loved her father, but right now, she wished that he sold washing machines or anything other than what he did.

"Isn't it true that you would do anything for your father?"

"Whatever I could."

"Including storing his drugs in your closet and kitchen so that he could ship them around the world?"

"No, that's not true. Believe me, that's not true," she exclaimed, leaning out of the seat and looking directly into the eyes of the jurors.

For two hours, he grilled her on her motives, intent and opportunity, the possession of drugs, and the sole control of her apartment. When she thought about it, a probable conviction was all there for Cavanaugh's taking. Her father had given her everything. She owed him a lot in return. In the eyes of the jurors, maybe even providing him with a hiding place for his drugs. Cavanaugh annihilated her. She was labeled a Mafia princess, and she would be tied to that world for the rest of her life.

When Pia left the chair, she was a good enough lawyer to know that he had a solid case for indictment. Her father led a shadowy life, with a restaurant as a front. He lived high and showered her with perks. She was her father's daughter, and it made sense for the government to say that the drugs found in her apartment were clearly placed there through a conspiracy between the father and daughter. The way Cavanaugh presented it, it all fit into a nice package. It wasn't true, but no one would believe her under these circumstances.

Cavanaugh next called on the building manager at Pia's co-op to further nail down his circumstantial case. Art Johnson told the assembled jurors that he had been the manager of the Dorchester for three years and that Pia Vassar was one of his tenants.

"Mr. Johnson, do you have a key to the Vassar apartment?"

"There are two deadbolts. I keep a key to the bottom lock and the tenant keeps both keys to the top and one to the bottom. That way, if the tenant wants someone to get in during the day, when the tenant is out, they can leave the top unlocked, have the visitor call me, and I can get a workman in with the bottom key. The rest of the time, the tenant is the only one who can access the place."

"Why don't you keep both?"

"We get new tenants about every 10 years. People live at the Dorchester forever. This way, if something goes wrong inside the apartment, no one can point a finger at management or anyone else, including me. If we need to get in, we can get permission from the owner easily enough. I know everyone in the building; there are only 80 units."

"Do you have any other way to access the apartments?"

"None, other than asking for permission."

"Did you ever enter the Vassar apartment since Ms. Vassar moved in?"

"No, Sir. It seems that she's a pretty busy lady. Sometimes, I see her leaving for work when I come in at 7:00 a.m., but when I go home at 5:00 p.m., she's never home yet. Those lawyers work a lot of hours."

Cavanaugh chuckled, and the jurors laughed.

"Have you ever been in her apartment at all?"

"No, Sir, never."

"How do visitors get in?"

"They buzz up to the apartment owner. If the owner doesn't let them in, or if they're not there, they can call into our office."

"Do you keep a log of people coming into the building through your office?"

"Yes, we do."

"Have you brought with you here today, a log for the last three months, starting in September 1998, pursuant to the subpoena I sent you?"

"Yes, I brought it with me right here."

"Do you have reference to any one single person on that sheet calling you or coming into your office to try to get into the Vassar apartment?"

"I looked. I read it over three times. Not one person."

"Have you let anybody at any time into the Vassar apartment since you became manager?"

"No, Sir."

"Have you taken anyone in with you?"

"No, Sir."

"Do you know how drugs could get into Ms. Vassar's apartment unless she brought them in or let somebody in herself?"

"No, Sir, I don't."

"Thank you, Mr. Johnson. That's all the questions I have."

It never ceased to amaze Cavanaugh, as to how easy it was to make somebody look guilty when nobody was around on the other side to cross-examine. He had direct evidence, the drugs found in her apartment, and he had plenty of circumstantial evidence to prove motive and intent. She was the only one who could get into the apartment, according to Johnson. Someone breaking in, coming in with a delivery man, or even bribing Johnson were subjects that Cavanaugh would never pose. Cavanaugh was the only one who could ask the questions, and now he was prepared to leave no doubt in these jurors' minds.

"Ladies and gentlemen, I have had the opportunity to take a sworn statement of a confidential informant, an undercover witness." One of the jurors grimaced, and Cavanaugh caught sight of him. "No, this isn't going to be three hours of reading questions and answers to you. It's short, very short." For the second time that day, the jurors smiled. "But it's important. It's going to show you why those drugs were in Ms. Vassar's apartment. This will give you the whole picture."

Cavanaugh just didn't call witnesses to ask questions, but to set the stage. He was there to make speeches and create any version of the case he wanted. Cavanaugh brought an assistant from his office to play the part of the attorney asking the questions of the confidential informant when the sworn statement was taken. Though a few days before, Cavanaugh had been the actual questioner when the statement was taken, he decided to now read the answers to lend a theatrical flair to the proceedings. Cavanaugh sat down in the very same chair that Pia previously occupied. This informant didn't just walk into Cavanaugh's office cold, sit down and answer questions. Cavanaugh grilled him for four hours, one to one, nonstop before the actual statement was started. When the stenographer started to take it all down, it all came out very nicely.

In the dress rehearsal, Cavanaugh covered every topic. "What do you do for the Pucchini's?" "Who did you know in the organization?" "What did you see while you were there?" "How often did you make trips and do errands for John Vittone?" "Did you go to his office in Garden City?" "Do you know the operation Vittone ran for the family?" The same questions were probably asked at least four times, regardless of whether the answers were the same each time. When Cavanaugh committed the informant, Vincent Noletti, to testify, he wanted him to be perfect.

A young lawyer, stood up and asked the questions to allow this informant, played by Cavanaugh, to proceed to give his long, colorful and detailed answers.

"Sir, who is John Vittone really?"

Noletti listened well to the family gossip, and he was able to paint a very convincing portrait of John Vittone. "Well, that's a good question. It's going to take a long answer."

The informant would do anything to avoid 15 years at the Marion Federal Penitentiary in Illinois, the same place where John Gotti was incarcerated. Marion was not going to be his home, and whatever it took to convict Vittone's daughter, he was prepared to do.

"John Vittone's a pretty sharp guy. If you see him on the street, you'd never know he was a wise guy. He brags about a beautiful home in the Forest Hills Gardens, right next door to a brain surgeon. I think the guy on the other side is a big shot for American Express. He wears $3,000 suits that are made at, what's the name of that store with the B's?" answered Cavanaugh, reading Noletti's written testimony and looking up to make eye contact with the jury.

"Brooks Brothers," piped in the intern at the live session.

"Yeah that's it, Brooks Brothers. He had that gold Rolex and a big ring. He drives big cars and keeps to himself. I've only seen his daughter once. Beautiful, a lawyer; she wore all the right clothes."

"Does Mr. Vittone work?"

"That's really something. He's not like the rest of the guys hanging out in some pool room or Italian club or in the back room of a dry cleaner. He's got an office you wouldn't believe in Garden City with all the millionaires, at the Garden City Hotel. You walk into the office, the carpet must be three inches thick, and there's mahogany furniture everywhere. The funny thing is though, there's nobody there. No customers, no employees. He's got a waiting room for 20 people, but nobody's in it. All he's got in that office are machines. Computers, faxes, phones and paper are all over the place. On the desk and the walls are cordless phones and cell phones. You name it, and that's what it's all about. He tells everybody he makes his living by running the Ristorante Roma in Forest Hills, but why does he need an office like that to run a restaurant?"

"That's the question, Sir, why?" the intern standing in front of the jury asked as he spurred on his star witness.

"Because that restaurant's only a front. Oh sure, he may own a piece, but so does Tommy Pucchini, and Tommy's son and the two under bosses for the family. In fact, they have a manager, Pete Calabrese, who really runs the restaurant. He spends about 100 hours a week there. It's all bullshit." Cavanaugh looked at the jury. They didn't blink an eye at this minor obscenity. "I'm sorry, it's all baloney," Cavanaugh intoned, as he rephrased Noletti's words. The jurors smiled.

"He's really the head of the drug business for the Pucchini family. He's got 40 guys on the road, all over the world, running around in planes and boats and cars running coke and horse, from out of the country into the big cities, like New York, Los Angeles, Philadelphia, wherever it can bring the most money. All those computers and machines keep track of where to pick up the stuff and where every one of those mules is every minute of the day."

"Is Mr. Vittone the mastermind?" the lawyer continued.

"He's got it all in his head. Every name, every contact, every place, but most of all, he knows how much he's paying, how much he's getting and where the money is going. The guy is really a genius."

"Would he have been able to get drugs from anywhere in the world?"

"Are you kidding? This guy controls a lot of the drugs in the world. Without him, the Pucchinis would be a bunch of hijackers selling TVs. He's the brains of the part of the family that makes the most money."

"Does he need a place to store his stuff, like in his daughter's apartment?" Cavanaugh never had to worry about another lawyer jumping up and objecting as to leading. This was a one man act.

"Sure, they always need a safe place to stash drugs, even if it's kind of a small score like this one. They get it in, they hold it a day or two and another guy moves it out. This goes on every single day."

"Can you think of any place better than his daughter's apartment?" Objections like speculation and relevance also never played a part in these sworn statements.

"One of the best, especially if she's a lawyer."

The statement was 12 pages in total. The mob rat described the millions upon millions that were brought in from every deal, and the ways that the Pucchini's and Vittone ran the operation. As Noletti in his statement explained it, all of the big money led back to Vittone. He created, from a few scraps of hearsay, a vivid narrative.

Cavanaugh made his case. There is an old saying in the legal system that in front of a grand jury, a prosecuting attorney can "indict a ham sandwich." Cavanaugh elicited from the director of the crime lab that the drugs were of the highest grade, pure cocaine, and two kilos in size, with a street value of about $180,000.00. The three federal agents had appeared and given their testimony about going to Pia's apartment and finding the drugs in plain view and arresting Pia.

But Cavanaugh was tired of standing in the middle of this bleak room for weeks on end, where the walls had dents and black scrapes. Eating tuna fish sandwiches for lunch and staring out at a bunch of old people in cardigan sweaters and making $60,000 a year was not his idea of where he wanted to be at this stage in his career. He wanted a lot more. Only the highest elected office in the state was on his mind and the mind of his gorgeous and ambitious wife. To get to that place would take something more, like calling a witness who he knows will give only one answer, which will be the same answer to every question and lend absolutely nothing to the case, but who will garner the attention this case needed to launch his political career.

"Mr. Marshall, would you bring in Mr. John Vittone from the hallway," Cavanaugh said in a loud voice, summoning the bailiff. The jurors changed positions and sat up in the jurors' box.

Bringing Vittone downtown to appear in front of the grand jury was nothing more than a grandstand stunt. Cavanaugh alerted all of the local television stations in New York to set up in the hallway to capture the Mafia boss entering the grand jury room as a possible co-conspirator with his daughter. The Mafia don and his child princess: Cavanaugh decided to play this theme for all that it was worth.

John Vittone wore the same black suit he put on the night Vining called. Again, Vittone prepared himself and his mind many times over the past 20 plus years for this moment that he once hoped would never occur. However, now that it had happened, he would do or say whatever it took to bring the whole matter to a quick, but successful, conclusion.

Vittone's attorney, James Gentry, accompanied him to the door. Gentry was, by everyone's account, the only criminal attorney in Garden City, since it was one of the richest communities on Long Island, and had only experienced one homicide since World War II. Gentry gave the same advise to Vittone as Pia's lawyer gave to her, except in her father's case, he heeded it. It was to be the Fifth Amendment straight down the line. It made no difference. Cavanaugh had the drugs in her apartment and for an indictment, he needed no more. Vittone was trying to avoid an indictment of his own and would live to fight his battle another day. The video cameras loaded with tape for the 6:00 p.m. and 11:00 p.m. news, and the still photographers backed down the hall as Vittone approached, popping as many photos as they could. Vittone held himself ramrod straight, and marched straight into the jury room, never looking one way or the other.

"What is your name?" Cavanaugh questioned in his most supercilious manner.

"John Vittone," came the reply.

"Where do you live?"

"On the advice of counsel, I decline to answer all further questions on Fifth Amendment grounds. You have made me a target in your prosecution of this case."

Cavanaugh would have asked every question known to man if the proceedings had been public, but as it was only himself, the jurors, the stenographer and a clerk, there was no sense in playing to the gallery. There were far too few Republican voters gathered in this room.

He asked the obvious, "Was he Pia's father? Was he a member of the Pucchini family? Did he command a brigade of drug runners who sold their wares to school children and addicted adults?" To each question, Vittone gave the same answer. After an hour, Cavanaugh tired of this game, and Vittone was excused. The proceeding recessed for the day.

As the jurors gathered the next morning, Cavanaugh strolled down the hall, chatting about the Knicks' game the night before with his young assistant. "Are you ready for the closing?" he asked to get back on track. "Jonathan, an orangutan could close this and get an indictment. Just remember, her old man had enough clout, or really enough money, to hire Leslie Gabrielson. Wait till you see her. She's brutal. She turns every case into a three-ring circus. That's where we are going to have to be on top of our game. This is not even a dress rehearsal. I'm going to keep it short and sweet, no overkill."

True to his word, Cavanaugh stuck to his game plan. In closing, his nerves were under control and the facts never so clear.

"Ladies and gentlemen, this will be short and to the point, because the testimony in this case speaks louder than anything that I could ever say.

"Two kilos of cocaine were found in the apartment owned, maintained and controlled solely by Pia Vassar. As the building manager told you, no one else had been in the apartment, and no one else had let anyone into the apartment. It's her apartment, her keys and her closet and refrigerator.

"If that were not enough, remember the words that we went over and over on the direct testimony of the former member of the Pucchini family. Her father, John Vittone, controls the sale, purchase and flow of more drugs than any other man in America. He's a made member of the Pucchini crime family. Those drugs give him an opulent lifestyle, a mansion in the Gardens and a suite of the best offices money can provide on the Island. He's got the computers, faxes and phones to orchestrate drug deals 24 hours a day.

"It's simple, very simple. She owes her father her life, her education, her credit cards, her law degree, and even her position at the top firm in New York. She owes him, and these men always collect, even from their daughters. Eventually, whatever he gives to her, there is always something to give back in return. He needed a place to store these drugs for a day or two, and he left them with the one person he could trust most, his daughter. Jeopardizing his daughter's life is nothing, absolutely nothing to such a man. Even though this is a harsh matter, she was a willing, knowing, voluntary participant, and she must be indicted and face a jury of her peers for these criminal acts. No man or woman is above the law, and we all must abide by the rule of law, even if we are lawyers, and even if we must pay for the sins of our parents.

"I implore you to do your duty. The facts are clear and speak volumes to you. There is no other alternative but to hand down an indictment on all four counts that the US Attorney's Office has presented, including the count under the Racketeer Influenced and Corrupt Organizations Act (RICO) which you have been provided with. You must indict on all four counts under these facts. Thank you."

The RICO Statutes comprised almost half of one of the volumes of criminal law in Cavanaugh's library. The most important part was buried deep within all of the legal wording. It read:

"Any person, found by the trier of fact to have engaged in the sale or distribution of illegal narcotics, which is part of a larger criminal conspiracy, shall be subject to forfeiting all of his property and possessions that may have been gained or derived from such endeavors."

If Pia is tried and convicted on any RICO charges, not only would the government confiscate her bank accounts, stocks, bonds, co-op and art collection, but her father would undoubtedly be indicted in the days after her conviction. The results could be deadly for the Vittone family.

The jurors were out less than 45 minutes. It was a finding of probable guilt, on all four charges, including possession, trafficking, conspiracy, and most importantly, violation of RICO. Pia Vassar, John Vittone's only daughter, was in danger of spending the next 20 years in a federal prison.

CHAPTER III

SARDINIA, MAY, 1940

OFF THE COAST OF ITALY lie two great Italian islands. Sicily has been the subject of books and movies, renowned for its ancient customs and as the birthplace of the Mafia. About 160 miles to the north is its sister island, the beautiful, but unheard of, Sardinia. The name conjures up the fish that make their home in the surrounding seas.

Most of Sardinia is a rocky isle, inhabited only by goats and sheep. The southwest corner, perched on the Mediterranean Sea, is blessed with fertile soil and just the right amount of rainfall. In the spring, the prevailing winds come from the western part of the Mediterranean. In the morning, the sky is often clear, but as the day progresses, the winds bring with them the rain clouds which deposit their moisture almost every day upon the lands and farms that make up the landscape.

John Vittone never forgot how, in the summer, the sea was usually deep green, calm and sparkling. Wild lilies and tulips, in vivid colors of red, purple and yellow, blanketed the fields that slid down to the waters rolling onto the beach. It was beautiful, and it was hard to believe when he sat as a boy in the knee high grass, dreaming of nothing other than what was on the other side of those waters and oceans, that his town was infested with a raw brutality not known to many other places in the world.

His father was a good man, a man who wanted nothing more than to provide a living for his family and keep to himself. The family sold anything that created a few dollars in profit. Newspapers, soda pop, games, stationary, anything that didn't cost much and that people liked to buy could be found in his small store. It was a simple life. John, his mother and father lived on top of the store in a one bedroom apartment that carried with it a 30-year mortgage.

However, there was some light at the end of that 30-years. The store and the small apartment would be free and clear of all debts. Not so bad in today's world, and John didn't mind at all sleeping on the couch in the tiny living room.

He enjoyed helping his father behind the counter every day except Wednesday. That was the day when the local enforcers from the society known as the Black Hand came to the business and each week, took from his father their envelope containing the 16,000 Lira, or $10.00 U.S.

Maurizio Vittone dreaded nothing more than seeing these men enter his store each week. They sauntered in, wearing expensive suits and hats with wide brims pulled down low over their foreheads. Their fingers played with the store's goods, as if they had an ownership interest in them, and they spoke with a sneer and an arrogance that told his father that if he did not follow all of their commands, they would exact the ultimate punishment, death, to be meted out without a further thought.

For years, the elder Vittone had paid and paid, but it was not easy. After the mortgage and the other expenses were met, very little profit remained. But this was protection money. Vittone paid his homage, and no harm came to his store or his family. It was humiliating, but a fairly satisfactory arrangement in this part of Europe where men were killed each day for the smallest transgression or defiance against the local crime don.

On the second Wednesday in August, the two men appeared, but they did not want the envelope. Instead they had a message to deliver. "Maurizio, the family can no longer take your Lira each week. It is just not working out. We need more because we have been good to you over the years, and you have prospered. We need to share in your good fortune."

Maurizio said nothing and kept the palms of his hands on the glass counter top and listened. "On Tuesday, you will go to the lawyer's office with your wife and sign the papers, turning over 25 percent of the business and the building to the family. After that, an accountant will figure out what you earn every month in profits and will pay you 75 percent. No more weekly payments. No more visits from us. Who knows, the family may even invest some money to clean the place up. This will work out for everyone; it's a good deal."

Like everyone else in Carbonia who was under the thumb of these thugs, Maurizio knew only too well what this really meant. In only a few months, the 25 percent would grow to 90 percent, if he was lucky. In a short time, he would be no more than a hired hand.

He pleaded, "I have always paid my money. Every week, my envelope has been waiting for you. I have done everything that you have asked. I cannot give you 25 percent. There will be nothing for me to live on."

"Maurizio, there is no sense in arguing. These are the orders. There is no alternative."

"I'll pay more each week."

"No. That's not what the family wants."

"I can't do it."

"Be at the lawyer's at 11:00 a.m. Besides, 25 percent is a lot better than losing everything." With that, they left the store and walked past the plate glass windows and were gone.

He could not wait for the day to be over. At 7:30 p.m. he climbed the stairs and opened the door to the flat above. His wife could see that something was on his mind and that it was not good. "Constanza …, the Black Hand … they came this morning. It's bad."

"What is it?" she asked holding a dish towel. She didn't want to know the answer, but whatever it was, it was inevitable.

"They don't want weekly protection money anymore. They want part of the store."

"How much?"

"Twenty-five percent."

"Why?"

"Because they want it, that's why. They don't have to give any reasons."

He slumped into the one chair in the room. It was hopeless. His wife was always full of ideas. Before this day, he had always been resigned to 30 years or more of working in the store, then having it free of debt, like a future pension. But now, there was no way out; he was being forced to take another route. "Remember the man, who last month wanted to buy this place?" She threw out the idea while her mind tried to find a solution to this puzzle.

"Yes."

"Let's see if we can sell the store to him. We'll sell for whatever we can get and then leave Sardinia. I can't stand it here anymore. You walk down the street, into a store, and some fellow from the Black Hand is always lurking around the corner looking for some way to steal from everybody. This is no life. We have family that went to America and they made it. We can too. I'll get tickets and we'll be gone. We'll just take whatever we need and start a new life. I don't want to raise our son here." She covered her eyes with her hands and wept softly.

His own people turned against him. The Italians treated each other like enemies. He did not want to be there, either.

"All right, I'll call him now. Right now."

Maurizio reached the buyer on the telephone almost immediately. "Senor Borcelli, my wife and I have thought about your offer for the business. We have decided we would like to try something new. If you still want, the store is yours."

Borcelli was only too happy. His daughter married a weak man with no drive. The store would be a perfect way for Borcelli to solve his problem. His son-in-law could stand behind the counter, and his daughter could cook the meals upstairs. The newlyweds loved each other and this was really perfect.

"I will have my lawyer draw up the papers. When do you want to close?"

"Two days would be good for us. We have an opportunity to buy a bed and breakfast on the other end of the island, and the seller really wants to move fast."

"Then that is the way it will be. Tomorrow, my son-in-law can do a quick inventory and that will be it. I have found that sometimes the best deals are made quickly."

Vittone and his wife were at first skeptical of their good fortune. Nothing had gone this smoothly for them before. However, they had no choice but to play this to a conclusion. Constanza packed a trunk for herself and her husband and a big suitcase for their 5-year-old son.

They would leave all the furniture. The china and flatware were store-bought and had no sentimental value. Any small family heirloom would fit in with the rest of the luggage. She wondered whether it was really possible to pick up and leave and start a new life.

The answer came two days later when the Vittones appeared at Borcelli's attorney's office, signed three documents and got their small amount of cash, which would carry them away from this land of threats and extortion.

The following morning, Maurizio and Constanza went to pick up their tickets for their journey. Three steamship tickets awaited them. Maurizio's black Fiat climbed one hill and then the next. At the top was a two-story building with two wooden double doors bearing the name of the agency. It looked more like a fortress than an office, and in this place, most businesses who did not cater to the retail public, selling apparel or other wares, preferred to be surrounded by solid oak walls.

Maurizio put the car in neutral and set the emergency brake. He and Constanza stepped from the car together as husband and wife and as his foot touched the sidewalk, two men moved out from behind the granite corner of the building, the same two men who, for the last four years, visited his shop every Wednesday.

They never stopped walking and each of them pumped three bullets into the proud little man, brushing past the young widow. The only man she ever made love with was now dead on the ground, laying in a pool of blood. The Black Hand would not allow him to have his own life. He belonged to them.

She stood over him with her arms dangling at her sides, still clutching her purse. These men robbed her of her heart and soul. She was determined that from that moment on, her son's life would be different. He would do things differently than his father. Power was even more important than respect.

Constanza had one sister and one brother. Giacomo Falcone lived in Caprera on the Emerald Coast of Sardinia on the northern tip of the island. Caprera was a vacation spot that looked over the straits that divided Sardinia from the French principality of Corsica. He never explained what he did for a living, but he made a nice life for himself. Emilia Falcone was like her sister, Constanza. She, too, had never left the life of Carbonia, preferring to live in a cold water flat, go to mass every morning and sell flowers alongside the road each day to survive.

There was no way Constanza could leave Sardinia now without her husband. She and her son moved into her sister's apartment, and she, too, sold flowers that she clipped from wild pastures and bought from the hot houses that were built on the bluffs overlooking the Mediterranean. The young John Vittone did manage to have a bit more income than that though. Each month, on the third day, a money order arrived, made out to the name of Constanza Vittone for the benefit of John Vittone. The sender, his Uncle Giacomo, wanted to make sure that the recipient knew the money was for the boy's welfare.

≈ CHAPTER IV ≈

CARBONIA, SARDINIA, 1950

DECEMBER 8TH WAS A special day in the life of John Vittone, for this was the day he was born in 1935. Vittone did not possess the typical heart and mind of a boy his age born in America. He was hardened from the brutal slaying of his father for the only crime of wanting a life of peace and freedom, away from the domination of the Black Hand.

At the time of his father's death, Italy had been aligned with Germany for more than three years, and his 5-years-old eyes watched the Germans strut around the town of Carbonia in their jack boots and swastika armbands like conquerors, patrolling the garrison that was waiting for the possible Allied invasion of Italy in 1943. The Allies chose instead the island of Sicily to establish a beachhead in Europe, but the German presence left a mark in his mind that power and force always prevailed, just as in the case of his father.

The war years were shorter for John than people in other parts of Europe, because Italy had capitulated on the second day of the invasion, leaving only the Germans to defend the peninsula and sending most of the intruders on the island to places on the mainland where they were more urgently needed. But still, food was a scarce commodity as he and his mother and aunt had to constantly use their wits to obtain whatever bread and vegetables were available. Meat was almost unheard of.

His aunt did whatever she had to do to keep the family fed. A young German officer found her attractive and frequently brought her packages of tin goods and food that were almost impossible to find on the street. Each night, they sat on the terrace of a café in Carbonia, under the umbrellas raised above tables that stood watch over the moonlit waters of the Mediterranean. While drinking a glass of Carbonia's world famous Cabernet, the drama being played out in the rest of Europe seemed far removed. German patrol boats occasionally sailed past, but the roar of their engines was barely heard on these patios.

Emilia Falcone knew whatever coins or food the German could provide might be the difference between living or starvation. She started to spend the nights with him in a small room originally built as a storage area in the basement of the eatery. In return for her sexual favors, the lieutenant gave her a few Lira a week in addition to the food parcels. John Vittone and his mother never spoke of where the aunt went in the evening, returning the next morning, but the activities of the German occupation troops were no secret in the town.

Even after the war ended, the fortunes of the family did not change for the better in any significant degree. The checks John's mother received from her brother grew larger, but it was still a day-to-day struggle. He wore trousers and shirts purchased at the parish rummage sales, and there was never any spending money for anything that was fun.

Constanza and John Vittone entered the Church of the Holy Cross at 8:00 a.m. on the feast day. They walked down the center aisle and knelt in front of the gold cross hung behind the altar and sat down to pray. Constanza asked God on this day, marking the beginning of her son's 16th year of life, to lead him into the sacred world where she thought he would be safe and respected. John, too, realized the significance of his birthday and asked that he receive whatever calling was planned for him.

The priest gave his sermon and spoke of how Christ's birth gave life to everyone, or at least to all those who believed. The 15-year-old sat in the fifth pew from the altar, and his eyes darted from one fresco to another as the Father's words cascaded through the great room. The gold gleamed everywhere, all the way up the wall which held the giant cross to the domed ceiling where fabulous painted murals covered the great arch of the sanctuary. Paintings, probably worth thousands, hung from the inside alcoves of each side altar. Each priest had his own gold chalice, and while most of the parishioners toiled in poverty, inside the church building, there was considerable wealth, accumulated from the Sunday offerings of its poor parishioners.

John witnessed wars, murders, sacrifice and poverty, and developed a maturity far in advance of his age. What kind of life lay ahead of him on this isle, a remote province, so far removed from the capital in Rome? His options were limited. If he left for the mainland, he had no contacts and no family. Most importantly, he had no prospects for a job. He knew that he did not need a calling from God to enter the priesthood because in reality, he had no alternative.

For almost two millennia, the church kept track of its parishioners from the day a male was born in the parish borders, and his birth was recorded not only on the thick bound registry maintained in a side room at the entrance to the church, but the priests also kept a book, lined not only with dates and months, but with years. When John Vittone was born, two entries were made in that log: one on the page marked 1935, indicating his birthday, and another entry for 1950, showing December 8th to be his 15th birthday. This was the age at which he became eligible for admission to the seminary, to embark upon a life of priestly respect.

John Vittone got up from his seat and went to the altar railing where he knelt to receive the wine and bread of communion. The priest lingered a second longer than usual when he placed the Host in his mouth, and John looked up at the man. In a town the size of Carbonia, both the priest and the communicant realized the importance of this morning and the fact that the church was always looking to gather as many fish into its nets as possible. On his way out of the church doors, the priest stopped him and said, "John, happy birthday. I remember when I baptized you thinking that you were blessed to be born on one of the greatest days in the church calendar."

"Thank you, Father."

"Why don't you come by the rectory at noon for lunch. We'll celebrate."

His Catholic high school was closed, so John accepted the invitation. "I'll be there at noon, Father." "Fine," smiled Father Quintera, as he started to shake hands with another member of his flock.

Constanza Vittone could not contain herself as they walked down the front steps. "John, you know why Father has asked you to lunch." He feigned ignorance. "Don't you?"

"I can probably guess."

"He wants to know if you're interested in the priesthood. You are of age now."

"I know that, but I don't know what I want to do."

"It would be a good life," she told him, thinking that it was the best she could give him. He would be a man of God, helping people. He would always have a place to live. "You know those priests never pay for a meal. The Sunday collection gives you all the money you need. Everyone will respect you and treat you as a man of honor. Perhaps you may even receive a large donation or at least a pledge for one over a period of time."

Yes, he would earn respect and a living. But he wanted more, or something with more excitement. Walking around in black robes and never touching girls really didn't appeal to him.

His mother could see the doubt on his face. "John, I don't want you to end up like your father." He turned to glare at her with his steel blue eyes. She went on. "We have no money. You can't start a business, and even if you do, without money, you'll be always under the heels of those terrible men. There is no way out in this place. We have no factories to work in. There's nothing to do except tend an orchard or a flock. What else do you have?"

John was not surprised by the reflections of either his mother or the priest. He thought about this decision for many years. It often was a topic of conversation amongst his friends in parochial school. They all knew that their opportunities were limited.

John felt that he had little to lose. It only took five years to graduate from religious school, and if he eventually decided to leave the seminary, he would still have a high school diploma. He guessed that he could suffer through a few years of celibacy.

"Don't worry. I know that I'm boxed in here. I'll try, but don't get your hopes up about my graduating." With that final statement, they silently strode back to his aunt's apartment.

At the luncheon, John didn't want the priest to be placed in the position of having to beg him to join the order. He had already made up his mind to placate his mother for the moment. The two sat down and the rectory cook brought in a hot stew with a glass of water for John and glass of wine for the priest.

"Father, I'm glad you invited me today. For a long time, I've been thinking about joining the Jesuits and I wanted to talk to you about that."

The priest was so happy at how easy it was to land John that he picked up the glass and clanked it against John's. "Let's toast to that. This is a good day for you and the church." They raised their glasses and the deal was reached, sending John off to a religious education.

Saint Anselmo's Seminary looked like a fortress. Its 14-foot-high stone walls, right in the center of the town of Carbonia, wrapped around an entire square block. A wooden door on each side was positioned in the middle of each tall section. Those doors were rarely opened onto the streets for the occupants inside. Saint Anselmo's required its students to rise daily at 5:30 a.m., attend mass at 6:15 a.m., eat breakfast and then attend theology, divinity and philosophy classes until dinner at 6:00 p.m. followed by a night of study and more prayer. For John Vittone, the subjects were not a problem. Behind the long, thin face and the long, straight Roman nose was a quick mind. He often surprised himself at how he memorized information, even the smallest bits, carrying everything around for weeks, even months. Historical dates, places and names just registered in his brain. Remembering events in the Bible was no problem for him. He had a photographic memory.

After the third year, at 18, John was sent back into the real world for six months to live at a parish lying in the foothills 10 miles north of Carbonia. The name of the town was Melici, and the 2,500 people who inhabited it were the descendents of those who had lived there for centuries. The wool sheared from its many sheep gave the families their existence.

John was sent as a deacon, a priest-in-training. He wore a collar and black clerical garb, and lived on the second floor of the dwelling quarters with the priest who had been assigned there for years. This was to be an internship, one more step to see if he was really cut out for this way of life.

Mass took place each weekday at 7:30 a.m., and after that, there

was little for a priest or his deacon to do for the rest of the day. .
Everyone in the town worked in the same sort of agricultural
endeavors, just barely eking out a living. John usually made his way
into a store that sold papers and groceries at about 9:30 a.m. Like
clockwork, John always bought a copy of the Carbonia paper, a cup
of espresso and a sugared roll, and sat at the two-seat table which was
in the corner, behind the door.

This particular Tuesday morning found him seated in his usual
seat, with his face buried in the paper hovering a few inches above
the lines that were laid down on the tabletop. The girl behind the
counter came over with some more coffee. "Father, I see that you
need another cup."

"I'm not a priest yet. I keep telling you that," he kidded her. "Just
call me John."

"All right, let's settle on Deacon John."

"If you want, but John is okay."

"Deacon, is there any way I can see you somewhere to talk to
you?" she asked with a serious look.

"Anytime, they don't give you much to do in this place," he
responded.

"How about at the fountain in front of the church at 2:00 p.m.?
It's dead in here around that time."

John obliged, "I'll be there."

The fountain in Melici was little more than a hollowed-out hole
surrounded by ceramic tile, with a piece of metal in the center
spouting water. But in a town of this size, it was the focal point. John
was sitting on the ledge reading a little pamphlet about pilgrimages
to the Holy Land in Israel. It seemed to him that nowadays everything he read and looked at was tied into religion. A trip abroad
would be nothing more than a tour of churches and cathedrals, all
narrated by a priest serving as a travel guide, who had been there
probably 10 times before. His life never varied, especially in this
outpost where they had sent him. The 19-year-old girl approached
him and turned directly to face him. "Can we go somewhere?"

"Sure, I have a cubbyhole office in the church."

"No, let's go over to an arbor behind the church." He never

knew this place existed, but he followed her.

"John," she began, no longer even bothering to try to call him Father or Deacon, "I have a problem. I can't tell the priest, and I can't tell my parents. You are the only one I can trust for help. John, I have sinned, and I am in a mess."

"It can't be that bad. Tell me what happened."

She blurted it all out. "For four years, I went to the high school in Carbonia with a boy, Domenico Ghirlandajo, from Carbonia. He liked me and I liked him. We couldn't see each other that much outside of school because I lived here. We graduated two months ago. He came into the hills to see me in his father's car. A couple of days later … I'm ashamed to tell you the rest."

"That's my job, to listen to people's problems," he told her in his most sympathetic voice.

"We went out," she explained looking at the grapes strewn on the floor of the gazebo below her, dropped from the grapevines that covered the lattices above the beams.

"He drove us up to a little lookout from where you can see down into the flatlands and out over the water. He asked me if I wanted to get in the back so we could lie side-by-side and touch each other. I should have said no, but I didn't. We laid down and he started to kiss me, and we kissed with our mouths open for a long time. He unbuttoned my blouse and turned me closer to him. Then he opened my pants and he started to touch me everywhere. I had never felt like that before in my life. One thing led to another. I could not help myself. I did it voluntarily. He didn't force me. He was really gentle as he put himself inside me. I wanted him, too. Two days ago, I found out that I am pregnant. I don't know what to do. I'm too young. If I get married, I'll have a lot of children before I'm 25. I won't have any life or any fun. I've never done anything or been anywhere. My life will be over. I'm only five weeks pregnant, but I can't have an abortion. It is against God to do that; I know it. Do you think I should move away for a while and have the baby and then put it up for adoption?"

John sat there, not moving or saying anything, but looking at the fragile girl next to him. He had rarely been this close to a girl in his life. When he was 14, the year before he joined the Seminary, he kissed an eighth grade girl on the cheek and maybe held her hand a few times. But that was it. This girl was the type of girl that he always imagined himself being with. Pretty, kind and inexperienced, a virgin up until her recent adventure. He wanted to put his arms around her and pull her close and do all the same things with her that Domenico had. It made him ache to think that another guy had been with her when she could have been his. He told himself that he would have taken her and made love to her gently and afterward, he would have laid down next to her for hours looking into her eyes. He wished that he had created the child in her womb.

"I'm not sure what to tell you. Obviously, in our religion, you must have the baby. You have no choice. If Domenico was a good enough man for you to trust with your heart and body, then I'm sure he is a good person."

"John, you are right, and if I tell him what has happened, he'll want to marry me. I'm just not sure I want to get married. I barely know him. What if we get tired of each other? I am thinking about going to a house run by nuns on the other side of Sardinia. They'll give me a place to stay and deliver the baby. I can tell my parents I want to explore the world. The sisters have a lot of good homes with good people that can't have their own children and are looking for a baby to adopt."

"Well, it sounds to me like you have your mind made up, but I think you owe it to Domenico to tell him. It is his child, too." That was the best advice he could give on such short notice, never having been asked to counsel someone before.

She pondered what he said for a few minutes. "Let me think about it. Can I talk to you in another couple of days?"

"Of course, I'll meet you anytime."

"John ... Deacon. I know you're not a priest yet, but everything I told you is in total confidence, isn't it?"

"Just as if you had told me in a confessional. You are my first confession."

"Thank you. I needed to tell someone," she said as she leaned over and kissed him on the side of his face.

They left the arbor separately because she felt it would be better if they were not seen together. It did not take too much to make tongues wag in this provincial town.

After that moment, John Vittone never again had the same feeling about his life in the Seminary or about his future life as a priest. This girl brought home to him all the feelings that he kept hidden and bottled up inside him. He wanted a girl to be with, to touch, to smell and to love. He also wanted a child. This religious life took all of that away from him. He was alone, with only the stars in the universe to contemplate. It was just too hard to think of spending 60 or 70 years without ever being in love. It was too much to ask of him, too much to give up. He knew that from this time on, his days in the Seminary were numbered.

The Seminary life is one of the most monotonous on earth. Each morning, the chimes from the belfry are sounded five times, signifying the time of day. Hot water is rationed, and a lukewarm shower is all that an aspiring priest can hope for. Morning prayers are conducted by an older priest, living his retirement years in the free bed that he has been assigned to by the diocese. Breakfast follows and then a full mass, preceding a day of studying the writings of the four Gospels, detailing the short life of Jesus Christ and the miracles he performed before his crucifixion. Paper after paper was written interpreting and philosophizing about those words that had been taken down almost 2,000 years ago.

Monsignor Pucci had been the director of the Seminary for 12 years. Over the years he had acquired an ability to tell when he was losing one of his students. The signs were telltale: fidgeting in the seat in class, doodling in a notebook with a wandering mind, daydreaming when called upon in class. A young man started to say the prayers and give the responses at mass by rote, with little thought or interest. In the philosophy classes, the answers came out as standard answers. A distraught look appeared in the eyes, a look that said the Seminarian was thinking more about what was outside the 10-foot-high wall surrounding the classroom and dormitory than what was being talked about inside. It was at that point that Pucci knew that his charge had lost interest, and wanted to return to the real world.

John returned after doing his six months internship at the parish.

Pucci approached him as he lingered in the school dining room, turning over noodles in his spoon, and staring into space.

"John, may I sit down?"

Vittone looked up at the older, gray-haired Monsignor. "Yes, Father, please sit down."

"In only another 10 months, John, you will be graduating." Vittone listened carefully. "That means that you will be entering a religious life for what, 40, 50, 60 years, maybe more, depending on how long you live. You'll be counseling people, speaking at mass on holy days and serving a lot of people who will be busy with their own problems and then departing this earth. Some will be poor, some will make a lot of money and live like kings. Some will be honest and some won't. The honest ones may not fare that well. But you, you will always be living where you're assigned, seeing people you're told to see. You'll be poor, with no property and a little salary from the collection. The parishioners will give you some money at Christmas and on the anniversary of your ordination, and maybe they'll buy you a meal, but you surely won't be rich, and your days will be all the same. There will be no life outside your parish. It's not an exciting life unless you have total dedication to the Lord—then it's the richest and most rewarding life there is."

The Monsignor had caught his attention. John heard every word and knew that they were true, because they mirrored all of his thoughts for the last year. During the past 12 months, he knew in his heart that this type of life was robbing him of any worldly joy, of any ambition or career. His life had been chartered and decided for him, and for him, it was a long, bleak road that was laid endlessly to the horizon. "Monsignor, I hear what you're saying. Are you trying to tell me something?"

"Yes, my son, I am. You don't seem like you have the calling of God in you anymore. You read the material, and repeat it back, just enough to get a passing grade and then you retreat back into your own world. You don't talk much to anyone, and you stay in your room. It's pretty obvious that this life is not for you. What do you think?"

"I think you're right. I'm not going to debate you."

A few weeks before, John had been on a rare excursion into the business area of Carbonia. At 9:30 a.m., on his way back to the seminary, a man about 20 was standing next to a plate glass window in front of a closed shop, with his hands on the hips of a girl John knew in grade school. She was 19, the same age as he. They were kissing each other, and she was holding his shoulders. As her hair blew in the wind, he wished that he was the one holding this girl and touching her face and dress, and feeling the soft lines of her body. This was what he wanted. From living this austere and loveless life he was sure that he had the inner strength to avoid the fate of his father, and not have to live under the heels of tyrants even if he left the Seminary. He had a stronger personality than Maurizio and would not let that happen to him.

"Father, I've thought about this for a year. I want out. I have decided to leave the Seminary."

Pucci didn't try to talk him out of it. "John, you will be of little value to God or his people if your heart is not in this. Take some time off, go out, experience things; if you want to return, you're always welcome."

The picture of the girl's tight floral dress, with the full breasts, tiny waist and curved hips and buttocks reappeared again in his thoughts, and John knew that he was envious of that young man. It was a vision that he could never forget as he told Pucci, "I am going to leave tomorrow morning. I want to thank you for your advice. Someday, I'll do something good for the church to pay you back for these years."

"You owe us nothing, John, other than to try to lead a good life."

CHAPTER V

CAPRERA, SARDINIA, APRIL, 1955

JOHN VITTONE LEFT at 7:00 a.m. the next day, and purchased a bus ticket that took him from the southern tip of the island to the very northern extreme. It was in Caprera that his future lay, for it was there that he hoped to find the love of his life and a way to make a living.

John's uncle, Giacomo Falcone, established quite a life for himself after knocking off a local crime baron, called the Fisherman, and taking over all the mob operations on the northern half of Sardinia.

Marriage had never been a part of Giacomo's life. The responsibilities of supervising 10 men who carried out his criminal assignments, seeing to it that his ship's cargo made it safely to the docks, and being responsible for those who worked for him was more than enough to keep him busy. For 30 years, this was his vocation, constantly giving direction to his people, and it made him tired to think about his future obligations.

The arrival of his nephew was a propitious event, beneficial for both of them. Giacomo needed a right hand man whom he could trust, and Vittone needed a source of income. Giacomo almost ran down his stairs when the butler announced Vittone's presence. The older man opened his arms and wrapped his barrel-like body around that of his nephew. The embrace was sincere on both sides. John's mother never told him, but it was the money from his uncle that had kept them from being beholden to the Sisters of Charity. It was Giacomo's check that paid for his clothes and his parochial school tuition.

"John, you have not been to Caprera since the day you went into the Seminary. Your mother sent me a message that you've now left the order. Is that correct?"

"Yes, Uncle Giacomo, that's why I'm here. I need to talk to you."

"You can talk to me all day and all night. Where are your bags?"

"I only have one. Seminarians don't need a big wardrobe."

Giacomo laughed and instructed his butler to bring in the bags that were sitting on the stoop. Giacomo poured John a glass of wine and opened the French doors that opened out onto the patio and the breezes blowing in from a western Mediterranean. Whitecaps dotted the shimmering waters and a group of seagulls flew over, occasionally diving in the water to latch on to a small fish for lunch.

"Uncle Giacomo, I will tell you right out. I put in more than four years at St. Anselmo's, and about a year ago, I knew that it just wasn't for me. It's too boring, there's no excitement, no life. I'm not that kind of person."

"John, you don't have to explain this to me. I wouldn't have been able to stay there one day, let alone for years. I'm amazed you lasted as long as you did."

"I need a job. I think I've got a fairly decent brain. For two years, I was number one in my class. I've got some good ideas, that I know. I want to be in business."

"You must know that to be in business in Sardinia and make money and live in a house like this, you must be a part of the family, right? Do you get my drift? I'm not shocking you?"

"No, I'm not shocked. The church knows that its biggest bene-factors earn their contributions in ways that we would rather not know about."

"Then you may be perfect for this life. You've already got the honest, boring life out of your system."

Giacomo chuckled as he poured another glass for both of them. "You've seen the perfect side, and now you've decided you'd rather live with the sinners."

"I am ready for whatever it takes."

"I need a man who can carry some of our friends' products over to Corsica. Corsica is a funny place. It's filled with smugglers from all over France, Spain and England. The poppies are raised in Turkey, and the Syndicate in Sicily refines the seeds into heroin. Sardinia acts as a middleman, a stepping stone from one part of the Mediterranean to the other. We have to take the least risks of all. I line the pockets of all our Carabinieri on the island. You're completely protected on this side of the Straits. Corsica is only a little trickier, because our colleagues also have greased the palms there, too. What it takes is a quiet, discreet man who keeps his mouth shut and stays to himself. A man who doesn't go into bars and brag about what he's doing and how much he's making. You can be that man."

"Uncle, I'm prepared to do whatever it takes to get on top. You know that I loved my father, but I don't want to end up like him." Giacomo nodded his agreement. His brother-in-law had been kind and a good husband to his sister, but weak. He was not a man who could control his own destiny. The Caprera Capo wanted more for his nephew.

"You can earn your wings on some runs across the channel. We'll see how it goes. But now, let's eat. You must be tired."

Giacomo led John to a bedroom on the second floor, which had a balcony and a settee from which John could look out to the west and see the last lingering light of the sun as another day ended.

John Vittone accompanied his uncle on his daily rounds to learn the routine. Giacomo moved like a god in his corner of the universe. Each morning, he met the men who operated his gaming warehouses and whorehouses, and the runners who carried drugs from the bottom lands of Sardinia across the mountainous terrain to the northern coast, and then on a 50 kilometer passage to Corsica. Each underling reported the take from the day before and was given his marching orders for the next 24 hours. Giacomo spoke in a whisper, giving orders and listening, with one ear turned to the voice of his loyal employee, and his eyes always looking off into the distance. The bosses in the capital city of Sassarri backed their Capos 100 percent, and every man working for Giacomo was required to give his complete and unquestioned loyalty. Total obedience was the norm. Giacomo's life proceeded each day in an orderly and disciplined manner.

After two weeks, the elder man gave his flesh and blood an initial assignment. John's first ferryboat ride with the lining of his jackets packed with heroin was probably the worst that he would make in all the years he worked for his uncle. The instructions were simple. Go down to the boat slip in Caprera, sit on a bench and wait for the boat to pull in. Walk on as a passenger, take a seat on top and then exit the boat when it gets to Corsica. Take a cab to a local hotel and switch jackets inside one of the rooms. Skill was not required, just calm nerves.

He took his seat upstairs next to where the captain of the boat stood at the wheel, in an adjacent room. Giacomo arranged for John to travel on a Wednesday, when the fewest travelers were going to Corsica. Just the week before, the three local Carabinieri from the district had been given their envelopes stuffed with Lira and went away satisfied. But now, as John looked out the window at a couple of fishing trawlers tied to the pier, two unexpected visitors walked up to the counter that an old woman sat behind, selling pastries and cappuccino.

Two French policemen must have decided to take in the sights on the Emerald Coast that morning. There was something about the two that made John wonder if they were only passengers returning from an excursion. They both turned with their backs to the counter, resting their elbows on the edge and scanning the few passengers who sat before them. The tiny cups of espresso that they ordered went untouched, and their watchful eyes seemed to follow John.

The captain sounded the horn to tell the deck hands to untie the lines. The gears of the boat meshed together, and the boat slid off the pilings, onto the open waters. After a distance of four and a half miles, the French had jurisdiction over the ship and its passengers, and a red buoy, with a flashing white light, bobbing in the waves, signaled the demarcation line.

The nine-mile ride took about 30 minutes at 20 knots, but that was enough time to question the six occupants who sat scattered around the room, all of them quiet and pondering the Frenchmen's presence.

Maybe he had a sixth-sense warning, but as John had surmised, after passing the buoy, the Provincial police moved away from the espresso bar and walked up to the passenger sitting closest to him.

"Sir, how are you today?"

"I am fine, Officers. How about you?"

"Very good. It's a beautiful day. What brings you to Corsica?"

"I'm going to see my cousin. We meet in the evening for supper now that we're retired. Old men have nothing to do."

The two officers asked, "Would you mind if we quickly searched your belongings? Unfortunately, people nowadays like to come to Corsica for more than supper." Chills went up Vittone's back.

"Be my guest, no one's paid this much attention to me in a long time."

"Merci."

The taller one smiled and the pensioner reached down, pulled up his satchel and gave it to them, revealing a special spool of fishing line and some lures packaged in with a light sweater. "My cousin loves to fish. It's a present." The officers nodded. "Please stand up, Sir, and we'll be finished." The passenger rose, and they patted him down, especially feeling in the area under his armpits all the way to the jacket pockets below. "Sir, we are sorry to have bothered you. We hope that you have a nice evening in France." "Thank you. Thank you," he bid to both of them.

John was sitting on the opposite end of the bench. He was a new recruit, and now about to be searched and arrested for carrying Sicily's biggest cash-producing export. Absolutely nothing had gone as his uncle predicted. These were not cooperative, bribed police, but men who apparently had not been paid, or paid enough by any contacts on the other side of the Sound. Obviously, Giacomo was dealing with amateurs, or maybe he was an amateur himself. In the two weeks that Vittone stayed with his uncle and accompanied him on his daily routine, the old man seemed fat, jolly and complacent, taking few precautions, always meeting with his henchmen in the same places on the same day and worrying little about who observed him. There was no guard at his estate and he walked like a man without a care in the world. But the burden of hearing the details of his father lying in a pool of blood on the street had instilled in the nephew a suspicion about life and the people around him. He was nowhere near as trusting as his mentor had become. Outside forces had crushed his father, and John had spent the last 10 years trying to avoid the same fate.

Dressed in a black jacket and dark pants, his hair blowing from the slight breeze kicked up by the boat's steady course through the water, John looked more like a midnight spy on an espionage detail than a tourist. The Frenchmen approached and gave the same salutation. "Sir, good day. Where are you going in Corsica?"

"Only to walk around and listen to some French. Should be nothing too important, I'm afraid."

"You have no traveling bag?"

"No, Sir, I don't." John looked both men directly in the eye and smiled politely. As the shorter officer was about to ask him to stand up and frisk the jacket lined with heroin, John pulled open his jacket and at the same time, pulled down the turtleneck on his dark blue sweater to reveal a clerical collar, the same one he had worn as a deacon at the Seminary no more than 20 days before and the same one worn by thousands of priests throughout Italy. "You know, even deacons of the Seminary have to get away sometimes," he told them as he pulled his wallet out of his pants pocket to take out a card bearing the Vatican seal and a large cross imprinted across the middle. He held up the identification which bore testimony to his deaconship at St. Anselmo's Seminary. The same officer who questioned him seconds before, asked John, "You are a long way from Carbonia, Deacon."

"I took a bus. Believe it or not, they pay us a few Lira. In a few months, I'll be a full-fledged priest and assigned to a parish in the mountains. I decided to get in a trip now. I may not have another chance for a year or so." John smiled languidly. He caught the two officers off guard. In Italy, in the1950's, priests were still treated as holy men, with great respect. To search a priest, even a deacon, would be inappropriate.

"Well, thank you, Deacon. We are sorry to have bothered you. If you need anything in Corsica, our barracks is located only three blocks from the ferry berth."

"Thank you. May God bless you all." He put the identification card back in his wallet as the boat slipped into the harbor. He realized for the first time that he was really his own man, with or without Giacomo.

Standing in Room 208 of the Horizon Hotel, John asked the woman waiting to meet him to open the lining of his jacket. "I can't switch jackets now," he told her as she held the blue blazer up for him to put on. "If I meet those two policemen again by chance, I'd better be wearing the same jacket or they'll know something is up and I will never be allowed to leave the island." After she removed the drugs from the lining, he suggested that she go down to the desk and get a needle and thread. "I hope you are a good seamstress so that you can fix the silk lining of my jacket."

"Sir, this was supposed to happen fast, off with one coat, on with another, and we're out of here. That's why this always works."

"Always works? You have no idea how close I came to being in jail for years. Now, let's move. You need to sew me back up quickly." John, who would be known as Mr. Chairman decades down the road in America knew how to give orders. The slight, dark haired woman did as she was told.

That night, safely back in the house of his uncle, he recounted the day's events. Giacomo heard what a close call John had with the authorities. He praised him profusely. "Nephew, maybe that's why God sent you to me. I'm probably getting too old and sloppy for this life. I need some young brains in the operation and from what you did today, it sounds like you are my blessing." From that day on, John became Giacomo's partner and, needless to say, the partnership prospered greatly.

≋ CHAPTER VI ≋

CAPRERA, SARDINIA, 1957

THERE WAS A TIME in the early 1700s, when Sardinia was a kingdom, actually part of a Duchy. Its center was the massive and dense alpine forest that arose above the Mediterranean Sea, blocking out any light that tried to infiltrate its canopy of vines and leaves. It belonged to the Duke of Savoy. The huge trees, rising over 100 feet in the air, provided an impregnable fortress for the Duke and his followers.

Every year, he would send his soldiers out from their secret hideaway to pillage and conquer surrounding farms. The men who tilled their plots were virtually forced into slavery or, at best, became indentured servants. Their wives and daughters were taken away for nights on end to be raped and made the playthings of his soldiers who had not seen the light of day, let alone any women, for months. When the militiamen had their fill, these matrons and young girls would be returned, defiled and humiliated. They were, from then on, considered damaged goods by both their husbands and fathers. It was a sad commentary, because neither the husband nor the father would have been effective against the Duke's soldiers, even if they tried.

These peasants toiled in a feudal system, growing crops and raising livestock for slaughter, to fill the tables of the Duke and his ally, the Marquis of Montferrat, and the barons, counts and noblemen who helped them control the men and women who worked the fields and raised the virgins that these royal rogues fed off of.

Not much had changed in 200 years. Huts or shanties lay scattered every mile in every direction from the original manor houses. In Sardinia, in 1955, electricity and all of its appliances and conveniences had come to Milan and Florence and the towns and villages in northern Italy. But Sardinia, was a backward society, inhabited by workers and their families who lived in the age-old bungalows and gave 60 percent of what they harvested to the aristocrats in the great houses that a 100 years before had housed barons who managed the day-to-day affairs of the Duke. The descendants of Duke Victor Amedeus II of Savoy still lived in the walled estates in Sassarri, the provincial capital and headquarters for the mob organization on Sardinia. Their tenant farmers were the offspring of serfs, living without plumbing, running water, heat or other modern-day conveniences.

In northern Sardinia, John Vittone quickly moved up the ranks in his uncle's regime. He took over the vast warehouse that held the beer, wine and liquor that was distributed by Giacomo's trucks to inns and bars and restaurants all over the northern half of the island. Giacomo and his colleagues to the south in Carbonia, had divided their world into halves, and not a bottle of booze was sold in the northern half from which Giacomo did not exact a tariff. Operating a monopoly was easy. Without competition, John only had to make sure that the deliveries arrived on time and in the quantities requested. There was one and only one source of bottled spirits, meaning he never had to advertise or spend money to buy a beer or a glass of wine for a bar owner. They either went to him, or they went without.

Giacomo reached a position in his life where he no longer drove a Fiat or a Renault. Only a Mercedes would do for him and his nephew. John was proud of his car, for it gave him the status that he craved when his thoughts turned to dreams each night behind the Seminary walls. He loved to shift its gears and listen to it climb effortlessly up and down the hills and inclines of the district where he sold his wares. In addition to liquor supply, John also was placed in charge of the craps and roulette game down on the docks of Caprera and the whorehouse established in the run-down hotel across from his gambling establishment. It bored him to go to these places, for every night, the bettors always lost their paychecks at his tables and then walked across the street and threw their money away on women who cared nothing for them, but who gave up their bodies for a few minutes of sexual pleasure without any emotion. His customers got for their money only what they wanted, relief from an existence that seldom provided anything but boredom.

Vittone's real enjoyment came from driving in the diesel Mercedes and paying social calls on his different bars and restaurants. They got something for their money and even made a profit from whatever he sold them. He was glad to sit down and share a glass of wine with these people. There was a business relationship between them, and he enjoyed their friendship.

The one-lane, gravel-filled road that led to the Genoa Café wound its way through the bottom land, the best growing soil in Sardinia, and into the foothills where the olive and grape orchards flourished and meandered through the same hills. In May, the high grass shimmered in the morning with the nighttime dew, and abundant wildflowers grew in the fields. The Genoa Café was a gathering spot for the local foremen and their families of hired hands. The foreman made sure each day that everyone in the family, earned his or her keep, and that they were out working the fields from early each morning until sunset. Anyone found shirking the work was sent an eviction notice and given 12 hours to collect all of his belongings. The disgrace of being forced to live in the woods, in either tents or flimsy huts, was threat enough to keep every husband, wife and child working hard for that person's landowner. Nothing changed since the Duke of Savoy settled the area years ago.

Living in the seminary taught John Vittone many things, one being that he did not want to live alone anymore. He was determined to choose a woman who would not only bring him love, but who would further his career and be there with him as he climbed the social ladder.

Virginia Cappello was a peasant girl in the truest sense. Since the time of her birth, she was the subject of a marriage contract, an agreement that her family had with another family down the hill in which Virginia would be betrothed to their son when she was 18.

Vittone first spotted her while making his rounds to all of his bars and restaurants that Giacomo sold wines and spirits to.

She was walking alongside the road, carrying a bunch of wild red and yellow flowers that she cut to take back to her mother. As John's Mercedes turned the corner, he saw her on the side of the road, with the bow of her dress tied tightly around her waist, showing off her good figure. Her dress was pale yellow, and her black hair rolled onto her shoulders and flew in the air as she stepped along the clay path.

He watched her in his rearview mirror, and her face was perfect and sweet in a way that he had never seen before.

Without even thinking about what to do, he braked and the car stopped some 50 feet ahead of her on the roadway. John got out and started to walk towards her.

"Can I give you a ride?"

"No, that's okay, my house is only a few meters away," the shy girl told him, not wanting to get into a car with a man she had never seen before.

"I insist, even if it's only a foot, you are too beautiful to walk it," he announced.

His statement was so silly, she smiled and laughed. "Would you carry me if I am so beautiful?"

"Absolutely, all the way to Caprera," he answered, making the motions to put his arms around her and lift her off the ground.

"Stop," she shrieked, afraid that someone would see her and that Roberto Gaspari, the other party to the marriage contract, would find out that she was in the company of another man.

He did not want to offend her. "I'm sorry. I was only joking. Let me take you in my car."

"Sir, you must not come up here much. Every girl in this town is signed away for and even riding in another man's car is dangerous. Someone might try to kill you."

"Will they? You've got to be kidding."

"Not really."

"What do you mean, 'signed away'?"

"When I was born, my parents signed a contract agreeing I would marry Roberto Gaspari who lives less than half a mile from here."

"A contract to marry? Now I know you're kidding."

The young woman noticed that he was driving an expensive car and knew that accepting a ride would turn the tongues in the town wagging, but something told her to accept.

They rode the quarter of a mile in silence, and John only understood too well that she was very serious about this contract.

Vittone received a frosty reception when he pulled up to the tenant farmer's shack that Virginia shared with her brothers, sisters and her parents, but two nights later, Vittone reappeared at her doorway. His Uncle Giacomo gave him some advice on these commercial endeavors. "John, buy out the contract. Pay the suitor 340,000 Lira and give the same sum to her father. I guarantee you, that will solve your problems."

It was hard to believe that in the 1950s, women could still be bought and sold, but the war was only a few years past and the wild 1960s had not yet begun. Vittone took the advice and asked to see her father alone. "Mr. Cappello, I want to marry your daughter." The man was shocked. He did not even know that Vittone knew Virginia.

"Are you out of your mind?" her father responded. "Who are you?"

"I'm John Vittone, and I want marry your daughter."

"You cannot, she's spoken for."

With that, Vittone pulled his bills from his pocket. "I'll make your daughter a lot better husband than this Robert Gaspari. I'll buy the contract for 340,000 Lira for you and the same for Gaspari."

The man seated in front of him needed that money to feed his family. He never put away more than $50 in any year. He looked Vittone over. He was educated and nice looking, and the man had some social graces. He came from a much bigger town and drove a very nice car. He knew that Gaspari would be happy to get more than two years wages. "Ask my daughter. If she says yes, you have my blessings."

The two young people, who had known each other all of a few hours, went outside and sat in her father's grape arbor.

"Virginia, when I saw you, I was struck by a bolt of lightning. Maybe it was Zeus or Cupid who thrust it, but it struck my heart. I came here to ask you to marry me. I know it's quick, it's unreal almost, but I've never seen anyone who made me feel the way you do. Say yes, and I promise you that I'll make you happy for the rest of your life."

"But I told you, I'm spoken for."

He took her hand and held it tight in his and looked straight into her dark eyes. "I've taken care of that. Marry me. Love me. Have my babies. We'll live in paradise."

When she said, "Yes," she thought the words came from someone else's mouth, but she knew her own voice. They kissed softly on the lips, and later that night, her father raised a glass and blessed their union.

Giacomo, looking quite elegant in his black tails, carefully picked his way across the back lawn to the head table, where a six layer cake, with a miniature bride and groom standing on top, was in the center of a small table. All the guests were milling around waiting for the bride and groom to cut the cake. The bride's eyes sparkled. She could not stop smiling at the groom, and then all the family and guests.

"I must have this dance with the most beautiful woman on Sardinia, maybe in all of Italy," the beaming Giacomo beckoned.

Virginia looked up at Giacomo and loved him like a father. He was the kindest and nicest man she ever met. He gave her whatever she wanted, without ever having to ask for it. He seemed to read her mind.

She rose up and came around the table to meet him. He took her hand and led her out onto the wooden dance floor as the band played his favorite love song, "La Contessa." He held her loosely as he two-stepped with considerable skill. The crowd chanted their approval, watching the elegant Don Giacomo enjoying himself with his nephew's bride. He knew that this day marked the end of one stage of his life and the beginning of another. He was past the age when men still worked every day and he needed to pass the torch to a younger generation.

The young bride was perfect. All the little girls at the reception wanted to be just like her, and followed her around in total adoration. The music stopped, and the crowd stood up and applauded. Giacomo took his new niece, and together they bowed to the pleasure of the crowd.

"I have an announcement to make. My nephew must be a very smart man, because he has chosen for himself the one girl in the world that I would have picked out for him." The crowd roared and clapped. Virginia's face became flushed, and John sat at the head table with a happy smile on his face. He had done well in choosing Virginia as a wife.

"Today is a great day for me and for my family. Today we have accomplished many things. Our friends have joined us in this celebration, not just to celebrate the marriage between these two great people, but also to celebrate all the happiness and goodness that we have all enjoyed together over the years.

"To insure that these good times will go on forever, or at least for a long time after I am gone, I am making an announcement.

"From this day forward, John Vittone will be my partner in all the affairs of the family. We will be joined together forever."

With that, the crowd again applauded. Giacomo's leadership over the years had been good for the family, and they had no problem in swearing their allegiance to this new leader, John Vittone. Giacomo would not put a man in power who was not able, well-qualified and a leader, not even his nephew.

Vittone made his way across the floor and came up and hugged his uncle and kissed him on both cheeks. He stood on the other side of his bride, and the three of them locked arms and waved to the crowd.

Before all of the guests had left, John and Virginia hurriedly retreated inside to Giacomo's villa and changed into the sport clothes they would wear on the private plane that was taking them to Venice, the city of lovers. They walked out on to the balcony off Giacomo's bedroom where John waved to the crowd of well-wishers and then kissed his bride again. While Virginia blushed, John acknowledged the huge crowd once more and then disappeared back into the mammoth bedroom.

That night, John's bride wore a sheer white gown with spaghetti straps and nothing underneath. The couple set down their glasses of champagne, and John put his hands on her shoulders, kissed her and pulled down the straps.

The French doors of the room were open to the Venetian Lagoon, and the breezes off the Adriatic softly blew in. They laid together under the top sheet and between their lovemaking, spoke of the many children they would have and the beautiful life that they would give those children. It was a wonderful world.

≈ CHAPTER VII ≈

ROME, 1962

FROM THE FIRST TIME John took Virginia as a virgin, they talked and planned about having a child, in fact a number of children. Why not? They were both in their 20's, and John would always have a good source of income while his uncle lived or was not assassinated by an enemy. But that was unlikely, because Giacomo made sure that all of his people were happy, and that they all received a share of the pie. None of his men had to worry about providing for their families. They were paid every Friday in cash, and it may not have been a great living, but on an island plagued by unemployment, it was more than adequate with the added bonus of no taxes. Giacomo was fair to all, and that, more or less, insured loyalty. The other insurance policy for loyalty was quick, painful and sometimes deadly retribution.

Virginia expected that she would bear many healthy children who would grow up and work in their father's business. Her fervent dream was that at least one of them would go a university on the mainland. John envisioned a day when one of his offspring would rule Giacomo's part of Sardinia, and at least one of his sons would join the world of legitimacy and become a lawyer.

Lovemaking would occur five, six, seven times in a week, but the months and then the years, passed, and still Virginia could not give birth to a full-term, healthy infant. Four times in the same number of years of their marriage she got pregnant, and then, only a few months later, she would experience a miscarriage. Psychologically, it was devastating. Each time, she got excited when she found out she was expecting. She would buy clothes and plan for an arrival seven or eight months down the road, only to be disappointed a few weeks later. Her husband pondered what they had done to cause these problems, but true to his religious background, he resigned himself each time to the turn of events and told his wife that this was simply God's plan for them, and sometime in the future, they would be rewarded in one form or another.

Without her husband's faith, Virginia was doubtful that she could weather these emotional storms. Not only did it distress her to see the fruit of her body destroyed, but she saw herself as a failure, not being able to give John the joy he deserved. He was doing everything that he could for her, and she wanted in the worst way to present him with children. After the fourth miscarriage, John decided that having a baby was like anything else in his life. He must use careful planning, covering all of the possibilities, not leaving anything to chance. The next time, he would do as he did in his business; study every angle and plot a reasonable course.

Maybe a change of scenery would help, along with some expert advice, he thought. Within a week after their last effort, John and Virginia were on a plane to the university hospital in Rome, where Virginia checked in for a series of tests and John took a room at the famous Excelsior on Via Venato. John made it clear to his uncle that if he were ever going to have an heir, money was needed for doctors and hospitals, and on the last major drug score before leaving, they divided the cash 50-50. Giacomo never so much as murmured when John explained how they were going to parcel out the money.

John brought along a lot of cash for the medical consultations and tests, but unfortunately, this was 1962, and research in the area of human sexual reproduction was only starting to develop in Europe. Little was known about how to correct a problem when it was discovered, and the medical journals devoted only limited space to the subject matter. The old school firmly believed that any red-blooded, Italian girl could have a child anytime she wanted one, and that getting pregnant was never a problem.

Dr. Navarra was the leading authority in Italy, and John went straight to the best in the business. The fact that John was connected held little influence in a country where anybody with a title or money automatically got respect. Cash was the tune that Navarra played to, and John had brought plenty of it with him, since he was determined to find the solution to the problem.

An abnormality in the uterus is one of the most common causes of spontaneous abortion, and that was the area where Navarra began his examination. He then conducted a number of medical tests. It did not take him long to determine the cause of the termination of Virginia's pregnancies. At the top of the vagina and near the base of the abdomen is the uterus, a hollow, pear-shaped organ. It is here that the unborn baby develops and it is in the lining of the uterus that the fertilized egg is received. A sample taken from Virginia's body revealed that the lining in her uterus contained a congenital abnormality that Navarra had seen a number of times before. Her chromosomes were such that blood vessels, glands, and cells could not attach themselves properly to the lining so as to receive the egg.

Navarra received the results from the laboratory and the bad news from the head pathologist at the hospital. They studied all the results together, and their opinions were the same. Virginia Vittone would never be able to bear children. All of her pregnancies would end in miscarriage. It was Navarra who broke the bad news to her husband.

"Mr. Vittone, thank you for coming into my office to meet with me. I thought it would be easier to go over everything here, rather than in the hospital."

"Thank you for seeing me, Doctor. What have you found?"

"Mr. Vittone, I must tell you straight out that it isn't good news. There's no way to make this easy."

"Tell me. I'm ready."

"One of the most common causes of miscarriages of women is a problem with the lining of the uterus. That is the area where the egg starts to develop into a child and that was the first area that I started to explore. I took a sample from your wife's lining, and the pathologist, and we have one of the best here, has confirmed my initial diagnosis. Your wife was born with a chromosome problem that is not that uncommon. There is something in the lining of her uterus that does not allow certain cells to form and then the egg cannot be received by her uterus. The egg is getting into the area but does not attach properly to her uterus, and is being discharged. This also happens to your wife in her monthly cycles."

Vittone was stunned, and after a few seconds said, "All right, Doctor. I think I understand what you have told me. The bottom line is that my wife can never have a child. Is that it?"

"I'm afraid that is the diagnosis, but I do have something I want to discuss with you."

Navarra knew of a new chromosome drug that was written up in the two major Italian medical journals. Ten women had already taken it, and eight had borne healthy children full term. One child was born deaf, but there was no way for the scientists to tell if this defect was related to the drug or simply congenital. Those 10 women, whose backgrounds were all tested thoroughly, came from poor circumstances, and if things did go wrong, they did not have the power to seek any type of legal restitution. However, sitting in front of Navarra was John Vittone, a well-dressed, distinguished-looking man, who came with large financial resources. He was obviously a successful businessman or connected with some powerful organization. Navarra decided to handle this very delicately because of the circumstances.

"Mr. Vittone, I am going to tell you some things and then let you make the decision without any medical recommendation from me. You came to me for advice almost four days ago, and after many tests on your dear wife, she certainly seems a likely candidate to take advantage of some recent developments in the field. There is a drug that has been tested fairly successfully on 10 women who had the same problem as your wife. One child was born deaf, but eight have been healthy births. On the 10th, the drug has had no effect so far. It is an oral pill that is intended to correct this chromosome problem. It could have huge side effects, including death for the mother or child or both, paralysis for both or mental retardation for the child. But it has worked in certain cases about 80 percent of the time. That's all I know. If you and your wife opt to use this drug, again, it is not with my blessings because of the inherent risks. Do you understand?"

Vittone nodded and softly answered, "I understand, Doctor."

For almost an hour, Vittone and Navarra discussed the discovery of the drug and the experiments that the researchers conducted during the past 10 years. Privately the men in the lab thought the

risks were small, but publicly, they were being extremely conser- ·
vative, and they wanted no lawsuits.

"Doctor, this is quite a decision for both of us to consider. Let me
talk it over with my wife and I'll get back to you in the next couple
days."

"Mr. Vittone, there's no rush. Give this a lot of thought. Take all
the time you need. It's an important decision for both you and your
wife."

"The one thing is this, Doctor. As you have suggested, if the drug
were that dangerous, you would not have put it on the market. While
you're obliged to tell me all the negative aspects of the drug, I do trust
you doctors implicitly. I'm leaning toward using the pill, but the final
word is up to my wife, obviously. Thank you."

During visiting hours, John and Virginia agonized over the options. It was basically her decision because she was taking all the risk.

After two hours, she had made up her mind. "John, I've decided.
I am going to take the pill and not look back."

John did not try to talk her out of it. The next day, they left the
hospital with a dosage of the medication to be taken once a day.

Two months after Virginia Vittone left University Hospital, she
met with her doctor and had received the news that, once again, she
was pregnant, this being the fifth occurrence in her rather short marriage. This time, when she heard the news, she was not ecstatic, but
fearful and apprehensive. Her gynecologist knew that she was placed
on the new drug, and he had no idea what the results would be. He
reviewed the literature and the warnings with Virginia and could
only hope for the best.

When Virginia gave the news to John that night at home, he, too,
was serious and quiet. Now they could only wait to see what happened and put their faith in God. The waiting would have to last
right up until the minute that the child was actually born. Then the
doctors would give a number of tests and make sure that both the
baby and mother were fine. During this pregnancy, they would wait
anxiously and hope for the best, making no plans to buy baby clothes
or even provide for a nursery.

John worked less and less as the baby grew inside Virginia's womb. At night, he would put his hand on her stomach, and he could feel the baby kick and change position. That was always a good time, and they slept well on the nights when the baby moved the most. However, as with all pregnancies, there are times when the baby was not active and for one reason or another, it seemed as though the embryo stopped breathing. Every time that happened for more than two days, the young couple would make an immediate appointment and drive to the doctor's office, where a stethoscope would again reveal a heartbeat and a very viable, healthy child. They would be relieved and go home; the next time the baby stretched, they would be besides themselves with happiness.

It was the beginning of the 1960s, and new theories were being developed every day on how to create happy and healthy children. Virginia bought every vitamin that her doctors recommended and ate nothing but fruits and vegetables and drank pure spring water.

In an abundance of caution, two weeks before the baby's due date, John took Virginia to Rome where John again took a suite at the Excelsior, but this time with his wife. The only place in the world that he was going to allow this child to be delivered was at University Hospital with the best doctors and equipment available. Each night, they would eat at a corner table in the glamorous dining room where the tables were illuminated only by candlelight. They became super-stitious and did not want to jinx the arrival of their child in any way. They studiously avoided talking about going to the hospital or having the baby and made casual conversation about anything that they read in the newspapers or had seen while on a shopping excursion.

At 8:00 p.m. Virginia started to feel a series of contractions which were coming in large intervals of almost an hour or so apart, but John was taking no chances. Her bag that she wanted to take to the hospital had been packed for weeks. Together, they hailed a cab and went directly to the hospital. It only took about 10 minutes, and they held each other close and prayed for a safe, healthy delivery.

Several hours later, Virginia lay on a table in the delivery room, with her obstetrician on one side and a nurse on the other. She had broken her water two hours before, and the contractions were coming faster and closer together.

"Doctor, I can feel the body moving. It's trying to get out," she yelled.

Dr. Barbone had delivered more than two thousand babies. The quickest delivery he ever had was 7 minutes from the moment the mother got to the table. Other times, labor lasted for 10 hours or even days. This one looked like it was going to be pretty smooth, but there was still some time before the delivery.

The first-time mother groaned with every contraction as they were starting to come every 30 seconds. Dr. Barbone positioned himself at the end of the table, like a baseball catcher ready to grab the pitch.

"Doctor, it's coming, and it hurts. A lot!"

"Virginia, hang in there. Everything's in good position. I can see the head. Keep pushing and take big, deep breaths. Every third breath, try to push. All this baby needs is a little help. It's doing a great job on its own."

"Doctor, I can't take it. It hurts so bad, you can't believe."

"Virginia, I believe, but it's all going to be over in just a little bit. Keep breathing and pushing. Deep breaths."

Dr. Barbone could see the crown of the head coming out of the birth canal.

"I want this over," she screamed, as Barbone placed his hands around the baby's head and gently steered the shoulders through the passage.

"It hurts! It hurts!"

"Virginia, you're doing fine. I mean it. The head's out, and the shoulders are coming. You're almost through the worst. Keep on breathing and pushing."

"I can't. I can't do it anymore."

"Yes, you can. Just keeping taking deep breaths."

"I can't."

"You are … You're almost there."

"Please, let's go."

"We're going, Virginia. Take it easy."

With that, the baby's chest could be seen, but the sex was still a mystery.

"Virginia, I can tell you, the baby looks great."

"Doctor, is it all over now?"

"Not yet, but I can say that it's a girl. Here come the legs. Just keep going 30 seconds more."

When the child was in Dr. Barbone's arms, he looked down at a full head of hair and a wrinkled face, with light eyes that looked to Virginia like they might remain green like her's. The baby was two weeks overdue, which accounted for the hair, and the eyes were a gift of genetics.

Virginia took the baby from Dr. Barbone after he had cleaned her up and cut the cord, and rested Pia on her chest. "Doctor, look at those eyes. I think they're green, just like mine."

He responded, "I know. I noticed them the moment I held her up. You Sardinians are blessed for some reason. Maybe it's the water," he laughed. "Let me bring your husband in. I've seen a lot of waiting fathers, but he's one of the most excited new fathers I've seen in a long time."

Virginia looked up at the doctor and said, "We both did a lot of hoping and praying to make this baby happen, Doctor. Four miscarriages and an experimental drug. I'm pretty excited myself."

"Well, you two did a good job," he smiled.

John walked in and sat down next to his radiant wife. "What do you think, John?"

"I think she's the most beautiful baby in the world," he replied, looking down at the jet black hair and the eyes that still had iodine drops in them to prevent infection. "I'm so happy you can't imagine."

"John, I can imagine," she answered, knowing that finally all of her dreams had been realized. She had presented her husband with the greatest gift imaginable.

The new parents sat with their baby daughter in total bliss that day. They talked about all the plans they had for her, and how someday she would either be another Maria Callas or Sophia Loren. They would do everything for her to insure a great future.

≋ CHAPTER VIII ≋

CAPRERA, SARDINIA, 1962

THE STEEP SLOPES ABOVE Caprera afford to any motorist a spectacular view of not only the Straits of Bonifacia, but also of Mount Lincudin in Corsica, a 7,000 foot peak, rising over the southern part of the French island. After Sunday mass, John decided to take his five-month old daughter and wife along the narrow road that twisted through these mountains and turned up to a vista, where they could park and enjoy the royal blue waters below. It was in the late summer, and the beaches around Caprera were full of sunbathers and far too crowded to enjoy with their newborn. Besides, the visibility was perfect, and Virginia brought along a set of binoculars that John bought her for Christmas a few years back. Pia was asleep in the middle of a number of blankets, and the proud parents had packed a picnic lunch and a bottle of the best red wine Sardinia produced.

Very few people, if any, settled in the mountains and rocky hills near the sea because the grades rose out of the ground at sharp angles, and in the winter and spring especially, heavy snows at the summit and rainfall below produced landslides and floods. A house perched on a ledge could easily be swept away into oblivion in a second.

When Mussolini came to power, he put to work every able-bodied man in the province, building some of the best roads in Europe. In some spots, however, there was simply not enough room for two cars to pass in opposite directions, and one car would stop to let the other one pass through. A guard-rail or a set of metal posts served as the only barrier to keep a car from going off the road and rolling down a thousand feet of foothills. The land under the pavement was mostly clay and, in some places, volcanic soil.

"Honey, what did you make us for lunch?" John asked his 25-year-old wife, who turned into a great cook during the first few years of their marriage.

"A little cheese, salami and ham and the best bread you've ever tasted. I found a new shop down by the docks that bakes its own bread. It smells wonderful."

"We've got all afternoon. I told my uncle that we're taking off, and nobody will be able to find us."

"Do you think he can live without you for a whole afternoon?"

"He'll have to. Nobody knows where we're going, and there's never any traffic on this road."

"We're like young lovers," she giggled.

"What do you mean, 'like' young lovers?" he told her as he took her hand and pulled her over to kiss her.

"John, watch where you're going."

"I am, don't worry, everybody's at the beach. We'll have the road and this place to ourselves."

"It sounds good. Pia can sleep in the sun a little. We'll put her on a big blanket I brought. Please be careful, John, the road is so narrow and dangerous, I'm afraid."

John was just about to answer her when a small truck hurdled around a curve, forcing them over the edge. The car spun out of control and careened down the side of the hill, twisting and turning until it finally stopped.

Hours later, at the local hospital in Caprera, John and Virginia received the bad news. The baby was safe, but Virginia's hip had not only been dislocated, her pelvis had suffered what the doctor called a comminuted fracture, or a splintering of the pelvic bone into many pieces. John's bruised cheekbone would heal normally, but Virginia was told that because her of her injuries, she could never have another child.

The couple took the news in stride. They were grateful that nothing happened to Pia. She was still fine and healthy, and they gave all their thanks for that.

CHAPTER IX

MIAMI BEACH, 1968

FOR HER FIRST SIX YEARS, Pia Vittone had lived like an average small-town Sardinian girl. Enrolled in Sacred Heart Elementary for kindergarten, she walked every morning with her mother the three blocks to the school that was built on one of Caprera's side streets. The reed thin girl wore her standard parochial school attire, and her plaid skirt fell below her knees where it met her white, knee-high stockings. Her mother always adorned her hair with a ribbon that picked up one of the colors in the skirt, either red, green or yellow, and her jet black hair was parted down the middle.

Miss Portia DeRossi had a class of 22 kindergartners, all about 5 years old. That first week in school, the kids sparkled in their new, shiny black patent-leather shoes and starched white shirts and blouses, and they all had new haircuts. During that first week, Pia particularly stood out with her brilliant, green eyes. Portia walked with Pia to the wrought iron gate that stood between the sidewalk and the green lawns of the school, and Virginia appeared promptly at 2:40 p.m. to pick up her child when the bell signaled the end of another day.

Portia was holding the 5-year-old's hand as she led the class to the front gate.

"Mrs. Vittone, I really enjoy having Pia in my class; she's very smart and well-mannered. You and Mr. Vittone can be very proud of her."

"Thank you," Virginia responded as she took Pia's hand. "She already started to read books on her own when she was 3. She'd ask me about the letters, and I'd go over them with her a couple of times. She caught on very quickly."

"So I've seen. She's the only one in the class who can read a sentence and spell all of the words; and her coloring is perfect. Who does she take after in the family, her mother or father?" asked the 25-year-old teacher.

This was the first time Virginia met any of her daughter's teachers, and she was pleased that her daughter was doing so well. What was the answer? She really didn't know which side of the family Pia favored. Maybe it was John's, since he was the smartest man Virginia ever met; so quick to learn something new, he never ceased to amaze her.

"I think she's got something from both of us," came the diplomatic answer.

"Well, you've done a wonderful job raising her."

Virginia and John had, in fact, done a good job. They lavished the child with nice dresses, patent leather shoes and the newest toys and dolls from the United States and games, not just play games, but ones involving numbers and words and puzzles. This little girl was already thinking, and they gave her plenty to occupy her mind with.

The Vittones did not have a lot of friends. John only socialized with his uncle, and when he met a business acquaintance, he did it at an office or a restaurant; he never brought anyone home. One or two of Virginia's girlfriends from the neighborhood might have stopped by for a cappuccino, but Virginia always made sure they were gone long before John got home so that she could have his dinner ready and waiting for him. Mother and daughter spent a lot of time alone together, with Virginia reading to Pia and practicing the alphabet with her.

To Pia, it all seemed very normal. Her father got up at 6:30 a.m., dressed each day in a dark suit, white shirt and patterned tie, and left the house at 7:15 a.m. to go to his office and work with his uncle in the family business, supplying liquor. His routine never varied, and he came home promptly at 6:00 p.m. to eat. Only once in a while did he go back to the office at night. Pia felt secure and loved. Everything was constant in her world, with her father leading a rather quiet life, if not a little mundane.

In early January, John received a long distance call from a man in New York. "Mr. Vittone, you don't have to say anything, just listen to me. I am calling from New York. I'm friends with some of your friends in Sardinia. We know your reputation for good work. We need your services on something important, and I want to meet with you."

John was caught off-guard. Was this a trick or a set up of some sort? Had somebody from Sassarri arranged this call? Why was a guy in New York calling, when he always took his orders from Sicily, the bosses in Sassarri or his uncle? He was only a local man, and just a small part of a much larger network. For 11 years, he quietly labored and developed a thriving business, but always kept a very low profile; this was one of the reasons for his success. He did not like any type of publicity.

"I think I need to know a little more."

"I'm not going to tell you anymore on the phone. I'm sending you some first class airline tickets for you and your family. I'll pick you up at the airport in Miami. Think it over. It will be a very good experience for both of us, I promise you. Don't look for me, I'll find you." The man hung up, and John was left holding a dead receiver.

The next morning, at the breakfast meeting with Giacomo, he related the call he received.

"It's obvious," Giacomo's said.

"What's obvious?"

"Somebody in the States wants to do away with some of the middlemen, and you caught somebody's eye as a man who can do a deal by yourself. Getting rid of an unnecessary layer is one of the oldest business practices in the world. Less people to cut up the pie with."

"How are the boys in Palermo going to like that?" John queried.

"Not too well," his uncle replied. "You can't cut them out completely, and everyone will know you flew to America before the plane touches down. If and when you do get a plane ticket, we'll talk to Dominick, our main man in Sassarri, and see what he thinks. Believe me, you can't keep a secret in this outfit, and he probably already knows that you got a call."

"No, forget the bosses for now. Let's wait to see what these people in America have in mind."

"John, you're taking one hell of a risk. This could be a set up in America. The DeMatos in Sassarri aren't going to be happy if they think you're trying to go out on your own and cut them out," counseled Giacomo, who may have been lax in his operations, but never forgot the ruthless business practices of the Black Hand, the secret organization, and progenitor of the modern mafia godfathers he reported to.

"If I can't take a trip without their permission, what am I, their prisoner, their slave? They don't own us. We're all part of an organization. They take 90 percent of our deals anyway. I'm tired of doing all the planning and putting my neck on the line every day, and what do we get in return? Peanuts!" stormed John who was tired of taking orders from two-bit hoods.

Giacomo hit the palm of his hand on the table. "Whoa! First of all, we can go anywhere we want to, but just let our guys know about it. Second, we get something … nobody challenges our authority, nobody tries to cut in on our turf and our men do what they're told. Sassarri keeps order and the leadership there give us protection. They make it a lot easier to do our work, and they're not crazy. They don't go around shooting everybody. Believe me, John, I see, I hear what goes on in Sicily and the United States. It could be a lot worse. We have peace, and we make money." Giacomo tried to calm him.

John countered, "Not enough. Nowhere near enough for what we do. I'm going to see what the deal is. I'm taking Virginia and Pia. It will be a family vacation. Even an underboss gets to take a vacation. Right?"

"I see that I can't talk you out of this, so just be careful. That's all I ask," Giacomo told him. "In the meantime, I'll tell our guys about your trip just to keep ourselves covered at all times."

"Uncle, who's more careful than I am? Have I ever brought us any problems?" Vittone said in a quieter tone.

"John, maybe you had some luck, but you can't be lucky forever."

"Don't worry. I'll be careful. Like always."

The tickets arrived two days later. They were issued in Rome and were three first class tickets to Miami, with a note telling him to go to the Fountainbleu Hotel on the beach and check in.

John flew with his wife and young daughter from Sassarri to

Rome and straight to Miami. In 1962, Miami Beach was America's greatest tourist attraction, and they were booked into its best hotel, The Fountainbleu. Frank Sinatra played its main showroom along with every other top entertainer. Jackie Gleason produced his show at the local convention center. The deep blue, turquoise waters of the Gulfstream were a pleasant invitation for the Vittones to relax and enjoy the sun while in America.

The red light on John's phone in his suite was already flashing when they walked into the room with the bellman. John dialed the operator and she gave him a number to call.

"Hello," came the greeting.

"This is John Vittone. I'm at The Fountainbleu and I'm returning your message."

"Mr. Vittone, the Sardinian Prince. I hope you like your accommodations."

"They're great. Very nice."

"That's good. Why don't you and your family settle in. Have a marvelous dinner, see a show tonight. Three reservations for the Palm Room and then the theater show are waiting in your name down at the front desk. The best table in the house. Just take it easy tonight. How about we meet in the coffee shop at 11:00 a.m. tomorrow? Your wife and daughter can get a cabana at the pool; it's already been reserved for you, and they can swim while we talk a little. Don't worry, we'll be done in time for lunch."

"Sounds good," John replied "How will I recognize you?"

"Don't worry about what I look like, I'll find you. See ya then."

John talked this over with Giacomo for days before his departure to Miami. Who would want to use his services, and why was he being extended this fantastic invitation? No matter how many times he mulled it over and went through the list of American mobsters, no answer was clear.

The show that night was sold out. January was the height of the season in South Florida. It takes a little inside juice to get a table in the front row, but that was where the Vittones found themselves sitting. Sinatra, the Chairman of the Board of the entertainment industry, was singing his rendition of "My Way," and the crowd was mesmerized.

"Dad, who is that man?" John's daughter asked in her own soft way.

"That's Frank Sinatra, sweetheart, the biggest singer in America."

"Sinatra. He must be Italian. Tell me, Daddy, is he Italian?"

"He sure is, sweetheart. A lot of Italian families have come to America, Pia. Who knows, maybe your father will even come here to live with our family someday. How would you like that, Angel?"

"Here in Florida?"

"I don't know. Maybe New York?"

"I've never been there."

"I know that, silly," he told her as he pulled her up and put her on his lap so that she could see the stage better.

Virginia's dream in life was to see Frank Sinatra in person. She was in seventh heaven. Nobody back in Caprera would have ever believed that she was this close to the pop idol.

"Are there any Paisanos here tonight?" Sinatra asked with a smile as he scanned the crowd.

Virginia looked at John and he prodded her, "Go ahead, tell him where you're from."

"I can't," she responded.

Sinatra knew more than he was letting on. The man who arranged this head table had more pull than John Vittone could imagine. "I see a beautiful brunette right down here. How about you?" he crooned to Virginia. She turned three shades of red and answered back in Italian, "Yes, I am from Sardinia."

"A Sardinian. The most beautiful women in the world. Did you know that my grandmother, my mother's mother, is from Sardinia?"

Virginia shook her head and whispered back, "No, I didn't know that."

"What is your name?"

"Virginia."

"Virginia. Very beautiful. Virginia, come up here and help me with my next song."

"No. No, I can't."

Despite her protest, a young usher in a blue blazer with the

Fountainbleu crest was already at her chair, ready to pull it out and help her up. The crowd clapped and Sinatra kept waving his hand for her to come up. She gained a few pounds over the years, but she still had a wonderful, full figure, with her black, shimmering hair falling in waves below her shoulders. John urged her on. "Go on. Get up there, sweetheart. You'll never get another chance like this." Pia was spellbound as her mother stood up and walked the three stairs up to the stage.

Sinatra put out the cigarette and took her by the hand. "What is your last name, Virginia?"

"Vittone," she replied hesitantly, first in Italian, then in English.

"Mr. Vittone, you are a very lucky man. Stand up and take a bow." John picked up Pia with one arm and rose and gave a small wave to the nightclub audience and sat down. Sinatra first acknowledged Pia as a beautiful young girl, and then motioned for his arranger, Nelson Riddle, to start the next number. "Virginia, this song is for you," Sinatra told her as he put his arm around her waist and swayed to the beat of, "Strangers in the Night." The lights were bright and the crowd was a dark blur. Virginia could not stop smiling. The song ended and Sinatra kissed her on the cheek and asked the audience to give her an ovation, then another round for the family. John Vittone stood up and pulled out the chair for his wife. She was overcome, and so was he, but for different reasons. Someone had gone to a lot of trouble to lay out the red carpet for him and his family. This must be a man with a lot of clout, John mused, as Pia sat in his lap with her bright red dress with a white bow tied around it and a red and white ribbon in her hair.

"Mommy, can you believe it? You were with Frank Sinatra."

"No, I don't think I'll ever believe it," Virginia said as she leaned over to kiss the joy of her life. That night, both of the Vittones went to bed dreaming of what lay ahead for them in this new country. Their decision to move to America had been made when Frank Sinatra called Virginia up on the stage.

When John Vittone approached the maitre d' at the coffee shop a few minutes before 11:00 a.m. the next morning, he was now prepared for anything. After that reception at the dinner show last night, all sorts of pleasant possibilities lay ahead.

"My name is John Vittone. I'm supposed to be meeting another party here," John told the tuxedoed man in his best English. "Yes, Mr. Vittone, your party is already here. Follow me, please."

The man whom Vittone was meeting looked more like a golfer than a crime boss. Vito "the Duke" LaDucci was a short man, about five feet six inches, and was dressed in black pants, tasseled loafers and a white golf shirt with the name of Essex Hills Country Club in Westchester County on the breast pocket. "Mr. Vittone, how was your flight?"

"Very nice," John replied , looking straight at the little man.

"And how about your room?"

"Equally as nice."

"And the show?" John laughed and the other man smiled, both of them knowing that everything was prearranged with Sinatra. "I don't think my wife has come down yet. Whoever arranged that really made her very happy."

"Arranged what?" LaDucci asked innocently, but with a touch of a smile.

"Mr. Sinatra brought her up on the stage. I didn't think that he would do that for just any stranger in the audience, do you?"

"You never know. Frank's a very nice guy," LaDucci answered quietly.

When he called him by the name "Frank," the message was sent, and received loud and clear. LaDucci had enough clout to get John's wife a personal acknowledgment from the biggest entertainer of them all. John took a sip of the fresh orange juice that was poured for him.

"What would you like for breakfast, John?"

"Melon and prosciuto is very good to start. Then scrambled eggs and Italian sausage would be fine, with some dark toast too, please."

A waiter appeared instantly and took John's order. Small talk had never been John's forte, and maybe that was one of the reasons he stayed out of jail these last 11 years. It was up to the New Yorker to break the ice. LaDucci took a sip of coffee and lit a cigarette.

"Mind if I smoke?"

"Please," John told him, with an open-handed gesture signifying his approval.

"You speak great English," LaDucci told him admiringly.

"Thanks. I work at it."

"That's an asset in our business."

"So far, it has been in my business as well."

"John, I won't bore you, and I'll get right to the point. Certain people have been taking a good hard look at you and they like what they see. More and more, stuff is being distributed through Sardinia because everything seems to be protected there, and you're the guy who they say makes these things run smoothly."

"I do my best."

"You do very well, let me tell you. There have been a lot less problems moving stuff out of Sicily since you came along."

"If you say so."

"I say so. That's why I asked you to come here. I've got a big deal, and I need a real pro to handle it."

"I think that you should be talking to my bosses in Sassarri. They are the reason my uncle and I have a nice life. We're not independent."

"Yeah, that helps in this business," he said with a smile and took another hit on the cigarette. "You don't have to worry about Sassarri or anybody in Sicily. We can square away all of that. You can keep working with the men in Sassarri, but you'll never get out of any of their deals what your expertise is really worth on the open market. And, I don't want you to go independent right now; I want you to be attached. This is my proposition. You make a deal all the way from Turkey through Sicily, Sardinia, Corsica and into France and then from France to Baltimore, and if it works, you'll get your little piece from Sassarri and your uncle will get his little piece. After you accomplish this, over a few months, I want you to move to New York and set up your own separate shop, do some big things and make big money. I'm throwing in a bonus of a quarter of a million dollars if this deal goes down the right way and you move to New York. Don't worry, I'll make it clear to Sassarri that you're too good to stay in Sardinia. The five families in New York need you more than they do.

You'll work independently, but directly for the five New York families. Sassari won't give us any trouble and they'll be happy because they'll get their cut on the deal. You didn't screw them out of anything. In fact, you'll be working with them on future stuff, and they'll even be making more money. The one condition is that, if you decide to work with us, you've got to move off the 'rock.' That's what the guys in New York call Sardinia, a tough place to make a lot of money. How's it all sound so far?"

John had not anticipated this generous offer. "You've kind of surprised me with this. I need a little time to think about it. I'd also like to meet the heads of the five families, informally of course. I just want to be certain that everyone connected with the deal is in full accord and happy."

"John, I can understand that. You're a pro. I can see that just in the way you look. I want you to think it over, and I want you to do your thinking right here in Miami Beach. Look around. A little nicer than the old country. You come here and all this will be yours. You'll be at the top, probably making $300,000 - $400,000 in the next year or so."

"Why me?"

"There just aren't many guys in the world who do it as good as you and still live to talk about it. Besides, you know all the routes, you know all the people. You're good at what you do. You've got the brains for a big job."

"All right, I'll consider it. You obviously know my wife and daughter are with me."

"Of course. I also know you don't involve your family in your business."

"That's right."

The Duke stood up. "I'm going to leave now, but here's my number. It's in Miami. Also, here's my New York line. When you get ready, call me, but I need to know in three days because things are starting to move. If it isn't you, it'll be somebody else, but I'll tell you straight up, I'd rather have you more than any of these other guys. Think about it!"

John started to get up. "Sit down. Sit down." LaDucci grabbed

John's arm and told him, "We would make a great team. I'll wait to hear from you." Then he left, and John looked out at the white sands, aquamarine waters, and huge frothy waves pounding in on the surf and saw dollars—big dollars.

≈ CHAPTER X ≈

NEW YORK AND SARDINIA, 1968

THE MAN WHOM JOHN met was Vito LaDucci, the Duke of Queens, the main advisor to Tommy Pucchini, the declared King of JFK International Airport. Tommy Pucchini controlled the smallest number of made men of the five great New York families, but he had a strangle-hold on one of the most lucrative sources of income: hijacking cargo from JFK and controlling the teamsters that hauled away all of the goods. It was a money-making combination. Pucchini, though, always took a back seat to the Gambino and Genovese families, because of his inability to make inroads into narcotics trafficking. Half of the players on Wall Street were paying a couple of grand a week to snort coke, and the bigger families were running the operation and siphoning off the profits.

Tommy Pucchini never failed to read the *Wall Street Journal* every morning and pick up whatever information he could. When a big oil company like Exxon needed new sources of oil, they didn't bother to explore and dig wells, but rather they acquired a smaller company with reserves. It was called Wall Street drilling. Like the corporate giants he read about, Tommy Pucchini didn't want to invest the money nor take the necessary time to assemble a stable of top drug runners. It was easier to buy a system that was already in place. Tommy Pucchini did his homework like any good investor, and he looked over a 100 drug runners in Europe and North America, like a Yankees' baseball scout looking for shortstops in the Dominican Republic. A couple had been successful for over 10 years, but along the way, there were losses and arrests, and the forfeiture of goods and assets. These guys could make millions for a while, but eventually they all became a little sloppy. One man however came to his attention, a guy who seemed to work in the shadows and keep to himself, and in a quiet way, brought home the big scores without a lot of fanfare—that man was John Vittone.

The Duke heard over and over how John was able to successfully ship drugs through Sardinia after taking delivery from Sicilians on the southern end of the Island and passing narcotics to waiting vessels that lay in the same northern harbor where Giacomo killed the Fisherman decades before. Vittone's history was known. He was a former seminarian, now working for his uncle. A real pro was the way LaDucci described him. Dressed in a quiet and understated but expensive suit, with his hair neatly combed, he didn't show his cards to anyone, which intrigued LaDucci. He was one cool, well-organized "customer." When Vito analyzed how many drug deals originated in Turkey that were refined in Sicily and moved through Sardinia and over to Corsica, he realized that this man was an integral part of the French Connection. LaDucci also knew that Vittone lived very modestly and that his uncle and the bosses in Sassarri were keeping the bulk of the profits to themselves.

LaDucci immediately flew back from Miami. LaDucci sat inside the cherrywood paneled office in Jamaica and explained the situation to Pucchini.

"Tommy, the way I see it, this guy has got contacts with everybody in Turkey, Sicily, Sardinia, Corsica and has the French route covered. He seems to know everybody on both sides. We've got the States covered. What more do we need?"

"He looks perfect for us, but what did he say?"

"He said he'd think about it."

"Do you think he's jerking us off?"

"No, he's not that kind of guy. He carefully examines the entire situation, and that's why he's so good. But, he does want to make sure that all the families are in complete agreement; he just doesn't want to step on any toes, here in the States or at home in Sardinia."

"Maybe he's shopping the deal around to the other families."

"No, no, that's not it at all. He's being careful, and I like that about him. I'm telling you, he's a good guy. He doesn't want to rock the boat in Sassarri or with his uncle. He likes to keep the peace."

"You'd hire him?"

"Yeah, I would, in a New York minute. You're never going to find a guy with his brains and his class. He's one smooth operator. I think he really liked the idea of big money and a nice life. I'm betting he calls us back in a few days and says yes."

"Okay. We'll just wait and see what he says," Tommy nodded, not sure what John's answer would be.

John weighed the pros and cons. This must be a dangerous deal with so much money at the end. A quarter of a million was more money than he ever dreamed of seeing all at one time. Giacomo needed him, but wasn't willing to pay him what he was worth. Sardinia was boring and isolated; the United States was fascinating, even though it was a little bit dangerous. The police there were probably not as pliable as the Italians, but he heard that even the New York cops had their price. There were more factors, including that, with assuming a higher profile, he stood a greater chance of getting caught. But above it all, he wanted to be more than just a small-time hood for his family. He also wanted the best for his daughter, but the opportunities were limited in Sardinia. The best a woman could hope for was to marry a laborer. It was only in the United States that he could possibly give her more, including a wonderful education.

John, sitting in a cabana with Virginia, watching Pia swim in the shallow end of the hotel pool, looked at Virginia in a quizzical manner, deep in thought.

"So, what do you think of America so far?"

"I love it. Who wouldn't? They have the best of everything, these Americans."

"Well, my love, how would you feel about living here?"

"And leave Giacomo and the business? I don't really know, Giovanni. Whatever is good for the family, but especially for you, let's do." In fact, it sounded like she wanted to move, but was worried that it would create problems for John.

"Giacomo has people who can help. Leonardo is a good man," he told her, referring to the man that ran the liquor wholesale business. Leonardo wasn't a genius, but John rationalized that he established such a smooth organization for Giacomo, anyone could run it, and Giacomo would take pride in the fact that the New York families tapped John for the job after getting his uncle's permission.

"And how will you make a living?" Virginia wanted to know, fearful of anything that would endanger her economic security.

"I can get a job in America. Lots of other Italians have." For the past 11 years, Virginia harbored suspicions about how her husband really made a living. His late night business meetings, carrying a gun in the glove compartment of his car and receiving the nods and salutations of people who passed him on the street made her question whether her husband had some link to the "Black Hand," the "Honored Society." When Sicilianos came to America, many went into crime because that was the only business they knew in the old country. John was a Sardinian, not a Sicilian, and he seemed to be so discreet, that whatever he was choosing to do in America, she was convinced he would keep his plans very quiet.

He asked her, with a slight smile, and a twinkle in his eyes, "Could you leave your family?"

"I could always fly back once in a while, couldn't I?"

"Yes, that would not be a problem, since we'd probably be living in New York, and it's a big city with all of the advantages and disadvantages that go with the territory."

"I think Pia would like New York."

The last statement really clinched it for him. He called LaDucci that night and told him he was interested. The Duke told him he would set up a meeting in New York soon. When LaDucci reported back to Pucchini, Tommy felt certain that now he, too, could soon have a drug empire to rival that of the other families in Chicago, St. Louis, Los Angeles or any of the other big cities.

≈ CHAPTER XI ≈

LUCERNE, SWITZERLAND, 1968

VITTONE MET WITH his new employers and decided to accept their offer. To make his mark with Pucchini and ascend to a position from which he could make millions, he needed to devise a way to get heroin into the United States.

There was a pharmaceutical company in Switzerland that sold antibiotics to the United States. It was Henri Capanos, a salesman for that company, whom Vittone met in the lakeside city of Lucerne. It was a cold, gray day with temperatures in the 30s, and the lake was steel blue as the snow-capped gray mountains reflected into the waters. The fireplace in the café roared.

"Mr. Capanos, it is a pleasure to meet with you. I have done some checking, and they tell me that you are a very successful man in the medical world."

"Sir, I'm only a salesman," he lamented. "I go to America with samples and literature, I make a sales pitch to huge distributors and drug stores, I get some FDA sanctions, and I sell my products for a company. That's my story. I don't make millions like the CEO's."

Vittone had done his investigation well. Capanos let it be known that he was tired of making all the connections on the west side of the Atlantic and feathering the nests of his superiors while receiving a relative pittance in return.

"Would you like to make some real money, Mr. Capanos? Enough money that you may not have to work again and for not very much risk?"

"What do you have in mind?" the cautious purveyor asked, having been contacted by a fellow drug dealer who was getting rich by helping the underworld.

"It's simple, really. You provide me prescription medication bottles, just like the ones sold in drug stores with the labels, and for whatever medications you sell a lot of overseas. Once you give me those bottles, I'll handle filling them and transporting them. All I need from you are bills of lading on LaRue stationary."

"What if your bottles were to fall into the wrong hands, or should I say the right hands, and end up on shelves in pharmacies? What if someone were to take what you're putting inside?"

"I will have my best men in harbors like New York and Baltimore. The man I work for controls the teamsters in those cities, and they make sure that the cargo goes exactly where it's supposed to."

"How do I get all the bottles and all the labels that you need? My company will ask questions."

"Again, not a problem. I'll pay you what distributors pay you wholesale. Your company will get what it always makes. That price is just a fraction of what we'll make through my resale. Cheap nickel and dime men always get hurt. I'm not afraid to see your company make its share. It's just that instead of sending your inventory overseas, you send the goods to me. I'll repackage them and ship everything with your documents on freighters I control. You only have to get the stuff to me and help me with shipping. I'll handle the rest."

"But, it never gets to the distributor."

"Yes it does. I'm the distributor. I'll set up a corporation this afternoon and I'll pay you on 30 day invoices just like anyone else."

"This seems too easy."

John reflected on that statement. In a way, Capanos was right, but when John thought about it, Capanos also was wrong.

If Pucchini tried to pull off this deal, he would have sent two goons from Queens or Sicily with all the tact of a sledge hammer. They would not want to pay LaRue and they would screw Capanos out of his share once the deliveries started. They would threaten to kill him if he wanted money. Vittone was able to pull this off with finesse, and this was why he would become a millionaire drug trafficker who avoided the inevitable jail sentences his compatriots always ended up with.

"It's not hard, it's sophisticated. It takes men with brains like you and I to pull this off. We can do what others never thought of and can never achieve. You and I are just better at planning and thinking."

They drank their cognac down and reached a deal. "You'll get $200,000 for every confirmed delivery, Mr. Capanos. That I promise you, and it will be in any currency you want."

Capanos had not made that much money a single year in his life, let alone for making a single shipment. Financially, he would be on a par with the men who sat in the executive suites and bore the fruits of his labor.

All Vittone needed was a good chemist for the refinery in Marseille that he commandeered. Tommy Pucchini paid to send the sons of his associates and friends to schools in the Ivy League, and Robert DeAngelo was one of those sons. He repaid his debt to Tommy by taking Vittone's dried juice of the poppies grown in Turkey and through his wizardry, turned that juice into a refined state, a brownish powder that traffickers call pure opium. The powder was again brought to an extremely high temperature, and it was poured into a glass tube through filter paper. DeAngelo was now left with a yellow powder called morphine base, from which, in the last burning process, the greatest bounty of all was created, heroin.

Now the easy part began for Vittone. He took his refined product and filled it into the containers that, only hours before, contained antibiotics and which still bore the batch numbers, listed ingredients and FDA numbers required for entry into the United States.

Vittone made so much money on his first score that he gave a bonus to Capanos and turned over more money to Tommy Pucchini than the Don had ever seen at one time in his life.

≈ CHAPTER XII ≈

QUEENS AND LONG ISLAND, NEW YORK, 1968

JOHN VITTONE ARRIVED in New York like a conquering hero. The cargo made its way to Baltimore Harbor without incident and was distributed throughout the whole country.

Tommy Pucchini experienced his first real taste of drug money, seeing huge piles of 10s, 20s, 50s and 100s stacked a foot high on tables in front of him. He was now convinced that the drug money would provide him with the source of capital that would catapult him into the legitimate business world. For the past 20 years, he wanted to build a company owning car dealerships, apartment houses or whatever else the men whose pictures dotted the society pages owned. The business itself really made no difference, as long as he would be accepted by the prominent families of New York City. Capitalism was an economic system run by people with money, and those people were respected. Pucchini wanted that respect in the worst way.

Vittone and Pucchini met after the first week the goods had actually arrived in New York and started to make their way onto the streets. "John, you did it. You really did it. You got that stuff in with no problems at all. I don't know how you pulled it off, but you broke through. Do you think you can do it again?" he almost whispered to Vittone, not wanting to let Vittone know how gleeful he really was. The more dependent he became upon Vittone, the more money John would want.

"Tommy, I can do it again, but it takes money, good men and planning. I need a good set up."

"I'll get you the men, the right men, all you want. Quiet guys who know how to travel in the dark. The money's available. It's up to you to do the planning."

"Then let me use my Sardinians to make some arrangements. They need to be paid, too. I will need some real first-class couriers. Men who know their way around Sicily, the States, England, France. No amateurs. Guys with some moxie, brains and good looks who can walk around without attracting attention. No bums. I'll direct them. They need to be able to take orders."

"I can probably start you off right now with maybe 10 men from our family and then maybe a few more of the kids of our guys that went off to college for a few years and now want to earn some extra money. We pay them more than they are making now."

"I just need them to pick up, travel and drop off," John said non-chalantly. "Obviously the key is to not get caught. If they do, they're on their own. If they go into prison on a drug charge, they'll never hear from us again. There'll be absolutely no connection, a clean break."

"I understand." Tommy realized the downside very well indeed.

Vittone continued, "And, there is to be absolutely no contact between me and them. I'm unknown. They go where I tell them and drop off money. I don't know them, they don't know me. They're just blips on a screen. Do you think you can do that, after running an organization where all the guys are like family?"

"We all don't need to have a love fest to make money. We can be cosmopolitan like our European friends when we have to." Pucchini got the drift that Vittone thought he was running loan sharking, prostitution and numbers, and he was willing to swallow it for now, so long as Vittone was capable of producing big profits.

"Good, then let me scout around for a house and an office. I also want a business to run my money through so it comes out nice and clean."

One of the places that Vittone first looked at was Forest Hills, Queens. For 50 years, Forest Hills was the home to the U.S. Open in tennis, which was played at the Tennis Club. Originally, the club was the exclusive domain of blue bloods. As fortunes were made in the city by the sons of immigrants, the doors had finally been opened to the moneyed set from Southern Europe, and a name ending in a vowel was not uncommon on the membership list.

John Vittone weighed his options carefully. The Vittones visited their new business associates shortly after their arrival in the Metropolitan area. John and his family were welcomed with some reverence, as it was recognized in Pucchini's immediate family that this was a very talented man from the old world. Distinguished and formal, with the manners of a landed duke, John Vittone carried with him the mystery of Europe and the old ways. To the Pucchini's, living in 1960's Queens rough and tumble world where everyone they met spoke with a heavy New York accent and enunciated their words in dems ands dos, John Vittone was the epitome of the cosmopolitan man. When he walked into a room, everyone took notice of his elegance. There was something about him that bespoke of his importance.

Even though he lived the life of a middle class guy from Queens, Vittone's boss also was a very sharp guy. Tommy Pucchini saw too many of his colleagues sent to jail, not for violent crimes or theft, but for tax evasion. This was still a time when an underling would gladly spend his life in jail to protect his boss, and the Fed's best bet for a conviction, just as in the Al Capone case, was to pin a charge of tax evasion on the Mafia warlords. The best way to prove that was to compare a tax return carrying a modest salary, with the opulent lifestyle of one of these criminal chieftains. A man making $5,000 a year had a very hard time explaining in front of a jury as to how he had paid cash for a mansion, parked a Cadillac and a Lincoln in the driveway, and sent his kids to Georgetown.

To avoid that problem, Pucchini maintained the same cottage that he lived in for the last 15 years in Howard Beach, a section of Queens populated by the firemen and policemen who commuted into Manhattan each morning. This house was purchased after the War for $9,000, and the taxes were the lowest in all of New York. Pucchini drove a Mercury and his kids went to public school. He kept his cash buried in places no one would ever look. As long as he didn't touch any of his illegal goods, the odds were high that he would never be indicted for either drug smuggling or tax evasion. A low profile had always been the key to his success.

Vittone came to America to get away from his austere lifestyle and to live the life that he was convinced he richly deserved. Besides, he wanted his wife and daughter to be proud of him. When he came home, he wanted to walk into a house that let the world know that he was a winner. For John, this was simple. The money the Pucchinis paid John for securing the biggest payday in their careers had been deposited into a bank account in Rome, for Italy had not yet enacted an income tax, and his money was his own business. He could trace his money back across the ocean if anyone asked, and they could never show that he had evaded the tax laws of the United States. He was perfectly free to do with his new found wealth as he pleased.

"John, we are very pleased to have you and your family with us for dinner," Tommy told him, sitting at the head of a table, which was adorned with veal, sausage, shrimp and sole, a typical Sunday dinner for a second generation Italian family in New York. Tommy's father, now 78, sat at the other end of the table. He was never able to acquire the language of his new country, and while he was successful in establishing a strong foothold as the leader of one of the five crime families, when the day had come that the members of the commission stopped speaking in Italian or a Sicilian dialect, he knew that it was time to retire and hand the reins over to his son who was born and educated in the United States.

After the second glass of red wine was poured from the huge carafe that sat in the center of the table, Tommy's wife, Angelina, turned to Virginia and asked her, "Where are you and John planning to live?"

"I don't know, we looked around a little bit the past couple of days," the rather shy woman told her.

"How about right here in Howard Beach or Breezy Point?" Angelina said referring to another seaside community that sat near the Bay and Atlantic Ocean, and which was home to a lot of Italian Americans in the trades.

John did his homework. He was thinking of someplace that was nice, but very quiet, where he would fit in. "We're thinking about Forest Hills. It seems like a nice place. Quiet."

"I don't know how quiet it is Mr. Vittone. There are certainly a lot of four-lane streets now," Angelina responded.

"Please, call me John. I was thinking about maybe near the tennis courts. The streets are narrow and I didn't hear any noise."

Tommy inwardly cringed a little bit. If his wife thought that one of his executives was living in Forest Hills, then she would want a bigger place, too. But a man like John Vittone was not going to fit in at a block party in the neighborhood, with a keg of beer, in the middle of August.

"John, are you sure that won't cause any attention or bring anyone in asking about where you're from?" Tommy inquired. His family never dared to mention any mob connections around their house since Tommy always held himself out as an owner of several gas stations and home fuel-oil depots. The fact that they were never to draw attention to themselves was plainly understood within the family circles, and this is what Tommy was trying to tell Vittone in a gentle manner.

"Tommy, I have given that a lot of thought, but I have saved my money in Italy, and I am free to bring it here. I too would like to live quietly, without any fanfare. I've been thinking about buying a restaurant here to invest in. There's one for sale, a big one near a house I'm looking at."

Pucchini thought it over for a few seconds. "You may be right. In Forest Hills, you will be just another successful businessman working close to home. Maybe it's better to stay with all those social register people," he laughed. "Who knows? It may be good for business. You probably know all about European art. We've been here too long. The only thing we know are the Yankees and the subway." His wife realized that the Vittones were a world apart from her family, and as long as this man was supposed to be some genius businessman who was going to make her husband a lot of money, what did she care. She, too, would benefit if Vittone brought in a lot of cash.

Pia sat at her seat taking it all in. These people were a lot different than those she grew up with back in Sardinia. They wore clothes that were cheaper and more colorful. They reached and grabbed for food around the table, and they talked with their mouths full and in loud voices. They didn't seem to speak the same kind of English that her father did. A meal here was a 15 minute affair, like a grab fest, not the two hours that she was used to. People in Sardinia were a lot more polite and not so bold. She was hoping that she was going to like school here, but she knew that it was going to be a lot different.

"What's Italy like, Pia? I've never been there," Tommy's youngest daughter inquired. "It's nice. We live on an island, Sardinia. We have a lot of flowers and the moon is big at night when we look at the Mediterranean."

"What's the Mediterranean?" the other girl wanted to know.

"It's a big lake; no, bigger than a lake, like an ocean. I don't know where it goes, but you can see it forever when you look out. There's no more land.'

"Is it nicer than here?"

"America is nice. You have nicer cars. They're a lot bigger. Your houses are bigger. And you have color TV. You have a lot more stuff than Italy. But I still like Sardinia. It's pretty."

"Prettier than here?" Pucchini laughed at his daughter's question. "Baby, Queens isn't very pretty. We have a lot of concrete. Everything's modern. Where Pia comes from, it's hundreds of years old, there's a lot of art. I promise you, I'm going to take you over there soon. We'll go with your friends here, and they can show us around. How does that sound?"

"Great, can we go this week."

"Not that fast. Pia's parents have to get a house and buy a business. They have a lot to do, but we'll go soon."

Angelina went into the kitchen, and her two daughters and Virginia helped clear off the table. She emerged through the swinging door with a white frosted rum cake, that even from a distance, gave off the aroma of the rich, dark liquor. Pucchini did the honors and took a sterling silver spatula and cut the cake into big slices and loaded them onto his wife's best china. He wanted to lay out the red carpet for their visitors, in honor of the success they enjoyed with John's drug venture and all the wheeling and dealing. If he had truly known all the brain power that had been involved in getting the drugs into the country through LaRue, he would have had the affair catered. Tiny espresso cups were set next to the adults' seats, and Angelina poured the thick coffee for the guests.

The Vittones thought that meals at Giacomo's were large, but this dinner was really heavy. Virginia dreaded the thought of having to cook dinners like this every day in America. Pucchini pushed his chair out from the table and announced, "John, why don't we go sit in my TV room and smoke a cigar and talk a few minutes. Bring your espresso," he said, as he started to walk away from the table. Angelina poured him a fresh cup, and Tommy drew the pocket door closed so the two could be alone.

"John, once again, I have to tell you how happy we were with everything that happened. I know that we are really going to make beautiful music together, and we're going to get stronger as we go. I never talk about business in my house, because over here, you never know who is listening. The Feds have these wire taps. You must be careful. The police are a lot more sophisticated here than in Italy. We have our friends, but not as many as back home. I don't think I have to tell you too much. You seem to be very savvy and very careful. That's what I like, a careful man."

"I've always been cautious, and I want to keep it that way. You last a lot longer."

"I want you to keep a low profile. I don't have a problem with your getting a nice house, but just remember, the government will be looking over your shoulder at every financial transaction you make. That's how they get at us. That's why I live so modestly."

"I know, I'll be able to back up everything. All my money back home is in legitimate banks, and the authorities don't have the power to question how it got there. But I need a business over here to show income so that I can live freely. That's why I'm looking at the Ristorante Roma. Do you know it?"

"Yeah, it's a roadhouse kind of place. Big as an ark and a lot of seats. The last guy who owned it didn't know what he was doing. You can't make a lot of money on dinners. You need catering. Get the Jews with all those Bar Mitzvahs. Those are really money makers. No matter what the price, they go all out. Maybe you can do something with it. Get yourself a good man to run it. We may have somebody."

"I don't want to offend anybody, but I was thinking about a man from where we live to run the place. Of course, you'll have a piece. Whatever I do, you're in on. You know that." Vittone was knowledgeable in the ways of his American counterparts, which was just like back home. The boss got a piece of everything.

"That's fine. Whoever you want. We trust your judgment. But remember, some of my under bosses and Capos may not be too happy with your sudden success. There may be some jealousy. Keep everything that you do quiet. I'll keep them away from you so you can be your own man. Your operation is going to be a low-profile secret for the most part."

"That is really the way I prefer. I'll be using my people in Europe for everything until things get set up here. Then you will have to give me some professionals to take over."

"Again, I'll take care of that. Salute!" Pucchini toasted as the coffee cups clinked together. A partnership had been formed that would make millions for both men in the years to come.

The day that the Vittones moved into their new home was very special. Virginia took care of the decorating, and the furnishings were from the best stores on the Upper East Side. The living room was massive, and John picked out two beautiful Italian paintings to place over the long sofa. The dining room table sat 10, and was carved from the finest mahogany. Behind its glass panes, a china hutch held the best Italian cut crystal glasses and bone china. Virginia made sure that her daughter's room would be a showplace. A brass canopy bed was placed in the middle of the room on top of a pale pink oriental rug. A bookcase full of the classics on the top shelves and games on the lower ones rested in the corner.

Pia was enrolled at the best Catholic elementary school in the Borough, Our Lady Queen of Martyrs, and was able to walk the six blocks from her house to the school on sunny days. The school was comprised of children of families who could afford to pay a $1,000 in tuition and whose fathers rode the train every day into the city to sit at executive desks for the great banks, brokerage firms and insurance companies of America. Many of these men wore horizontally striped school ties, signifying their status as graduates of Harvard, Yale and Princeton.

John Vittone did not have a school tie to wear, and when he appeared at the social gatherings to raise money for the school that first fall semester, he stood awkwardly in a corner of the school's gymnasium, talking to his wife and holding a glass of champagne punch. When he looked around the room, he saw men and women with pale complexions and ruddy cheeks, with light brown, straight hair, dressed in dark business suits bought at Lord and Taylor, and their wives wore dresses to the knee with pearls looped around their necks. They spoke with a quiet reserve and a great confidence, and they were very sure about their places at the top of American society. Even his successful fellow Italian Americans assumed the bearing and style of their WASP counterparts, and through their education at places like NYU and Rutgers, they gained their entry into the comfortable world of corporate America, where jobs were guaranteed for life, as long as you played golf on Saturdays at the right country club.

John was making an assessment of what it took to enter these circles. He already had come a long way from Carbonia, begging for bread on the streets during the war. He knew that no matter what he did, he would never be 100 percent accepted by the people in this room, but he could still make sure that his daughter moved into their ranks. All it took was money and brains and the right appearance.

Each year, Pia's school sponsored a big dinner and dance, a black tie event that brought in enough money to keep the school up to the highest standards for any private institution in the city.

John Vittone did not tell his wife, but on this spring night, at the end of Pia's first year at Our Lady, he would bring them some respect.

After dinner was finished, Horace McManus, the chairman of the board of trustees, took over the microphone. "I would like to thank all of you for coming tonight. This has really been a great success, and we're going to give more than $50,000 to the general development fund." The parents and friends of the school applauded.

He went on, "I also am pleased to announce that five scholarships have been established to fund entire tuitions each year for needy students. This will be a 20 year program, and I'd like the donors to stand up and take a bow." He found John and Virginia at a center table and said, "Mr. and Mrs. John Vittone, would you please stand up so that we can acknowledge you."

Virginia felt her face flush, but John was rising to his feet and helping her pull her chair out. "Mr. and Mrs. John Vittone, we want to thank you for the gift, and we want to make your scholarship the centerpiece for an entire program here at the school." With that, and without a microphone or planning, John made a statement loud enough for everyone to hear. "It's a great pleasure for us to be able to do this. Our daughter has been going to school here this year, and we thank you for all your friendships." He gave a little wave, as the crowd gave him an ovation and the couple sat down.

In bed with his wife that night, he told her, "Now, when you go to that school, those people will look at you a little differently. They'll know you're somebody, and Pia will be a somebody too." He was proud for what he had accomplished.

≋ Chapter XIII ≋

NEW YORK CITY, 1984

Marymount College sits high on the bluffs, overlooking the mighty Hudson. Located 30 miles north of Manhattan, it has traditionally educated well-to-do Catholic girls, whose fathers made money manufacturing clothes or operating giant bakeries in the five Burroughs. It had virtually no scholarships to hand out, so its student body was comprised of rich girls looking not only for a good education, but also a job that would put them in the right position to land the right husband, one who came from "the right family," and was already starting to climb the executive ladder.

Sister Clara Malone was the dean of the school of liberal arts and doubled as a career counselor. She spent much of her time placing her girls in the best jobs in downstate New York. Three months before she was set to graduate, Pia met with her to plan her future.

"Pia, you have really accomplished everything that a student can at Marymount. I think the world is yours for the asking."

"Sister, from what I read in the papers, good grades aren't the only criteria in today's marketplace. It's hard for a woman to become successful in a major corporation. It's still an all-boy network, and they don't accept women that easily."

"But not you, Pia. You have brains, beauty and elegance. You can't miss."

"I don't know anything about corporate life. I need to be even more secure before I start out on a career path. One of those big companies could eat me alive before I knew it."

"You think you need something more substantial in the way of education?"

"Yes. I really do. My dad spoiled me all my life. I don't think I'm ready to go out and make a living just yet. I guess you can say my confidence level is still low in view of the horror stories I've heard from some of the girls who graduated last year," she said with a thoughtful expression.

"Well, you took all the right graduate exams. You got 96 percent on the LSAT, a 3.9 grade point average and you were president of the senior class. Every law school in the country would love to have you."

"But getting up in front of people, juries, other lawyers ... I don't know ... is that me?"

"Of course it's you. You're quick on your feet. Just do it. Don't worry so much. If you stumble once in a while, that's okay, we all do."

"The admissions office at Columbia Law called me and wanted some more biographical information."

"Call them back. Tell them they're really missing out if they let you go. Tell them you'll be the champion on their moot court team in two years. Promote yourself." *The old nun should have gone to work on Madison Avenue in an advertising agency and not into the convent*, Pia thought. She was really feisty for someone who lived such a secluded life. Pia decided to push her application some more with the admission's office.

John Vittone came a long way since his days in Sardinia, but he knew only too well that no matter how many donations he and his wife made, nor how many scholarships he created, he would always be considered part of the Mafia—feared, but respected, something like one of the Gambino family. Maybe he would be a rich man, but always living the life of a gangster, looked down upon by the same corporate giants who stole legally from Wall Street. For his daughter, Pia, he wanted more.

When Pia received over 1,400 on the LSAT, Vittone decided to use his "clout" to get her into one of the best law schools— Columbia. If he could be accepted in the Gardens, then getting Pia into Columbia would not be a problem, affirmative action notwithstanding.

Pete Calabrese was a great choice as the manager of Vittone's restaurant. Smooth, charming and good looking, he lived all of his life in Queens and his father had been a Democratic committeeman in Flushing for years. The father and son seemed to know everyone, including Mayor La Frontera, on a first name basis.

In early January, during Pia's last semester, Calabrese and Vittone took the subway to Morningside Heights on New York's west side. Columbia was surrounded by the tenements of Harlem, but the Ivy League bastion was made up of old brick buildings that bespoke fondly of the intellectuals that labored inside.

Vittone arranged an appointment with the dean of admissions of the school through the highest levels. Dean Winthrop told him that morning, "Mr. Vittone, Mayor La Frontera told me that I was going to be meeting with you this morning concerning the application of your daughter, Pia. I have looked over your daughter's transcript from Marymount, and I see that she's done quite well." Vittone had been proud of his daughter every day of her life, but this was one of his highs, sitting on the other side of this highly polished desk with the dean of a renowned education institution like Columbia. Pia did everything during her undergraduate years, including being editor of the college yearbook, and that should have practically insured the right to attend any law school in the country.

"Mr. Vittone, your daughter's grade point average is good, but I must tell you, there are more than 100 applicants in New York City who scored over 1,450 on the LSAT and who are in the top 5 percent of their graduating classes, and, I must unfortunately say, from schools more prestigious than Marymount. They include Harvard, Yale and Stanford. One of Pia's problems is that she lives in the city, and we only take a certain number of students from New York."

Vittone did his homework. Calabrese warned him in advance that this man was a snob, the product of an old WASP family who had members on the faculty at Columbia every year, for more than 100 years. Why should he give an entree to one of the top law firms in New York to this greasy Mafia Don? Dean Ethan Winthrop would let this newcomer know that "making your bones" just didn't count at Columbia. But John was prepared.

"Dean Winthrop, I know that every student in your school is as good or better than my daughter. I know that only the cream of the crop gets accepted to Columbia. I am prepared to do anything I can for Columbia, to offer any assistance I can give. I know that I am only a restaurant owner in Queens, but maybe there is something I could do to repay your kindness for admitting my daughter?"

With a wave of his carefully manicured hand, Winthrop was dismissive. He was determined to put John in his place and crush his dreams. There was no doubt that this girl could succeed if admitted, but she stood little chance in the face of this admissions officer.

"Mr. Vittone, Columbia has an endowment of four $4 billion. So there is just nothing you can do for us. I am sorry," Winthrop told Vittone, looking at him with his cold blue eyes.

"Dean Winthrop, maybe there is something I can do. Just the other day, in the local section of the *New York Times*, a reporter wrote that Columbia wanted to expand, but that it was land-locked. It wanted to take over an apartment building in Harlem, but the black political leaders were screaming that this was just another case of the rich taking from the poor. The building was rent controlled by the city. Only the city can condemn property and not a local, private entity like Columbia. I know people who would condemn that building and have the city sell the building to the college. All you'll have to do is devote a portion of the new complex to civil rights law and name the building after a famous African-American leader. I would be happy to sponsor a petition before the city council leaders to acquire the building."

All his life, Winthrop sat behind this desk, meeting with the admissions committee and reviewing reams of applications submitted by brilliant students. Nobody knew who he was or what he did. There was only one way he could leave his mark at Columbia, and that was by building something that would stand forever as a monument to Ethan Winthrop. He could see the prominently displayed plaque with the president's name and his name on it.

He answered quickly, "Mr. Vittone, you are correct. Columbia is interested in taking over the Heights Apartments. If you could accomplish that, I think that Columbia would be very much in your debt."

Vittone assured the dean, "It will happen at the next general meeting of the city council. Anything you could do for my daughter would be greatly appreciated." Dean Winthrop was a practical man.

He was not going to accept the girl until the deal was sealed. "Mr. Vittone, I'll be watching that meeting personally and very closely. We'll talk after that."

Vittone wanted nothing for free. He understood the rules of the game. "Very good, we'll get together after the meeting," Vittone answered as both he and Calabrese stood up and shook Dean Winthrop's hand.

On the way down the elevator, Vittone looked at Calabrese. "Well, Pete, what do you think?" Calabrese knew that this would be a tough job and told Vittone, "Winthrop wants his building. He wants to be a hero. If you deliver, Pia's in. But this is politically explosive."

"Not really," John responded. "We just need the blacks behind us. You know Congressman Connors from Harlem. I lined him up. Columbia will admit some African-Americans and develop its civil rights courses and name its building after him. He's friendly with a majority of the council members. You just make it clear to the mayor that a couple of strings are attached, and that Harlem is virtually getting its own law school. This will be a tremendous public relations coup for La Frontera. Columbia will be happy; Connors will be honored for an eternity, and Harlem will finally get some lawyers of its own. Just explain it to La Frontera that way. I've already got a group of Harlem labor leaders ready to buy into the program, and they've converted Connors to our cause. It's like a row of dominoes. They're all beginning to fall into line."

"John, I'll talk to the Mayor, but it sounds too simple."

"Most of life is, Pete. Just keep it simple and you'll win every time."

The city council of New York City met at 10:00 a.m. every Tuesday. On this Tuesday, a new item had been recently added to the agenda only a few days before at the specific request of the Harlem Congressman, Lionel Connors. A motion was going to be made for the city to pursue by the age old rights of eminent domain, the Heights Apartments complex. Sitting in the front row that day was Ethan Winthrop.

When the motion was called up by the council president for

deliberation on the floor, Connor's chief of staff rose and made his proposal. The city would take the building and sell it to Columbia. Columbia would house its civil rights unit in the complex and train local college graduates, who would be given preference in the admissions process. Additionally, the building would be renamed The Lionel Connors Center for Civil Liberties. This would be the cornerstone of a whole new learning community in the heart of Harlem. The mayor sent a memo to the council, expressing his total commitment to this matter and reciting how it would benefit the lives of every man, woman and child who lived in the upper part of Manhattan. The motion passed without any opposition.

John Vittone took the call an hour later from Pete Calabrese, telling him that the motion passed seven to zero. Vittone then placed his call to Winthrop.

"This is John Vittone. May I speak to Dean Winthrop?"

"Please wait. We'll see if the Dean is in," she answered imperiously.

Instantly, the other end of the phone came alive. "This is Dean Winthrop."

"Dean Winthrop, this is John Vittone."

"Mr. Vittone. I have some good news for you. The admissions committee has unanimously recommended your daughter for admission to the school of law for the fall term."

"Dean, that is wonderful news. Thank you for all your considerations."

"And, Mr. Vittone, thank you," the dean responded.

≈ CHAPTER XIV ≈

MANHATTAN, 1986

THE GREAT LAW FIRMS of New York historically prided themselves on recruiting only the brightest graduates from the top law schools. An editorship of the *Law Review* was almost a prerequisite. Pia had not only been an editor at Columbia, but she was the second in command. "Brilliant and beautiful, graceful and chic." This was the way one headhunter for the top agency that lined up superstars for the best corporate firms described her.

In Pia's last year at Columbia, Virginia went back to Sardinia when her brother died. John kissed his wife goodbye at JFK International Airport, and she flew back by herself for a two-week stay. John and his daughter remained home by themselves. She was completing her last year of law school and was extremely busy, not only with her law classes, but all her other activities.

La Motique had become the most popular restaurant in mid-town Manhattan for anybody who could afford $75 for an entree. John made a date with Pia that morning before catching a train to Garden City to meet her there at 6:00 p.m. at a table for two. The place was dark, and it had only a limited number of tables, discreetly separated from one another. It was the perfect kind of quiet place for him to broach the one subject that always had been taboo between him and his beautiful daughter: his true vocation.

At 6:00 p.m. the limo pulled up to the canopied entrance, and John Vittone strode out of the car in his elegantly tailored black suit with the pearl white shirt and gold and diamond cufflinks. His black hair was still as full and thick as ever, and he combed it straight back. The doorman looked like a Swiss Guard while he held the door open and John made his way toward the maitre'd.

While John always kept a low profile, and his daughter had no real idea of who he was, his demeanor spoke for itself. Here was a man of importance. Everyone who met him knew that he was a success.

"I am meeting my daughter here at 6:00 p.m. A tall, attractive 25 year old …" The maitre'd interrupted politely. "Yes, sir, your daughter has been waiting for you. Please follow me."

John was led to a table in the far corner. He instructed Pia to find them something out of the way where they would not be disturbed. She sat on one side of the booth. John took the man's hand and pressed $20 into his palm.

"Thank you, sir. Have a nice dinner," he appreciatively told Vittone.

"Thank you," John replied, and told his daughter, "You look great. Thanks for making the time for your old father."

"Dad, how could I resist. I'm with the most handsome man in New York."

"Pia, I don't know exactly how to say this, so I'll just get it out. As you realize, I have never, ever discussed my business with you. There are reasons for this, and it is better that way. You know that I own the Ristorante Roma, and that it's done well, but you're a smart girl, a very smart girl, and you read the papers and you hear people talk. You have probably assumed that there is more to me than Ristorante Roma, unfortunately, a lot more."

"Dad, I still don't need to know all your business. Things have worked out fine the way they are."

"Well, maybe you don't need to know everything, but you know that Uncle Giacomo and I were important men in our world in Sardinia, and when you were little, I wanted bigger and better things for me, for you, for your mother. So, we came to New York. I did what I had to do to give you the good life that anyone would want. I may not have done it the right way, according to the book, but I did it." He paused for a moment and went on. "You are going into the legal world now. Every firm in New York will want you."

"Don't be so sure about that. First of all, I'm not a man."

"Pia, times are changing; in fact, firms are now looking for women, for bright women, and you are one they will all want. We don't need to debate that."

"Dad, don't count your chickens so soon."

"Forget it. I counted them and scrambled the eggs already. Listen to me. From time to time, the papers have written about me, some good, some bad."

"Dad, it's okay. I don't even see it. I don't listen."

"You see me as your father, your loving old man. But not everybody sees me the same way. The newspapers see me differently and so does the establishment."

"What are you getting at?" she asked as she could not take the suspense any longer.

"You are going to become part of the justice system, a part of the vested interests. You need, along with your degree, a clean start. I want you to legally change your name so that at least you will have an even chance of making it on your own."

She was startled, and the words were blurted out. "I'm proud of your name. I won't change it. I'm proud of you. I love you," she told him with fierce determination.

"Pia, I know that, and I love you, too. But there is too much baggage being John Vittone's daughter and having that name. It will haunt you for the rest of your life."

She did not continue to protest. She knew it was true. Even though she was prepared to bear the burdens of her father, she knew that her father was right. "All right, if this is what you want, then that's what I will do."

"I have given a lot of thought about a new last name for you, one that has some class. How does Pia Vassar sound? Very traditional and distinguished, don't you think?" She smiled, "I like it as long as I know you chose it for me."

"I christen you Pia Vassar," John announced, holding up the stem of his glass. They drank to her new name. Several weeks later, the surrogate court made it official.

Pia now sent out resumes to about a dozen of the best firms in the city. One of those, Chesney, Starcloth and Vining, had been advising foreign nationals wanting to do business in the United States and Americans entering the foreign markets for over 80 years.

An old line, silk-stocking firm, it had been an all-male fortress for the first 75 years. This gradually changed, though, and women were now being accepted into its ranks.

Over the years, the firm's secretaries quietly accepted the sexual innuendos and salacious comments by the male attorneys, but female lawyers would simply not put up with these indignations. Surprisingly, it had not been hard for these neanderthals to adjust, and it was nice once in a while to be able to bounce courtroom tactics off of somebody who knew how female jurors were likely to react.

The law firm did not interview its applicants for associate positions like some other firms. Applicants were not required to send in resumes and appear for an interview; the process was too unsophisticated for them. This firm first reviewed the transcripts of the top 80 percent of the graduating classes of Michigan, Harvard, Yale, Columbia and Stanford. CSV differed from a lot of firms. It was more important for them to enlist people who had family connections and could bring in big business, rather than to mindlessly look exclusively at grades and activities. Some students might be smart, but they would never be "rainmakers," or those lawyers who could bring into the firm new clients. Secondly, there were no office interviews. Hours, days and weeks were spent developing a list of top prospects. These prospects were extended invitations to fly into the city and first see the offices of the firm and then to meet with partners and junior partners at the best restaurants like Twenty One, Top of The World and the Palm Room at the Plaza Hotel. There, under the scrutiny of the firm members, a young man or women about to be admitted to the Bar, was gently interviewed to see whether this person could be a team player.

Pia Vassar was nervously looking forward to her meeting with one of the named partners, Ronald Vining, and two aspiring junior partners at Ranato's, the best Italian restaurant on the Upper East Side. The dinner had been set for 7:00 p.m. Pia walked out of a cab about 10 minutes before the hour. Vining's group got there about a half an hour before to have a drink and talk about a case.

Pia was wearing a white linen Armani pants suit, which didn't totally reveal her long legs, but showed off her perfect curves. In black high heels, and with her dark hair flowing down to her shoulders, she cut an impressive figure.

When the doorman escorted her into the bar, Vining instantly guessed that she was looking for him. Unless she turned out to be incoherent or crazy, he made up his mind in that moment to hire her.

"Ms. Vassar," he both stated and asked.

"Yes. I'm Pia Vassar."

"I'm Ronald Vining," he said, shaking her hand, "And this is John Harvey and Doug Witherspoon, two other members of our firm."

"It's nice to meet you," she said, greeting all three with a soft smile and eyes they had never in their lives seen before.

"Let's go over to our table," Vining instructed and a server led them toward a private corner where they could talk without interruption.

"Pia, what kind of law do you want to practice? An office practice with tax and estate planning, trial law, research and writing?"

"Well, everybody at Columbia dreams of standing up in front of a jury and making a fabulous closing argument that wins a big case, but dreams and reality are two different things. I'm looking to go to work for a firm that will let me move into the position that best suits my talents."

Wow, brains, poise and cockiness, Vining thought. *She's not going to give the standard answer, like the rest of them.* The other two men nodded their approval.

"Well, at CSV, we'd let you experience every facet. We're not trying to pigeon-hole anybody. We want your talents to be used to the utmost."

They carried on a spirited conversation for the next 45 minutes, while having a glass of wine and munching on some shrimp and crabmeat appetizers.

"Pia, we'll get down to brass tacks here. John, Doug and I have looked over the papers you sent out about yourself. You have done it all in college and law school. We're looking for the best people, and it's silly to question you. You deserve better than that after what you've achieved. This may seem a little quick and forward, but I've found that some of the best deals I ever made were done quickly. I think I speak for all three of us when I say that we want you to join our firm. I think we'd all be a good match. You're a hard worker, a quick study; you make a good appearance, and you are a great writer, judging from the samples that you've sent us. We'd offer you an associate's position at $75,000." This was a huge salary to be offered in 1986, and she was surprised. She checked around, and this firm was not a sweatshop like a lot of others. They expected her to put in 10 hours a day, but not 20, like some of the other Wall Street firms. Vining also had a reputation around town for being a ladies' man, but on the other hand, he was known to be faithful to his wife and only flirted outrageously. He actually listened to what the women in his law firm had to say and gave them a lot of independence, treating them like equals. After only the first 15 minutes of the meeting she made up her mind to accept a job if they offered.

"Mr. Vining, I'm going to be frank with you, Mr. Harvey and Mr. Witherspoon. You might think it's a little presumptuous, but I did a little checking on my own, and everybody tells me you're the firm I should go with. I'd like to accept your offer." The three men were a little surprised at her quick response. Vining was not really sure if those were his own words coming out of his mouth, but he reached over and shook her hand. So did Witherspoon and Harvey. The wooing and courting was over almost before it had begun.

The group ordered dinner and a 40-year-old Rothschild. Midway through the meal, Vining had the wine steward bring a second bottle. Harvey and Witherspoon never saw the firm make such a quick play for an associate before, and they were both perplexed. Beauty and brains were not the only parts of the equation at CSV. Money still played a part, a big part. But Vining saw what he needed to see. *The money that she could make for the firm could be staggering*, he thought. Northern Italy's economy was starting to boom, and Pia would make the perfect link to that business. She lived in the Forest Hills Gardens, so she had to be rich. The only thing missing was that Vining could not put his finger on any of her family's relationships. It was almost like the entire family just suddenly seemed to appear on the local scene, especially Pia Vassar. The name Vassar, when plugged into his computer network, pulled up nothing. Little did he know that when Pia got her new name, she changed her birth certificate and school records under New York's laws requiring all official records to be changed to reflect the new status. But her academic and university background check was perfect, and he decided he did not need to investigate any further.

After passing the Bar exam, Pia was moved into a small office on the 18th floor of the newly-opened glass and steel building adjacent to the World Trade Center that housed the firm of Chesney, Starcloth and Vining. The carpets were gray, and the furniture was black with chrome fixtures. Ash trays and glasses carried the monogram of the firm, which was a CSV made in the form of a triangle. Cocktail napkins had the name of the firm written in blue letters on a white background. The firm brochure, which was in the lobby, carried pictures of all the partners. The senior partners were shown in posed informality, seated behind their desks or sitting on their credenzas. The associates had headshots only, and the junior partners were all grouped together, sitting around a conference table in a room with book-lined walls.

The young, female lawyer moved up quickly, learning the trade faster than most, and becoming a junior partner after five years. The case that made her a senior partner and a star in her own right had gone to trial four years before.

A man named Mike Chiang was charged with bringing illegal immigrants into the United States on freighters from Hong Kong. He was accused of stowing away 20 people in hidden compartments and charging them $10,000 each, netting himself a tidy extra $200,000, not counting what he made on his legitimate cargo. For years, Chiang was one of Ron Vining's biggest clients, and together they had fought battles over excise fees and tariffs and the city surcharges that New York charged Chiang and his import-export corporation. One of Vining's immigration partners made a living off of successfully getting green cards and visas for Chiang's family members who wanted to leave Hong Kong before the British Colony was turned over to the Chinese. But, since the take-over by the Communists on the mainland, it became an easier practice to simply smuggle cousins into this country.

The problem facing Chiang was not typical for the kind of activity that he was charged with. Normally, he would pay a fine of maybe $100,000 for smuggling these people. But in this case, the federal government wanted more. Under forfeiture laws, they wanted to confiscate Chiang's assets, and shut down his businesses here and deport him to Hong Kong. On one hand, the Feds weren't seeking prison time because Chiang never applied to become a U.S. citizen and that was good. The bad part was, if he were found guilty, within 72 hours, he could be returned to a place where his life, for all practical purposes, would be over. He had few rights as an alien if he were convicted, and this case was going to make or break him.

The trial went fairly well. The burden of proof was on the government, and Chiang stuck to his Fifth Amendment rights and did not take the stand as Vining and Pia advised him. The ship that was caught was flying a Liberian flag and was owned by a corporation registered in the Cayman Islands. The Caymans were notorious for their secrecy laws, and the government could only circumstantially tie Chiang to the boat. Title papers did not reflect that the Delaware corporation he owned had a hidden ownership interest. His name was not on the wire transfers into the bank accounts and was not on the corporate documents or the ship's registration. True, his goods and containers were found in the hold of the ship, but it was not a crime to hire a company to carry his cargo across the seas. The Greeks did it for third parties for centuries, i.e., the oil tankers roaming across the seven seas.

Vining was forced to pick an unusual jury. A number of prospective jurors candidly told him in voir dire that they were tired of people entering this country illegally and then taking jobs away from Americans. Two jurors said that Chiang was Chinese, and so were the immigrants, and this created bad feelings in their mind about his involvement.

These were tough days to be a trial lawyer, and unfortunately for Vining, he really looked the part of a slick lawyer. Vining did a good job in cross-examining the prosecution witnesses and exposing the fact that nothing directly linked Chiang to the crimes being heard. But Vining wasn't getting good feedback from the jury. Every time he looked over at his jurors, he was met by arms folded across the chest and blank stares.

The last prosecution witness had been called, and Vining announced that the government had not proven its case. As a result, the defense was resting without calling a single witness. Vining also made a motion to dismiss at this time. While the motion was denied, the judge would still instruct the jury that it was up to the government to prove its case beyond a reasonable doubt, and Vining knew that he had blown huge holes in the case. After court, he and Pia went back to their offices with Chiang.

He told his junior partner, "Pia, you did a great job cross-examining that expert on foreign shipping. You proved that he didn't have a clue as to who owned that steamer. It was all assumptions and voodoo. I thought the judge might throw the whole case out after what you did, but I guess he thinks that they got in enough facts to present a case."

"Ron, thanks for the compliments, but the jurors just didn't seem receptive," Pia replied.

"I don't know, Pia. They seemed hard-boiled about attorneys and the judicial system. But they lightened up a little when you got up there." Turning to Chiang, he said, "That's why I think Pia needs to do the closing. She's sweet, honest, innocent, and she looks like she's fighting for the Constitution and all that other stuff. She's not some high-priced looking lawyer like me. What do you say? We let her make the last pitch. Besides, there are a couple of guys on the jury who may be rooting for her because she's a lot better looking than I am."

Without any hesitation, Chiang agreed, "Ron, I'll go with your recommendation all the way."

She turned to the two men sitting around the table in front of her and said, "Okay. I'm ready. Let me put it together tonight, and I'll meet you in court tomorrow morning. I think we can win this thing." She folded all of her files into her briefcase so that she could take them home and work on her closing probably until about 4:00 a.m.

On the way out the door, Vining told her, "You'll do the closing completely and I'll just sit there and give you moral support. Mike will keep his fingers crossed and no matter what happens, we'll know that we made the right decision and won't look back."

Chiang got up, and as he went out the door, he turned to Pia and said, "Pia, I've got a lot of faith in you, and I don't want you to be nervous tomorrow. No matter what happens, I know that you did your best."

The next morning, Pia got out of a cab carrying a huge black briefcase and proceeded into the federal courtroom where Judge Halverson was holding session. She took her place at the counsel's table between Vining and Chiang and listened to the prosecution's closing argument. The government made its best pitch and told the jurors how Chiang was a man of commerce who was looking to make a profit and had strong ties to both Hong Kong and the United States. He had the motive, the opportunity and the intent to bring these people in and make hundreds of thousands of dollars at a time. After all, he was a business man, and it made no difference to him whether he was carrying shirts sewn in Hong Kong or human bodies; all he wanted was a profit. The circumstantial evidence was simply too much, the prosecutor told the jury. The entire hold of the ship was filled with Chiang's retail wares and it was admitted that they belonged to Chiang and his company. Who else could have gotten these illegal aliens onto the ship, and who could have provided them with food and water and enough comforts to make the journey alive? The prosecutor turned and pointed his finger at Chiang and told the jury that he was the guilty one, as he was the only person with enough involvement to ensure the success of the project. After 30 minutes, the young prosecutor sat down, confident that he put together enough of a case in the jury's mind to convict Chiang beyond a reasonable doubt.

Pia then took the floor. She carefully looked all the jurors in the eye. Did they believe in the United States Constitution? Did they believe that everyone, no matter where they were born or where they were from, had protection under the U.S. Constitution while they were in this country? Did they believe that everyone was presumed innocent until proven guilty? Would they follow the judge's instructions as they had promised to do when they were initially interviewed? Would they specifically follow the instruction that says that the government had to prove its case beyond each and every single reasonable doubt? As she explained, under the law of the Constitution and the court's instructions, there was enough reasonable doubt in this case to drive a truck through. Not one single shred of evidence showed that this vessel was owned by or connected to Michael Chiang. In fact, the government had not proven by one iota of evidence, what person or entity owned or controlled this ship.

She paced up and down in front of them, pounding away at her themes. None of the immigrants had ever seen or talked to Chiang. They could not identify him. They had given their money to an unknown man in Hong Kong. Chiang was not in Hong Kong when the boat took off. The boat was registered to a company that had no ties to Chiang. The crew had no connection to Chiang. In New York, the illegals were led to Chinatown by a woman, who they didn't know, and never saw again. Chiang's goods simply were loaded on by stevedore, and Chiang paid for the transportation just like any other customer.

"There's no proof of anything," she explained. As she outlined it, not one person testified that they gave money to Mr. Chiang. Not one person ever met or knew Mr. Chiang. He was in Florida when the boat came in. The captain never met him.

To convict a person on that evidence wouldn't just be inconsistent, it would show that America is not a place where all men can get justice, where all men are equal before the law. To convict Mr. Chiang would be to say that he's guilty just because he's from another country, and that's not the way it works here, not in our system. America is a lot better of a place than that.

Pia sat down and the prosecutor got up to rebut her, but the damage was done. Too much doubt was placed in the jurors' minds.

The jury had returned a verdict of "not guilty" in less than 30 minutes. Pia now had the corner, senior partner's office.

CHAPTER XV

MANHATTAN, JANUARY, 1998

MONDAYS WERE ALWAYS the toughest day of the week in law. During the weekends, clients would go to cocktail parties or weddings and invariably meet a friend or a cousin who was a lawyer, or who knew a lawyer. The client's case would come up in conversation, and somebody would always have some advice or opinion, and say that this case was a surefire winner and the case should be handled in a certain way. At 9:00 a.m. Monday, the switchboard would be lit up at CSV, with clients wanting to talk about some strategy in their cases that they learned over the weekend.

Pia's day was particularly tough. She had two motion hearings before noon, and one was with a judge who thought that all foreign businessmen were in the United States to take advantage of the U.S. statutes when it was to their benefit, and to evade U.S. laws when it was in their interest. She couldn't win that one. At 5:30 p.m., she was to attend a partners' meeting where, as usual, the major topic of discussion was money and fees, and the need to generate more.

One of the young paralegals in the firm was a woman named Alexandra Morariu. Her father was a Romanian refugee who worked hard enough to put his daughter through two years of night school for an associate's degree. Even though Pia was 14 years her senior, Pia and she looked like young sisters, and with their style and grace, the two turned a lot of heads when they walked into a gin-mill.

Pia ran into Alexandra before the partners' meeting, and they made a date to go to PJ Clarke's that evening after work. Clarke's was the bar where the up-and-comers hung out. Pia knew that she was going to need at least a beer—maybe even something stronger—after this day.

For 11 years, she successfully labored in the hallways of a powerful, corporate law firm, and in courthouses where victories were won by the most able and best prepared lawyers. It consumed her, and in ways, she knew that it had tarnished her laid-back attitude, and in part, her happiness. She would wake up in the middle of the night thinking about her pending cases and worrying about the next day's calendar of events. She felt sure that she was always walking through a field of land mines, knowing that eventually she would hit one, and that she would have to scramble like hell to repair the damage. There was never enough time to catch up, and she was always behind schedule.

This life left little time for a normal relationship with a man. Guys would come up to her if they were bold enough, or would be introduced by law partners or CEO's of the corporations she was representing, and they would seem interested. The face, the body, plus the brains, were all overwhelming, and they always thought that they had been struck by a bolt of lightning.

They would ask her out, but often she couldn't go for dinner because she had to work late at the office or had to be home early because she had to be at court early the next morning. The weekends were taken up by trial preparations and reading and writing memoranda. There was no time for a social life when you were on a fast, professional track.

When she did go to bed, it was rarely, if ever, with one of her suitors. To be touched by someone who barely knew her made her turn to ice, and she could not bring herself to respond.

One guy recently made dinner for her at his apartment, and had ordered the most beautiful flower arrangement from the top florist on Park Avenue; it was one of the nicest bouquets she had ever seen. The flowers were in the middle of the table and he lit the candles that flickered in the small dining room where he turned off all the lights. The dinner was catered in by the 21 Club and was superb. He served a 20-year-old bottle of dry, red wine with the dinner.

After they finished supper, they sat on the couch sipping brandy, and she talked to him about her life as a child and where she grown up. All he could tell her was that he had lived in suburbia, out on Long Island, in a nice house just like all of the other ones around it, and he studied hard and had been pushed by his parents. With a little over-achieving, he went to the University of Connecticut where he had earned an MBA. He never took the time to smell the flowers or walk in the surf or climb the mountains. The man had no heart, no memories, no feelings. He was just living a life that his parents charted for him years ago, and he was playing a role, without even thinking whether it was really for him. He wanted a girlfriend to become a wife because that was in the script that had become his life. There was no love left in him to give to that person. He didn't love himself or anything around him.

When he moved closer to kiss Pia, she kissed him lightly on the lips and told him that they would have to save the end of the evening for another night. It was perfect, really, but she had to go, because tomorrow, she had a big case and needed to be ready. Maybe over the weekend they could get together.

He was dejected because he set the stage for a grand finale. He walked her downstairs and hailed a cab for her, and she sat alone in the back, on the ride back to a night of solitude.

When she and Alexandra entered the glass-paneled door of Clarke's at 7:30 p.m., the place was pretty busy for a Monday night.

They both wore camel's hair-top coats, and every man in the place instantly realized that this was a very good-looking twosome. Pia ordered PJ's famous cheeseburger, french fries and a Heineken and her friend had a piece of fish, which was unusual for the most famous, upscale burger place in the city. Pia casually scanned the bar. A lot of guys were standing up with one foot perched on the foot rail and an elbow leaning on the bar, talking to someone seated next to them, all the time checking the place out for possible dates.

In the corner next to the window, in the last seat, was John F. Hampton, the Pulitzer Prize winning columnist for the *New York Daily News.*

John went to Princeton, where he played lacrosse and belonged to one of its best dining clubs. His father had, from his birth, planned a future for him, where he would go to Harvard, get an MBA, and then join an investment banking firm, to be posted for a few years overseas and then return to a major position and a million dollar salary. Hampton rejected this program. Growing up in a ten room, Manhattan co-op, he developed a love for the city, with its quick pace, sophistication and late nightlife. He had a feel for the people who would tell you "fuck you" to your face, but whom could be trusted; and, the ones who stood in dark corners, sipping a martini, waiting to stab you in the back.

John had the ability to get people to talk to him, tell him their life story. He told his father that he was going to use this ability and have a little fun with his life. The senior Hampton also was looking for some good times himself, and felt restricted over the years by being a stockbroker, working under huge stressful conditions. He told the son that he was giving up a lot of money, but that money couldn't buy him love, and that he had his blessings for whatever he did.

There was only one job for Hampton, and that job was journalism. Normally, a Princeton grad would have worked for the *New York Times*, but the paper, at that time, had a reputation for being "too stuffy." The real people read the *Daily News,* and unfortunately, it was those people who ended up on the front page with some adverse publicity.

Over the years, Hampton, established his own column, captioned "The Town Crier." It appeared five times a week and on Sundays. He wrote about celebrities, corporate titans and politicians. He made a name for himself, and won a Pulitzer Prize several years before for an expose called, "The New York Mob's Pact with the Mayor."

As he checked out the action at the bar, his eyes locked onto Pia chatting with her girlfriend, and he knew immediately that he wanted to meet her. It was one of those rare moments that inevitably leads to something bigger. She stared back for two seconds, and then returned to her conversation with Alexandra who was seated across from her.

She whispered something to her friend, "There is the best looking man over there at the bar. Right out of a magazine, and he looked at me several times during the past few minutes."

"How are you going to meet him?"

"I don't have the slightest idea. I'm lousy at this. I always get nervous and say something stupid."

"Tell the waiter to send him a drink."

"Forget it. With my luck, he's going out with Claudia Schiffer and she'll walk in right about now and pour the drink on my head. That's way too risky."

"Pretend to pass out. Maybe he'll run over and do CPR," Alexandra giggled.

"Will you stop it. He probably makes eye contact with every girl in this bar. Maybe he's gay, and I can forget the whole thing."

Alexandra turned her head slightly over her right shoulder, trying not too look obvious. She caught a glimpse of him, and whipped her head back. "I can tell you one thing, he's not gay. He's gorgeous. I'll just walk over and tell him you're in love. All he can say is forget it."

"If you move one inch out of this booth, I'll kill you," Pia said half-kidding, half-panic stricken that Alexandra would do just that.

The waiter brought the dinners, and Pia did something that she usually never did. "I'll have another beer. In fact, she'll have another beer too," Pia told the server pointing to her gorgeous girlfriend. Alexandra murmured, "This could be an interesting night."

The burger was huge and sloppy. They poured on tomatoes, grilled onions, melted cheese and ketchup. Since she didn't want to look like a slob in front of John, Pia took out a knife and fork and carefully cut the bun and ate little pieces. "You're very meticulous with that hamburger," her friend noticed. Pia murmured, "I don't want to get this all over me in front of Mr. Wonderful."

"Just wave at him or something. What do you have to lose?" Alexandra prodded.

"If he ignored me, I'd have to crawl out of here. No, I'm just going to play it cool."

"Then he'll get away. You're going to kick yourself tomorrow morning."

"Yeah, I know, but it's better than being humiliated tonight."

Hampton decided to make the first move. He stood up and walked down the aisle between the bar and tables, going as slowly as he could, trying not to look too concerned. About five feet from Pia's table, he glanced over and she looked back. Her reaction surprised even herself. She giggled as he went past.

"I blew it. I acted stupid. He's going to think I'm a nitwit," she lamented to Alexandra.

"No, he's not. He's going to know you're interested and it didn't cost you anything. What did he do when you laughed?"

"He just smiled and kept going."

"That's great. He could have looked at you like he was rejecting you. He gave you an in. Now follow it up."

"How do I do that?"

"Send the drink."

"I can't. I don't have the guts. I'd rather die."

"Pia, this guy's got it all. Don't blow it. Go for it."

"It's not me. I don't know what to do."

They sat there and ate while Pia thought of every possible option. Hampton took a seat and struck up a conversation with someone who looked like he was talking about some sort of football game going on that night.

"Well, I guess we've got to be in the office early tomorrow," Pia told her companion.

"Pia, this is your last chance. You'll never see this guy again. It'll be over. And you know that there's an attraction between the two of you."

"Forget it! There's nothing I can do. He didn't make a move."

Pia put on her coat and slung her pocketbook over her shoulder. At the last second, while passing in front of the bar, she reached in and plucked a business card out. Slowing down for a second, she passed Hampton and leaned over the bar and placed her card down in front of him and walked out. Neither one made eye contact with the other.

Sitting behind her mahogany desk at mid-morning the next day, Pia and Alexandra were putting the finishing touches on a brief that had to be handed in to the New York Appellate Court that afternoon. The deliveryman knocked on the open door to her office, while holding a vase filled with a dozen yellow roses.

"Is a Miss Vassar here?"

"Yes, she is," Alexandra piped up. "Put them right here in the middle of the desk," she told him excitedly.

Pia's pulse quickened a couple of beats and she leaned back in her chair.

"Go ahead, open the card," her paralegal coaxed her.

"I'm too nervous. With my luck, my father sent those to me."

"If you won't open it, I will," Alexandra went on to see if Pia would let her.

"Go ahead. Don't keep me in suspense," Pia replied almost holding her breath.

The young woman couldn't wait. The card read, "I'll see you at Clarke's tonight at 8:00 p.m. John Hampton."

Alexandra was happy for her friend. "You hit the jackpot. He loves you. He wants to marry you and move to an island in the Caribbean."

"He probably wants some free legal advice. He fell down skating at Rockefeller Plaza and wants to sue," came the sarcastic reply.

"Come on, you know he's interested. Anybody who looks that good doesn't need to send flowers. He could have a lot of people in that bar just by standing there. You did it. You got him."

"Now I'm more scared than I was before. I shouldn't have dropped that card."

"Pia, if you walk away from this, you're crazy."

All that afternoon, she couldn't think about law or cases. What would she wear? Should she change or just keep on what she wore to the office that day? She didn't want him to think she needed him. Should she get there early or late? Was it better to keep him waiting a few minutes—just fashionably, not too long?

She decided on the straight-up approach. She'd wear her work clothes and be there at 8:00 p.m. on the dot. It was windy outside as the cab pulled up and let her out at the curb. Her hair got blown all over the place. Great, she thought, he'll think I'm a mess. She got through the door and looked over to the corner. He was sitting there. He waved and flashed that full smile and his eyes twinkled with a sort of mischief in them.

"Hi! Mr. John Hampton?" she said quickly. "I assume you're the person who sent me those lovely flowers. If you're not, just tell me now and I'll just run out the door and leave the city."

"No, I'm the one," he happily told her with delighted body language.

"Please excuse my hair. I almost got blown over out there."

"Believe me, you look good whether it's windy or not. Sit down."

He pulled out the stool and she sat next to him. Hampton saved a spot for her which wasn't easy. "What do you want to drink?"

"A glass of white wine, thanks." Her mind was a blank.

John ordered the drink and turned back to her. There was something about this guy that she trusted. "I almost didn't come tonight. I didn't think I had the nerve to do it, until I walked through the door."

"I was scared you wouldn't show. I should have called you, but I chickened out. The flowers were safe for me. I'm sorry I made this hard for the both of us."

"That's okay," she said, drinking a little wine to calm herself.

"By the way, I don't know what I'm thinking, but let me formally introduce myself. I'm John Hampton," he said, holding out his hand.

"I'm Pia Vassar."

"Pia, it's really nice to meet you. What do you do?" he asked, trying to make small talk, having already looked at her calling card.

"I'm a member of the second oldest profession in the world," she said kiddingly.

Hampton knew that she was talking about her life as a lawyer, and responded, "It's nice how so many times the members of the second oldest profession come to the aid of the oldest profession," he joked back.

"Yes, it is," she laughed.

Pia broke the ice. Hampton asked if he could hang up her coat, and when he slipped it off her, he realized what a gem he found. *Brains, charm, beauty and a body, all rolled into one,* he reflected after looking her over carefully.

They could not stop talking to one another. The words poured out. She grew up in Sardinia, and her father had a small retail business. He wanted a better life for her and her mother, but she missed the water and the beaches and the Straits of Bonifacia with its purple waters and the pastel colors of the houses. She really missed the food too. She'd gone to Marymount and Columbia and worked for CSV.

He was impressed. All he really told her was that he was a writer for the *New York Daily News*. He left out the part about a wealthy father and a Princeton education and the Pulitzer Prize. This was a girl who was looking for more than money and prestige and he could sense it. It amazed him in the face of these money-hungry times that there was a girl like Pia still around.

The next two nights, he took her to the same great Italian restaurant. It was his favorite, and it gave them the privacy they wanted. The couple was in its own world, oblivious to anything or anyone else. They wanted to know everything about each other. Pia had never in any way felt like this in her life. If he had asked her to marry him on that third night, she would have said yes, without any hesitation.

On the fourth date, John chose a different venue. Gifford Hampton's partners for years kept an apartment at the Waldorf Towers. Located on the 36th floor, it had both a southerly and an easterly exposure. The lights of buildings and bridges were scattered throughout the most populated island in the country, like stars in the Milky Way. Pia and John ate at the Peacock Alley downstairs, and he was not sure what her answer would be, but he broached the subject right before they finished their coffee. "When we finish, do you want to see the view from my father's firm's apartment upstairs?"

She looked at him calmly.

"You know, that's kind of a gentle way to say it," he told her. "How about if I just say it for the both of us? Will you spend the night with me tonight?"

She didn't have to say anything further.

"Pia, you are the one woman I am looking for. I fell in love with you the first night I saw you. This isn't just some sort of fling." He was flustered. He could have any woman he wanted, and he was sinking fast.

"John, this probably would have been better if you hadn't asked me, but I think it's nice, kinda polite. As long as you don't think I'm easy, my answer is yes."

"If I thought you were easy, I wouldn't be going upstairs. You're special, and I mean it."

They didn't say a word to each other during the elevator ride and they walked into the suite. He turned on the lights. The apartment was decorated with great modern art that was hung from every wall. Abstract and modular pictures made any onlooker stand there and think for minutes or even hours.

John took her over to the mammoth windows that let them see out for miles. "It looks so beautiful from up here, so placid and perfect. It's when you get down on the streets when things get interesting. Up here, it all looks so simple. People live in apartments and drive cars, no problems ..." he mused.

"Do they all have to have problems? Do you think you can be happy in a relationship?" she asked.

"It's hard. Very hard. You've got to have two right people, and they have to be good to each other. I'll be honest, I haven't found it yet."

His candor was refreshing, but surprising. If she went to bed with him, there were certainly no guarantees. If things got bad, he'd leave; it was obvious that at this stage of his life, this was his way.

"Let's try really hard to make this relationship work. Okay?" she responded.

"I promise you," he said as he kissed her. When he put his hands around her waist, he could tell that she was scared; her body was tense.

"Do you want to watch a video?" he asked, trying to relax her.

"No, I want to be with you."

He opened her blouse slowly and it slid off her shoulders. The top of her breasts spilled over her black lace bra. He unhooked her bra and her bosom was bare. Her breasts were firm and round. Hampton put his mouth on her nipples as her head dropped back and she began to breathe hard.

The zipper in the back of her skirt opened easily, and he pulled her slip down along with her pantyhose. The only thing that was left between Hampton and her glorious secrets was a pair of little white panties. The plan was to lead her into the bedroom, but he could not contain himself. He put his hands on her round bottom and pulled her underwear down to her knees. There he stopped, and put his mouth between the apex of her thighs.

"John, I want you to take me now. Please. Right here. Now."

He undressed and laid down on the thickly padded rug in front of the wide open windows. She lowered herself on top of him. He filled her inside and they moved to the rhythm of their bodies.

They both felt each other erupt in one gigantic climax. Her whole body shuddered in complete satisfaction. She bent down and kissed him all over. He took her in his arms and pulled her tight to him as she laid on top of him.

"John, I don't want to wake up tomorrow and hear that it's over. That's not going to happen, right?"

"You've been hanging around the wrong guys, Pia. You're not ever going to be able to get rid of me. I just wish I could have spent the last 20 years with you."

"John, I love you. I know that this has been fast, but I know that I love you. Hold me tight all night long."

"I will, but let's get into bed," he smiled, and they turned down the blue and white sheets and settled in amongst the huge pillows.

Pia and Hampton became an inseparable couple. In the middle of the day, they would rendezvous at the Towers. At night, their bodies were entwined at his place or hers. On weekends, they went to the Pocono Mountains or out to Montauk Point. No longer was her practice the paramount thing in her world. Her life could not have been better.

~ CHAPTER XVI ~

QUEENS, NEW YORK, MAY, 1998

FOR 30 YEARS, John Vittone's partners, the Pucchinis, maintained order in their crime family and throughout their world. If a man got nabbed, they hired him a great lawyer, he went away for three years, and they gave an envelope each week to his wife. The soldier did his time, and when he got out, he was handsomely rewarded for his silence.

But things changed, and the changes came quickly. Wiretaps were placed in the cars, bedrooms and meeting rooms of the Mafia gangsters. These tapes became devastating evidence. The captains of crime were caught detailing their many escapades that they master-minded, and all of the grisly, blow-by-blow descriptions of beatings, murders and burglaries became part of court evidence. There was enough on these tapes to send these higher-ups away for life.

The most chilling episode occurred when Sammy "The Bull" Gravano turned on John Gotti. Gotti eluded the best prosecutors in the U.S. Attorney's office for years, through influencing jurors, tam-pering with witnesses, and just an outright lack of direct evidence on the part of the government. No one ever came forward to implicate him in a major crime, and to do so would have been suicide for them. Any potential witness for the government had to be mindful of the fact that Gotti was a man who apparently ordered the killing and dis-memberment of a neighbor who, by pure accident, drove over Gotti's son who was riding his bike on the street. Gotti ordered that the innocent man be quartered; what would he do to someone who intentionally came after him?

Gravano had been Gotti's right hand man, carrying out all of his orders for executions. As it turned out, Gravano personally directed the murders of between 20 and 30 enemies of the Gambino family.

He did it all for his boss, Gotti.

When the feds finally gathered enough evidence on Gotti and Gravano to charge them with multiple murders, they rounded up and arrested the boss, Gotti's underboss, and a number of other mobsters, all part of the Gambino family. Gravano stood solidly behind his boss, John Gotti, until Gotti asked him to take the fall. The feds had engineered a rift between the two, and when they approached Gravano with an offer to turn state's evidence, he readily accepted.

The look on Gotti's eyes in the courtroom when Gravano took the stand has been captured on TV, and broadcast over and over again on the evening and late night news shows. Vittone watched intently, and he clearly saw the hurt, disappointment and rage in Gotti's eyes. Gravano testified that Gotti ordered over 15 killings, and he recited the details of each one over a period of 10 days on the witness stand. Gotti sat through every word emotionless, but with the realization that he probably would have walked again, if not for Gravano. Sammy "The Bull" rolled over on the man whom he had sworn his loyalty to many times before.

When Gotti was transferred to the federal prison in Illinois, Vittone read the newspaper accounts of how he had been placed in perpetual isolation, in a cell, two levels beneath the main floors of the penitentiary with only a TV, a toilet and a fold-down cot. This was where Gotti would now live out every single minute of the rest of his life.

Sitting alone in his study on a Sunday evening, watching the show, "60 Minutes" Vittone knew that it was only a matter of time before he, too, would be "put away" by the feds, regardless of his care and insulation from the drug activity.

Sure, Vittone insulated himself from the low-level grunts that actually did the work, but he also placed calls to his capos to follow every deal, and they in turn would call the contacts who made the agreements between all of Vittone's runners. Vittone's name would invariably come up somewhere, sometime. His name would inevitably surface in other layers of conversation. All it took was one stupid soldier who turned on his boss, who then, in turn, would rat on Vittone, and it was over. The feds could offer too much, and the

Mafia was now upper-middle class. Capos had families and vacation homes and their kids went to college. They would turn on Vittone in a heartbeat to maintain that kind of lifestyle.

After thinking about it for several months, Vittone wanted out of the rackets. He knew that he could not be lucky forever, and that someday his good fortune would end. He began to plan the life that would set him free from the constant fear and anxiety of imprisonment and possible death. The only other person who mattered in his life, his daughter, now had a great job and had made it into the top level of corporate law. She was set, and now he could plan for his future. What he longed for was the one last great score that would bring him enough money to put Tommy Pucchini and himself on easy street, free of problems and worries. Maybe he'd even go back to Sardinia and live out the rest of his days peacefully.

However, the nightmare that John Vittone now faced was Sal Alegri. Alegri too, had come to the United States from Italy, but from Sicily, the fierce island to the south of Sardinia. In Sicily, you were either a peasant or connected to the mob. Even the most honest businessman had to deal with the mob in order to stay in business. There was no alternative.

Alegri was a hood from the time he was 12, being an errand boy for the local Mafia chieftain in his small town of Doprera. When a truck needed to be stolen, Alegri did the footwork. If a good beating had to be administered to send a message, Alegri gathered up a couple of punks and administered the punishment. His superiors saw no future for him other than as a low-level hustler.

Alegri left Sicily in 1993 to join a cousin who wound up with the Pucchini family in Queens. He worked the streets, collecting on loans and carrying coke from one corner of the Borough to the other. He had been warned by his cousin from the first day: keep your mouth shut and just do the job. For once in his life, Alegri heeded the advice. He had hated being run around like a kid by the bosses in Sicily, and he was determined to do better in his new home, New York.

A man like John Vittone did not pay much attention to Alegri, but twice, Sal was called on to pick up a good stash of cocaine from

JFK airport and drive it to a place in Newark. Things went off without a hitch, and Vittone stored his name away as a guy who might be developed.

Alegri worked his way up and was given a relatively safe assignment. Each Monday and Thursday morning, he would go to a different spot at Kennedy and pick up a package, drive it down the New Jersey Turnpike to Camden, New Jersey, right outside Philly, and deliver his package to an unnamed man. There was no more to it than that. He would drive back, and the problems about who got the final delivery and who got paid were not his concern. The rest of the time, he paid off numbers players and kept to himself.

Five years passed, and in 1998, Alegri was making $750 a week for his efforts. It was barely enough to cover the rental payments on a walk-up in Long Island City and a used Audi. At 35, with a paunch and the dark beard that he could never completely shave off, he was going nowhere. He made the move to New York and kept his act clean, and done everything he was told. But in his heart, he knew that he did not have the appearance to be a world-class courier, like one of Vittone's top men who traveled the globe in supersonic jets, staying at the best hotels and handling the biggest deals. With his Sicilian face, muscular body, hooked nose and large ears, he stood out as a hood, and nothing more than that. He was a smart guy, who didn't screw up, and he paid his dues. He was entitled to more, and he was now out to get it.

A bar almost directly outside the subway station in Long Island City, opened at 6:30 a.m. to serve shots and beers to its patrons who could not make it much longer without a drink. Men in flannel shirts and denim jackets were lined up when the bartender opened the front door, and they would sometimes stay there until late in the afternoon. The windows were tinted, and the sun never shone directly in. It was here that Alegri met with two other men who worked for Tommy Pucchini. They were Rocco Datale and Izzy Marucci. Alegri thought for a week about what he was going to say, and had rehearsed his speech so that he was ready.

"Gentlemen, I've got something I want to go over with you," Alegri announced, trying to sound like the chairman of the board.

Marucci and Datale never heard him speak with such concern in his voice.

"When I came to the United States, my good friend and cousin here, Rocco gave me some tips: keep your mouth shut, do your job, and you may go places. You've got to agree with me that I've been a saint. Whatever the boss told me to do, I did and I did it right with no problems or questions, just got the job done. You gotta agree with that."

Datale and Marucci shrugged and nodded. Datale piped in, "You're a saint. What's the point?"

"The point is, that I proved that I've got a brain, some experience and I can get a job done."

"At least you got the job done," Datale teased.

"Don't be funny," Alegri responded. "Listen to me."

"You two are the same—loyal, trustworthy, good soldiers. But do we get anything for what we do? Diddley squat, that's what we get, $750 a week. No more, no less. We got no life. And you know what Pucchini and Vittone live like? I drove by Vittone's place one time to see for myself. A three-story house sitting on a beautiful lawn up on a hill. All fancy streets. Dogs running around in little plaid jackets with maids holding the leash. The maids probably live better than we do and so do the dogs. Pucchini's in Vegas in a hotel that he's got a piece of. He's got a tan that's like bronze. He's got it made. He's got punks like us doing all the work and he's making all the money. Same with Vittone. He hides behind that restaurant front. That bitch daughter of his spends more for clothes than we make in a year, and she's not spreading her legs for guys like us."

"Sal, you're going crazy here. What's the point of this whole conversation? We know they got money, but what's the deal?" Datale asked, now showing his impatience.

"The deal is this, Rocco. I go to JFK and pick up a sealed bundle twice a week. I do it with no problems. I drive over 100 miles, no problems. I deliver it, no problems. You don't have to be a genius to figure out what's inside, and you know Pucchini and Vittone are making huge bucks. It's easy, because I do a good job. I'm a smart guy. So are you. We know half of Sicily. This is it! We get our friends to send some packages, and I do the same thing. Drive to Philly. Except, I get paid, and paid big dollars for doing the deal. Same car, same road, same everything. It's two deals at a time; one is for them, one is for us. Think about it. What's so hard?"

Marucci had not said a word up to this point, but he jumped in. "Sal, it's not as easy as you make it look. A guy like Vittone handles every angle. He knows the growers, the manufacturers, the refiners, the guys in the airports and the docks, the planes, the boats. He's got an organization, you've got nothing. Just your dick. You can't pull it off! Besides, what if Vittone finds out about it? He'll cut off our dicks and stuff them up our ass."

"You think too small. That's always been your problem. To make big money you've got to think big, take big risks. Pucchini does. He isn't any smarter than us. He's just got bigger balls. Your remember Louie back in Quasari. We call him up and get together. He can supply us with anything we need."

"We know him. He's a local kid. Never been out of that town in his life," Datale rebutted.

"I don't care where he's been," Alegri answered. "He can get his hands on all the coke we want, and he can stow it away on a plane to New York. All we got to do is to get the guy I leave the drugs with in Camden to come in with us and pay us. He'll love making the extra money. And you guys will love the money, too."

"Sal. Sal. Slow down. If word gets out that you're dealing for yourself, your life won't be worth two cents."

"Who's gonna know? The three of us aren't going to tell anybody and the guy in Camden, it would be suicide for him. No way anybody knows. We can get rich like those fuckheads we work for."

His buddies reluctantly agreed, but luck was never Alegri's friendly companion, and Datale was worried about this side dealing. Sal's boyhood friend delivered the goods via a Sicilian woman who swallowed the small cellophane bags and carried them inside her stomach. They would be discharged along with her other bodily waste when she reached New York. It was a dangerous assignment for her, because if the bags ruptured, she would be poisoned and quite possibly die. She was well paid for her efforts, and passed her packages to Alegri right on schedule.

It was on the other end that things went haywire. About 10 days before, Alegri approached his point man in Camden. The exchange of conversation between them seemed strained this time when approaching the subject that he discussed with the boys.

"You know, I don't even know your name," Alegri told the man in Camden.

"Its Bill. That's what everybody calls me." Alegri never in his whole life met a connected guy named Bill, but it made no difference to him. His name could be shit for all he cared, as long as they could make some money together.

"Listen, Bill, twice a week I bring you a package. I make a couple of bills, but not much. How bout you? Are you getting rich off these deals?"

"No, but I don't do it for the money. I do it because I love the business."

A comedian, Alegri thought. "I know you want to make some more bread, Bill; everybody wants to make more money. Am I right?"

"Maybe." *Getting an answer out of this guy was like getting blood out of a rock,* Alegri thought.

"Bill, listen, do you want to make some money? Are you interested in money, yes or no?"

"Maybe."

"For Christ's sake, are you interested?"

"Yeah."

"Good. Here's my proposition. I can score some coke and drop it off with my weekly package. If you've got somebody to buy it, you get their money and we'll split the profits."

"How much?"

"We'll start kind of small and see how it goes. We'll start with a quarter of a kilo. I'll get it for $30,000 and you get us $90,000 and we'll split the $60,000. That's not bad for a day's work. Who knows how high we can go. Deal?"

"Deal," Bill suspiciously replied, but didn't say anything more.

It all went as planned on the first try. Sal's Sicilian girl had come through as always, and the ride down the turnpike was beautiful. It was a nice fall day, in the 60s, and he was listening to a south Philly station that played hits from 20 and 30 years ago. Bill turned over the money, and Alegri was farther ahead of the game than he had ever been in his life. What the Pucchini's didn't know wouldn't hurt them, he figured.

Less then 24 hours passed after Bill's sale, and Vittone was summoned to a meeting on top of the Italian-American club in Ozone Park, one of the Queen's villages that was an endless stream of low-cost housing developments. Big street lights were stuck in the middle of the medians and at night, the roads had an eery, dim yellow illumination to them. Burger wrappers blew up against the curbs, and cans rolled around in the gutter. The place was light years removed from the stately homes of the Gardens.

It was a brick building, and it was really a fortress. The oak door was solid, and when somebody walked in everyone looked up to see who he was. Upstairs was off limits to the public. This is where Pucchini went when he had business to conduct with more than two or three wiseguys.

Bordering on the paranoid, Pucchini went to greater lengths than any of his rivals to keep security tight. Every other morning, the place was de-bugged by a nationally known security company that came by with big rods connected to what looked like Geiger counters. If any listening device was located within 500 feet, the machine would start to buzz like crazy. Pucchini never found anything planted, but he wasn't taking any chances. Twenty minutes before his meeting started at 2:00 p.m., the security company called back, doing the same inspection it had done at 10:00 a.m. Why take any unnecessary chances, Pucchini explained, for a measly few hundred bucks.

Vittone made it a point to come to this place as little as possible. He didn't want to be caught on video tape by the police, who he was sure had the place under surveillance, and he didn't want anyone to be able to link him to the organization. This was only the second time that Tommy called a meeting at the club in the past several years, so Vittone knew it must be serious.

Pucchini set up a comfortable place for them to sit upstairs for the meeting. A T-shaped table ran 12 feet lengthwise and around it were chairs for his associates. At the top of the T, Pucchini built a judge's bench on a platform, raised three feet higher than the table in front of it. He sat like a king, in a high-leather seat that swivelled, so that he could turn to face his subjects, or when he wanted to, rotate his back to his associates and ponder the wall, appearing to be studying all of the options that his guys had laid before him.

Vittone sat at the other end of the slab directly across from his superior. Between them were underbosses and capos and the group's counselor, called by some *consiglierie*, in the traditional form, but simply called Vito or "The Duke" by Vittone and Pucchini.

Pucchini started the meeting. "Thanks for coming over, and listen, if anybody wants anything special to eat, they'll bring it up. Food or beer, it's on the table in the back." He started the real business of the meeting. "Everybody here knows that we try to run a tight organization, fair but disciplined. If everybody does his job, all goes smoothly and everybody makes a living and we don't have any problems."

"Problems happen when people get greedy and try to take advantage of the family. One guy wants more than somebody else, the next guy gets jealous, and he starts grabbing, and everybody gets pissed off at everybody else and wars break out and people get killed. That's all bad for business and bad for all of us."

He continued. "Guys get paid for their rank and for the risks they take; the more risks, the greater the rewards, just like any business. Bill Gates makes the most money for Microsoft because his ass is on the line. When the government sues Microsoft for antitrust, they go after him. He's the one responsible for everybody else, and he gets the biggest share, but he also makes sure that everybody has a job and that their kids go to college and their wives have money in the bank."

Nobody in the room needed to be able to read tea leaves to figure out what was coming next. Someone in the family had stolen from Tommy, who had to get things in order and set matters straight.

Vittone had to admit that this was a good speech for this group. Pucchini made it sound like they were all corporate executives at General Motors, and everything would fall in line, if they followed the corporate line.

"One of our members has gone out to deal on his own. Why, I don't know. We pay him well. We make it easy for him to do his job. We shield him from the police. He has a nice life, but he is a newcomer, and may be not familiar with our ways. The man I speak of is Sal Alegri."

Vittone's heart sank. Alegri had worked his way up to working for Vittone, and he was now John's responsibility. John checked this guy out so carefully, and he seemed good. Quiet, unassuming and with no wife, no kids, meaning he had no financial problems. All he had to do was work a couple of days a week and he didn't even have to think.

Alegri was stupid. The "Bill" he met appeared to be a guy working for the Philadelphia group with no ties to Pucchini. He looked like a small cog, like Alegri, who could use a few extra dollars a week. Alegri did not know, though, how far Pucchini's long arms extended. It was true that Bill was a nobody like Alegri, but a nobody with an ace in the hole. Bill was really Carmine Lupo, a three-time convicted felon on larceny charges for robbing either gas stations or convenience stores. Each time he was apprehended, he became hotter and nobody in the organization would touch him.

Pucchini was stuck with him because he was married to Pucchini's favorite cousin, Patricia, whom he had grown up with. At Christmas and Thanksgiving, they were the two who would always sneak under the dining room table loaded with food and tie the shoelaces of their uncles together. She loved him more like a brother, and when her husband had no job, Pucchini ordered Bill to do pickups and nothing more.

Lupo realized his own limitations, and knew that without Pucchini, he'd be driving a truck for a South Jersey farm probably loaded with beans or some produce and getting paid minimum wage. The job he had now was like heaven. He was a gopher who made a good living with no responsibility, and he worked only a few hours a week. At his age, he was not going to do anything to jeopardize this, and he was aware of Pucchini's nickname, "Boots," because he put his rivals in concrete slabs. Pucchini was not a man he would ever cross, and besides, Pucchini was good to him.

It took all of an hour for the severity and shock of Bill's deeds to sink in and for him to contact Pucchini after his deal with Alegri went down. The call was short and to the point. "Mr. Pucchini, I don't know if you remember me, but, I'm Bill. You know, Carmine Lupo, Patricia's husband. It's been a while."

Pucchini could be a charmer when he wanted to be. "Bill, what are you talking about? I saw you two months ago at Pinky's wedding. How have you been? How's Pat and the kids?"

"They're great, real good Mr. Pucchini. Thanks for askin! Mr. Pucchini, you've done a lot for me, and I want you to know I appreciate it. I would never do anything to hurt you."

"Bill, what's the problem?" Pucchini asked, hoping that he wasn't going to need to make bail.

"Mr. Pucchini, there's a problem. I don't know how to put it."

"Just say it. Get it out," Tommy implored. With that, Lupo spilled out his guts and told the whole story about Alegri and his self-dealing.

Pucchini, to his anger, now had to relate what Bill told him. "We have a fink amongst us," Pucchini solemnly pronounced.

Pucchini could be overly dramatic when it served his purposes. Guys had been doing side deals from the beginning of time, but when Tommy caught them, especially cutting in on his lucrative drug trade, he was determined that it had to be nipped in the bud immediately. Drugs were the lifeblood of his personal empire, and gave him the economic strength to keep his rivals at bay. Once he found out how much money he could make from the narcotics trade, he was not about to let anyone cut into his business.

"Who is this Sal Alegri, anyway?" Tommy inquired, thinking maybe he wasn't really part of the family.

"He's been around about five years; he came over from Sicily," Angelo Guerra, an underboss, spoke up. "He's a driver, a bag boy. He keeps to himself; he's never complained and always seemed loyal. But who knows what's buggin' him now. We can't have guys working their own deals against us. He'll get himself busted, and we'll all go down."

The family members turned very quiet. Everybody knew that

Alegri was one of Vittone's soldiers. It was now Vittone's responsibility to deal with the matter. The eight men around the table did not have any idea what Vittone's response would be. Since coming to New York, absolutely no one held his cards as close to his vest as Vittone. He never tipped his hand once. He didn't socialize with any of the other capos. He didn't go to their baptisms or confirmations, not even to their weddings. The only one he dealt with was Tommy. He was the biggest money maker in the family, and all the men at the table knew it and respected him. Not one amongst them wanted to screw up a good thing. He did as he pleased, and as long as he produced the big bucks, no one else dared to look any further.

But now, he was being questioned by Pucchini. Vittone never said one bad word about Pucchini, and Pucchini knew that John had no aspirations to take over. Tommy was tired of always being the lead man; he wanted John to take some of the heat for once all the way down to his balls.

Pucchini had gotten as far as he had by knowing his men. He knew how John would react, and it was textbook material.

"Tommy," Vittone responded, with a low, throaty voice from the far end of the table. "This is my man, and he's my problem. I wish that I uncovered this first, but it's not important. We found out and we're a family. This is my responsibility, and I'll deal with it. No one here has to think about this again."

That was the end of John's statement. He owed the group only that much. It was his brains that turned them into the biggest narcotics outfit in the five Boroughs, and he made them richer than their wildest dreams. This was Vittone's problem, and he would handle this his own way.

Pucchini scanned the room. His guys were quiet.

"All right, we've said our peace. The matter is in good hands. I'm going back to Jamaica to go to work. Have a nice day, gentlemen." With that, Pucchini got up and walked past his group and down the stairs.

The meeting was over, and Vittone walked out to his car. Vittone got into the front seat and put on his seatbelt. Calabrese had driven him over and didn't ask any questions, but pulled away from the curb and drove through the wide avenues of the newest part of the city.

"You know Pete, the one thing you can't ever plan for is human nature—the greed factor. Some guys want more, even when they have it good. You just can't satisfy them."

"It sounds like somebody turned fink, huh. Is that why Tommy called the meeting?"

"Yeah. A guy that you never even heard of got awful greedy with our money."

"Who's that?"

"Some guy … Sal Alegri. You know, I thought he was a good fit. I asked around. Nobody to support and he didn't need a lot of money. He didn't have a big mouth. He stayed to himself."

"And now what?"

"I guess he decided he could make some bucks on his own. I don't know the facts, yet, but Tommy and the guys upstairs have already put out the hit, so it doesn't make a difference. I've never had to whack anybody out over here. We've been lucky up until now. It had to end sometime. I guess I'll have to take care of it myself." Vittone took a deep breath. He was tired of all this nonsense. If this were a Fortune 500 corporation, he could have just fired the guy and been done with him. But in his world, things had to be handled differently. Vittone had to make an example of Sal Alegri. It would be slow and painful.

Sal split his bounty with the two men who helped him gather the drugs from the mule who had carried them inside her stomach, and the three of them had made sure that everything went smoothly. Alegri was a newcomer, but Datale and Marucci had been around for a long time.

Within two hours, word was out on the street and Datale and Marucci knew that Alegri's life was not worth a nickel and if anybody found out that they had been part of it, their time would be up, too. The men gathered in Pucchini's upstairs club were not good at waiting for more than a day or so for extreme retribution. The co-conspirators plotted their course in the back room of a newspaper store where they made bets on the races at local tracks.

"Izzy, Sal's a problem for us. A big problem," Datale explained.

"I'll tell you I'm really worried about what happens if Vittone's goons get their hands on him. They're gonna wanna know who was in this with Alegri. Vittone figures that Sal ain't smart enough to do it alone. They'll break him down in about 10 minutes with either an ice pick or an electric prod on his balls."

"Nah, Vittone's too laid back. He's not that kinda guy," Izzy replied, apparently not worried.

"Are you crazy? That's just a show, part of the act. Vittone's one mean sonofabitch. He makes the huge jump from Sardinia. Right here, into the middle of the action, and takes over the whole show and makes millions. He's smooth and he's tough. You've got to be a tough mother to pull that off. Don't let him fool you. He had to get tough with guys along the way to make it this far. Nice guys don't get where he is. He's gonna break Alegri and then kill us all. Wake up. We're in deep shit."

"What can we do? Vittone's going to get to Sal in 24 hours, maybe sooner."

"There's only one way out. We tell Alegri to get himself back to Sicily and quick. He's got family there. He'll be safe, and Vittone will leave him alone. Why should he chase him around the world for what's only peanuts to him. Once he's out of the picture, Vittone can tell Tommy he took care of it without firing a shot. They'll both be happy."

"It sounds good, I guess. I hope he does what we tell him. We'll go see Alegri. Rocco, I give you credit. In this instance, you're smarter than I thought," Marucci commended in glowing terms.

The two hoods made a beeline to Sal Alegri's apartment. He was happier than he had been in a long time. Alegri took his $20,000 and went to a luggage shop and purchased a suitcase in which he carefully laid all of the wrapped money. His goal was to stash this money away in a safe deposit box, but for now, he wanted to spend some of it. Now, he was truly an American, a consumer, and no one would be the wiser.

A doorbell in the apartment sounded. When Alegri looked out through the peephole, he recognized the faces of Datale and Marucci staring back at him.

Since no one in the outfit knew where he lived, and these types of guys didn't drop by to watch a football game, he immediately became suspicious. He warily opened the door and invited his visitors in, "Hey Roc, Izzy, come on in. I'll make some coffee for us."

Rocco shook his head. "Sal, I've got some bad news. Tommy knows you did a side deal behind his back. Both the man and Vittone are looking for you and when they find you, you'll be whacked. That's what's out on the street."

Alegri turned ashen-faced. He knew that they were deadly serious.

"Sal, it's not over. Don't look like you're gonna pass out. I've got a plan. Listen to me. Stay calm," Datale suggested, worrying that the Alegri was going to faint right on the spot. Sal didn't move an inch.

"Sallie, listen to me. Use your head for a minute," Datale pleaded, trying to shake him out of his temporary paralysis. "You've got family in Sicily, right?"

"Yeah."

"A big family, right?"

"Yeah, pretty big," Alegri uttered.

"It's easy. Get on the next plane back there right now. Pack a bag. We'll drop you off at Kennedy. Business here is over for you. You're out of everybody's hair. They don't see you; they don't think about you. You go into exile, and nobody will bother you. You've made enough money during the past 10 years; you'll live a great life and be happy. You made a mistake. That's it. It's over."

"I made a mistake … What about you guys?" Alegri asked incredulously.

"Why do you want to take us down with you? What the fuck did we ever do to you? We'd rather live in Sicily than this dirty fucking Queens, but we gotta stay here and make some money. After all, you'll make 10 times more than we do. Come on, pack your bags. We're driving you out to the airport."

Alegri had no choice. They would kill him if he didn't go, and Datale didn't want to be forced to do that. To kill Alegri would be a sure sign to Vittone that there were others involved, and Rocco had more fear of Vittone than Marucci did. Alegri knew he made a mistake and got caught. He pulled his suitcase out from under the bed.

When Izzy pulled up to the Al Italia check-in stand on the sidewalk outside the terminal at JFK, Datale jumped out and opened the rear door for Sal.

"Sal, go on, run in, get in line and purchase a ticket. There's a flight out at least every three to four hours. I'll carry your bags. Izzy, park the car and meet us inside," Datale directed.

There were no non-stop flights open to Rome, but there was a direct flight to London and then onto the Eternal City. Sal booked himself on that one, silently cursing the day he got greedy and turned to cross the family.

"Sal, in a few minutes you'll be up there in the sky and everything will be good again," Rocco promised.

"Yeah, great. What do I tell my relatives?"

"Tell them the truth. You got a little careless, nutty. They'll understand and forgive you. The word will get passed around. Sal is gone; he won't be a bother to anybody anymore. You'll live in peace."

"I guess so. I hope you're right."

"Of course I'm right. Pucchini just needs you out of the picture. He doesn't care how."

Marucci and Datale sat in the front row of seats next to the gate the whole time that it took for passengers to board, and they stood up and shook Alegri's hand as he walked past the stewardess and handed her his boarding pass.

"Sal, good luck. We'll call you when the coast is clear to see how things are going. Stay low. We'll cover everything here."

Alegri nodded and said nothing. The two men waited for him to disappear down the ramp and sat looking out the tall windows until the plane left the departure deck. Only then did they walk through the terminal and into the parking garage.

Izzy mumbled to Datale, "I hope nobody finds out that we're in on this."

"So do I," his partner answered.

For John Vittone, Alegri's being sent into exile was not enough. After his two henchmen returned from burglarizing Sal's apartment and finding all of his clothing gone, John obviously knew that the smart place for Alegri to make his retreat was to Sicily. The easy play would be to tell Pucchini that Alegri was out of their hair and in Europe; the problem had been solved. But John needed the respect of everybody in the family, for without it, those from within would move to unseat him. The eyes of the entire family were on him, and they were waiting to see what his response would be. To let Alegri fade away would send a message that John Vittone could be challenged, and he would not react in the traditional manner—swift and violent retribution. Vittone knew only too well that Giacomo took over the Fisherman's place in Caprera when his predecessor became lackadaisical, and the same fate would befall Vittone if he did not act immediately.

Thirty-six years passed, but Giacomo still had all of his faculties, and his regime was stronger than ever. In such a small place, where people never moved and lived their entire lives in the same houses, everyone knew that Giacomo acquired his position by lethal force, and that he killed over the years when the "death penalty" was called for. Anybody who tried to remove him from his position of family head would be making a mistake because Giacomo's reaction would be brutal. John now turned to his uncle once more for help in this new hour of crisis.

Giacomo knew every player in Sardinia. One family ran two regimes on the island, which they divided into a northern and southern territory. On Sicily, however, things were more complicated. Almost every town had clans that fought each other for centuries and one day, one was in power, only to find itself decimated the next. Keeping track of where the strength lay was a tricky business for an outsider who did not want to be caught in the wrong place.

Alegri's family was small, with maybe 10 members, and his uncle ran the show. They presided over a tiny corner of the former kingdom of Sicily in a town 10 miles west of Palermo, called Doprera. It was there that Alegri's father took orders from his uncle, who was the brains of whatever organization existed. The family operated a vineyard, and whenever it sold wines, it often sent heroin or cocaine or marijuana along with the wooden case holding the bottles. From the sale of grapes, the family got the cash to lend out at usurious rates. It was really the reverse of Vittone's operation. The legitimate business brought in the main source of income and the rackets were a side line.

Vittone decided not to place the call to Pucchini to tell him that Alegri ran off to Europe. His only call was to Giacomo. "Uncle, it's John." Giacomo thought that this was only a repetition of the weekly calls he received from his boy for over 30 years. "John, when are you going to come see me?" As Pia got older, the visits to Sardinia became less frequent. If John made it over once every two years, he was doing well. So Giacomo was surprised by the reply.

"I'm coming now. I'll be there tomorrow. Please, listen to me. There's an Alegri family outside of Palermo, some town I'm not familiar with called Doprera. Do me a favor, but quietly, no one is to know. Please, check them out for me. I leave tonight. I may need a couple of your men."

"John, I'll be honored to have you. Bring Pia."

"Not on this trip uncle, not on this one," he answered, his voice trailing off. Giacomo knew from his tone that there was trouble and inquired no further. "Call me from Rome so I'll know when you're arriving. I'll have a car meet you at the airport in Sardinia."

"Te amo," John told him sincerely.

"I love you too, nephew. Watch yourself."

More than 90 percent of Giacomo's drugs that were picked up in Carbonia, on the southern end of the island, and driven across the mountains to his stronghold, originated in Sicily. Giacomo's man who was on the receiving end from Sicily lived in Carbonia. It was still a boring ride down to the southern tip, through endless hills, but Giacomo decided to have his driver take him there. He felt it would do him good to see the goats and sheep and olive trees once again; who was to know … at his age, he might never get to view them again.

The man in Carbonia, Don Nino, was Giacomo's counterpart for decades. Giacomo talked to him very intently. "I have a very private matter that I need your help with. Do I have your assurance that my inquiries will go no further?"

"Giacomo, after all we've been through? I cannot believe that you need to ask me, but the look on your face tells me you're worried. I also know that you did not make this trip to see Carbonia. Of course! Anything you say is between us. What is it?"

"Have you ever come across an Alegri family outside Palermo in a dot on the map called Doprera?"

The man shrugged his shoulders and his mouth turned down. "Small timers. Two bit men. Once in awhile, they send something over to be sold. Usually, it's not worth the trouble, but I package it with bigger bundles. They're always afraid someone is going to steal their money. You can't tell me that they are a stone in your shoe. I can't believe it. They're nothing."

"If I needed to find them, to get on the inside, you could help me?"

"Surely. But I wouldn't waste my time on these penny pinchers. It is not worth the effort. The trouble would outweigh any gain."

"Don Nino, that's all I need to know. I need you in my corner on this one. I'm afraid that tomorrow a call will come for me. Any assistance you can render will not be forgotten."

"Giacomo, don't waste your time. If they have caused you trouble, we will just not do business with them. That will be our revenge."

"I'm afraid it is not going to be that easy, my friend. Good day."

On the long ride back to his estate, Giacomo thought of why Vittone would travel thousands of miles to find the Alegris. He came up with no answer. How could these people be so important to his nephew when he never heard of them and his fellow capo dismissed them out of hand. He would have to wait until his nephew was back home to get the answer.

After Vittone arrived at the small local airstrip and was driven to the secluded estate with the vines of bougainvillea growing on tressels, John met in the same study where he spent five years learning his trade. "Uncle Giacomo, I have been betrayed, and I must avenge this treachery," John related to the old man seated across from him.

"What has happened, Johnny?" the patriarch asked with lines of concern etched on his face.

"One of my runners went into business for himself, and Mr. Pucchini has decided to make an example of him. Normally, something less drastic would be done. This man would walk into his apartment and be beaten or have a finger cut off. The matter would be finished. But now, Pucchini is testing me, as you were once tested by your rivals. He has put me on the spot, and the capos and the underbosses are waiting to see how I react. I must send my own clear message, and do it in such a way that these men have fear in their hearts. Without fear, I won't last a year."

"John, it is unfortunate, but in our line of work, you are right; fear is our power, our sustenance. We can't exist without it. But don't kid yourself. In the corporate world, they rule by fear, too, the fear of taking away material wealth and positions, and putting a man back in the place where he came from. To some, that is worse than death."

"But this is stupid, Uncle. He carried my drugs to New Jersey. He brought along some of his own stuff and sold it, too. Alegri was dumb. One of the men on the other end was related to Pucchini through marriage. He ratted. Pucchini is jealous of me, I think, not worried or threatened, just envious, and he wants me to feel the pressure. If I can get to Alegri, I can return the challenge and let him know that I am a man to be reckoned with. I want to make sure that this is the last time that Pucchini will play with me."

Giacomo mulled it over. "The way you describe it to me, I agree. This Pucchini needs to have respect for you and your connections, as well. What is your plan?"

John picked up his wineglass, carefully swirled the red liquid around as the glass caught the lights of the chandelier and the wine turned different shades. "I am not 100 percent sure. Someone was in this with Alegri. They may become my enemy and act against me or go into hibernation. I don't know. But I want to know who these men are. Killing Alegri is probably simple, but I want him to tell me who the men are before he dies. That will take some doing."

≈ Chapter XVII ≈

SICILY, 1998

THE WALLS OF ALEGRI'S uncle's house were built to resist an invasion. Twelve feet high, with metal shards and broken glass placed on top to repel any would-be climbers, the house inside was crumbling, but was hidden from the outside by sturdy gates. Sal was holed up inside, waiting for things to blow over so that he could go back to eking out an existence in this very poor part of the world.

Two days after the meeting between Vittone and his uncle, a private plane was flying Vittone and two soldiers to Doprera, the village on the north coast of Sicily. Giorgio Caruso, a Sicilian runner who now worked for John, already made the arrangements at the direction of Don Nino so that Vittone could make a clear statement: treachery would not be tolerated and would be met by fast retaliation.

A day before, Caruso, at a small café, met with Alegri and told him that word was out that he was back. Caruso explained that a major Palermo family needed him to take some drugs to Canada for what was a relatively risk-free venture. The only thing Alegri had to do was to appear in one of the warehouses on the outskirts of a large vineyard that covered three townships along the Sicilian coast and be handed the goods.

It was in this antiquated, musty building that Vittone and his men came to end the threat to Vittone's drug empire. Casks lined the huge oak-paneled room, and as Alegri stepped in, Giorgio walked out from the shadows to greet him.

"Sal, thanks for coming," Giorgio announced, clasping Sal's hand.

"It's my pleasure, Giorgio. I'm glad you thought of me for this job. I've been looking for some work now that I'm living back here."

"Sal, I've known you, your uncle and your father forever. I'll throw whatever I can your way. You know that."

Giorgio summoned up his best smile and for a second time, extended his hand to Sal. Once again, Alegri extended his and Giorgio squeezed the smaller man's hand in his bear-sized paw and drew out a gun, which he stuck hard and fast into Alegri's ribs.

"Giorgio, what's up. What's going on? What are you doing with that gun?" Alegri asked, more scared than he had ever been in his life.

"Sal, it's just business, nothing personal, stay cool. Everything'll be okay. Just stay cool."

Caruso led his quarry over to a table. "Lay down on here. You're gonna be okay, Sal." As Alegri lowered himself back on the solid wooden table, two of Vittone's accomplices appeared.

"What's going on?" Alegri exclaimed in alarm, sitting up and looking at the men who were now alongside the table on both sides.

The one grabbed him by the throat and threw him back down. The other took what looked like an extension cord, and started to wind it over and over across Alegri's chest and legs and under the table, until he was completely bound like a mummy. Still, Alegri did not have any idea as to why these three men would want to hurt him.

It was only when John Vittone stepped out from between two tall wine containers that it all became clear, and Alegri knew in his heart that his fate was sealed.

"Mr. Alegri … do you even know who I am?" Vittone asked, in a quiet tone, hovering imperiously over the terrified man.

"Mr. Vittone. Sure, I know who you are. I remember when we talked, when you interviewed me. What's going on?"

"Sal, remember our conversation five years ago when you were a quiet guy, a loner. You kept to yourself. You had no aspirations, no ambitions. You just wanted to make a nice, quiet living. Remember me talking to you about that?"

"I do. I do remember. I stayed quiet Mr. Vittone. I minded my own business."

"Did you? That's not what I'm told. I hear you went out on your own. Started doing your own deals. Cutting the family out. Making your own money. Shoving it right down the family's throat. You say to hell with the family, when we gave you everything—money, clothes, a car, protection, respect. Nobody ever fooled around with you. Did they?"

Alegri's eyes were as wide as they could become. There was no good answer, either he was an ingrate or a liar. Either way, Vittone was going to do something terrible to him. He looked straight at Vittone without speaking.

"Sal, you didn't just fuck the family, you fucked me. You're one of my guys and you turned. You spit in my face."

Alegri knew it was useless to pretend. To bluff would just insense Vittone and drive him to more vicious acts.

"Mr. Vittone, I swear, I only did it once. I made a mistake. I could get the stuff from my old contacts in Sicily so easy. It was so easy. I'd deliver your stuff with mine. You'd get your money and I'd make a little. What's so bad about this? All I wanted was a couple of extra bucks. I didn't want to hurt anybody. I didn't want to make you look bad. Nobody would know, and it wouldn't cause no trouble."

The guy was crying and in his brain, Vittone knew that he made sense. To kill a guy for scoring a few bucks for himself was completely disproportionate to the crime. If the family killed everybody for skimming on their own, there wouldn't be anybody left. But there was more to this. For some reason, Pucchini made this a cause celebre in front of the whole family, and everybody was waiting to see what Vittone would do. If he didn't whack Alegri, he would appear to be weak, and the sharks would circle in on him and eat him alive. Pucchini wanted to make Vittone jump, and Vittone had to show him that he would not flinch. In fact, the manner in which he dealt with Alegri would establish their relationship for years to come.

Alegri was a guy caught in the wrong place at the wrong time. He was the victim of a bigger political battle than he could ever envision, and he was the pawn of these two men with clashing egos. Alegri would be slaughtered so that they could dominate those around them.

The whole room was quiet, and the thoughts were ricocheting around in Vittone's brain. Alegri was stupid and if not for his greed, he would have not gotten himself into this mess. This was of Alegri's own doing, and now he would have to pay the consequences. Vittone was talking himself into the violence that was to come.

"Giorgio, let's go," Vittone ordered. Under the table was a battery with wires. Giorgio pulled the wires up from underneath and the two assistants pulled Alegri's pants and boxer shorts down.

"What, what are you doing?" the bound man screamed. "I don't deserve this. I didn't mean to screw anybody. I'm just a punk trying to live. I didn't hurt anybody," he wailed as the wires were applied to his testicles. Vittone inched closer and dropped his nose a centimeter from Alegri's nose. "Sal, I know you're too dumb, too small to do a deal from Sicily on your own. I don't care about the guys over here. They're just selling goods and making a profit. Who was in this with you on our side?"

Alegri had his own code of honor. He never in his life ratted on another guy, and Datale and Marucci came to him when they knew his life was in danger and got him out of New York and into safety for a moment. He owed them a lot, and besides, they were his friends.

"Honest, it wasn't nobody else. Honest, I picked it up at the airport and drove to Camden by myself. There's nobody else for me to give to you."

"Sal, you're too fucking dumb to do it alone. I don't believe you." With that, Vittone raised his index finger and Caruso applied the juice. The volts weren't lethal, but excruciatingly painful. He felt like his genitals were on fire or like they'd been hit by a grenade. His ass jolted off the table, but he hit the restraints and sank back.

"Sal, we can do this all day. I don't care. These guys have all the time in the world. Who helped you?"

"Nobody. Honest to God. I swear on Jesus. Nobody helped me." Beads of sweat covered his body.

The index finger shot up and again, the electricity surged from his scrotum into his pelvis, up into his neck and right into his brain. The jolt raised him up, and he didn't know how many more of these he could take. The pain was as bad as if he had been knocked in the crotch 10 times at once in a soccer game.

"Why, why are you doing this to me? Anybody else would get a beating, a broken nose and be done with it. I never screwed you, Mr.

Vittone. Never. Why are you killing me for this? It's so small; it's nothing. I'll give you the money. Anything. Why so much for this?"

Vittone rationalized that it was either himself or Alegri. To come back to New York after flying thousands of miles and teaming up with his uncle, whom he made into giant proportions through his stories that he told in the States would be a sign of weakness, of a man who could not take care of his own business.

Vittone raised his finger again, and before the third charge ever hit him, Alegri made up his mind to give him the names. For this charge, he almost numbed himself to the inevitable pain, and when the electricity hit him, it felt like he had fallen off a roof. He screamed again and again, echoing off the walls of the warehouse.

"Mr. Vittone, you're making me go against everything I believe. I'm not a rat. I keep my mouth shut. Always. People trust me. But I can't take this anymore. It was Datale and Marucci," he said, and the tears started streaming down his cheeks. "All they did was help pick up the stuff, and I gave them a third each. They're not bad guys. They wouldn't hurt you. Can't you just let this be the punishment for all of us?"

"Sal, I gave you my total trust, my total loyalty and you violated it. You know what the penalty has to be for that."

"Mr. Vittone. No. I'll make it up to you. I'll work for nothing. I'll take the most risks. Anything. Please. I didn't violate you. I only wanted a few extra dollars."

Vittone was fed up with Pucchini and what Pucchini forced him to do. He was tired and decided to play this all the way through. When the bullet flew into Alegri's brain, he rationalized that he was not killing Alegri, but telling Pucchini, "I'm a bad guy. If you ever screw with me again, the next bullet will be in your brain, Tommy. Don't ever pressure me again."

John dropped the gun down to his side with his eyes stuck wide open. "Get him out of here. Put him someplace," he instructed his men.

CHAPTER XVIII

SICILY, 1998

THE ADRENALINE WAS FLOWING fast through Vittone's veins. It was not enough to avenge Alegri's treachery and ingratitude for all that Vittone did for him, but Vittone decided that he also must have a slice of Alegri's bootleg money as well. Once he had that, he could return to America, having saved face with the entire Pucchini family.

Vittone looked around, and the room was silent. Alegri lay on the table with his arms dangling toward the floor, with blood caked all over the side of his face and in a pool next to his head.

Vittone's heart was racing. "All right, stuff him into one of those empty barrels over there. Pour some wine over him and the bastard can ferment. They won't smell him for awhile."

Giacomo's men hoisted him up and threw Alegri into a giant cauldron used in the first step of the aging process.

"Now, I want my money," John pronounced grimly. "Where does his father live?"

Caruso spoke up. "In a small place on the other side of the vineyard. He's the quiet one in the family. He does what his brother, Sal's uncle, tells him to do."

"Let's pay him a little visit," Vittone directed.

Giorgio knocked on the door of the cottage. No one answered. He pounded harder. This time, the door opened a foot, and an old man peered out with a dog, some type of shepherd mongrel, staring out from between his legs.

"Yes?"

"Mr. Alegri?" Caruso asked.

"Yes."

"Mr. Alegri, we're friends of your son, Sal. We were supposed to meet him on a job, but we can't find him. Do you know where he is?"

In every small town in Sicily, the arrival of strangers was most often an ominous event. A man like the elder Alegri, who lived through the murders of countless neighbors, knew that the less said, the better. "I don't know where he is. He went out several hours ago."

"That's okay, we'll wait for him. You don't mind if we wait, do you?" Caruso said, forcefully applying pressure to the door.

Vincenzo Alegri realized that these men were coming in whether he wanted them to or not. Maybe his son would stay out all night and that is what he hoped for, feeling in his gut that this surprise visit involved his boy.

"That's fine. Come in."

The door opened and the dog stayed at Alegri's side, growling softly.

"Why don't you tell your dog to go inside, Mr. Alegri? We're not here to bother you. We just need Sal for a few minutes. Something came up." The 70-year-old Vincenzo muttered a phrase in a Sicilian dialect, and the dog put his head down, loped over to a corner, and sulked.

The four men were now inside. "Would you like a glass of wine? I've got some from the vineyard next door," their host inquired pleasantly.

"No thanks, Mr. Alegri. We'll make this quick. Your son has some money put away here in the house. That's what we're after and then we'll be gone. No problems," Giorgio told him.

"I don't know anything about money. My son's a poor boy. I doubt he has money. He's looking for work."

"Mr. Alegri, let's not do this the hard way. Tell us where the money is and we'll leave."

"I swear to you, I don't know anything about any money," the white-haired father protested.

Vittone had enough. First the kid screwed him, and now the old man was doing the same thing. Stupidity must be hereditary, he guessed.

"Mr. Alegri, you don't know me. I'm from America. I knew your son over there. Your son's in a little trouble, and if we get the money, he can get out of trouble. This is not hard. It's simple. Hand over whatever Sal gave you. We know he put it in here somewhere."

"I don't know what you're talking about," Vincenzo responded defiantly.

John was livid. He grabbed the old man around the neck with both hands and threw him back into the wall with all his weight.

"No more bullshit, you old bastard. No fucking more. Give me the money, or I'll blow your brains all over this shack."

He was throttling the man back and forth, and Vincenzo's head kept hitting the wall. "Now! Tell me now! Or I'll be done with you, and you can take your money with you to hell!"

Vittone's veins were popping out of his strong neck, and his eyes bulged out of their sockets. He became a lunatic, a man who could not be reasoned with.

"All right. Enough, you win," Alegri cried out. Vittone stopped beating his head into the cement, but did not loosen his grip around Vincenzo's throat.

"In the back is a porch. Under the floor boards. It's there. Take it and leave us alone. We have done nothing to you. Take all your money and go."

Vittone flicked his head toward the two enforcers, and they went out onto the woodframe addition. Vittone almost dragged Alegri with him by the scruff of the neck. A shovel lay outside, and they put the edge of the metal under a board. Like a fulcrum, the blade lifted the rotted board loose from the rusted nails. The accomplices grabbed the planks that lay on either side and hoisted them up, exposing a suitcase lying underneath. The bag was pulled out and unzipped. There was Alegri's $20,000 all neatly stacked in $20s and $50s. A man could retire on a sum like this in this town where a few thousand dollars a year was a good income.

Now, Vincenzo Alegri would not only never get to spend the money, he would never live out his retirement.

His son lied to Vittone and so had he. They treated John with no respect, and slighted him. They stole from the family in the eyes of both Vittone and his mentor, Pucchini.

Vittone took his gun out from behind his back and told the old man in stark terms, "Your son is dead. He had no honor. The same is true of his father. You, too, have no honor. You'll both end up where traitors go to die." With that, Vittone put a hole in the center of Vincenzo's forehead. The old man's eyes opened wide for a second, his head tilted back and his spine arched like a cat's. He lurched forward onto his knees, his face met the floor and this branch of the Alegri clan came to an end. There would be no more double dealing. The dog ran over to Alegri and started to whimper and lick his face.

Vittone's men gathered his money and walked out single file. To John Vittone and Tommy Pucchini, the matter was settled. A man had gone bad, he was punished and order was restored. This affair was between John's crime family and the two Alegris and no one else. Unfortunately, for Vittone and his boss, it would not be that simple.

Chapter XIX

NEW YORK, 1998

BRUNO ALEGRI, VINCENZO ALEGRI'S older brother, was awaken at 2:00 a.m. The howling of the dog, locked inside the house, awoke Vincenzo Alegri's neighborhood, and the police finally came after two hours of phoning from neighbors trying to get some sleep. The Carabinieri were used to commotions and noise, for Sicilians were a loud people. A death got their attention in about half an hour, but to get them to come for what seemed like a local nuisance was almost impossible.

The patriarch of the Alegri clan walked into a crime scene. There were police everywhere, taking pictures and dusting the furniture for fingerprints. In the middle of the chaos lay a body, face down. Bruno could tell from the white hair and the bald spot on the back of the head that this was his younger brother, the one he always looked out for.

To see him lying there like that was unbelievable. Vincenzo never did anything to anybody in his life. Vincenzo did whatever Bruno asked him to do, which consisted of no more than collecting money from vending machines in bars and selling clothes that had been hijacked from the mainland at local stores.

"Why in the world would anyone want to hurt my brother?" the surviving brother pondered in his mind. Vincenzo was now retired from doing the minor and innocuous tasks that he did for his brother, and he was a threat to no one. The older sibling looked around the room and saw that the gold crucifix was still on the mantle, and the color T.V. that was bought for his brother for Christmas had not been touched. Robbery was not the motive, and outside of that, Vincenzo's life had no meaning to anyone else.

Vincenzo's brother, the local crime boss, wandered to the back of the bungalow, both stunned and unbelieving. There, he noticed the floorboards of the woodframe porch were torn up, and below lay only the raw, clay-colored earth. It was readily apparent to the police and anyone else standing there that this killing involved whatever had been hidden below that floor.

Bruno could not imagine any riches that might have been buried there. His brother was not a wealthy man. He lived off the stipend that Bruno sent him each week, and as he thought it through, the clouds slowly passed over Bruno's head. It had to be Sal, his morose and sullen nephew, who rarely uttered a word. The boy had always been slow, but yet, Sal saw himself as someone greater than his intellect allowed him to be. This horror was somehow related to the kid, who never did anything for his father or his uncle. Bruno could only imagine what stupid blunder had led to the death of his brother.

Bruno walked out of the house without saying anything to the police. When he had entered, he told them of his relation to the deceased and gave no more information. If he found the nephew, he would find the killers; that he was sure of.

For days though, Sal was nowhere to be found and by this time, John Vittone was long gone, as was Caruso, who was pushing Vittone's drugs across the skies and oceans between Europe and the United States. The two bag men were making their usual runs between Caprera and Carbonia at the bidding of the elderly Giacomo.

John Vittone, on his arrival at Kennedy Airport, was taken by car to Tommy's house, where they met in the book-lined, walnut-paneled den as was their custom. The TV was turned a few decibels higher, and the two whispered while CNN's report from the Mideast blared from the black box.

"Tommy, I have fixed matters. Alegri will never be heard from again, and I have retrieved the money that this thief took. Only you and I will know what happened, and the word will slowly leak out that Alegri is no longer of this world. Our message has been sent loud and clear. The matter is closed!"

"John, you have done well. This incident will play itself out, and our friends and our foes will know that we are men to be respected and not to be played with. I knew that you would handle this with your usual precision. Let's get back to business now and make more money for many years to come."

"Tommy, you have all my loyalty. We will prosper together."

The meeting was short, as Vittone liked to stay in his own world, separate and apart from anyone who could bring him down by mere association. Vittone and Pucchini kissed each other on the cheeks, and Vittone went back to his office.

CHAPTER XX

SICILY, 1998

THE SICILIANS LIVE TO retaliate, and Bruno Alegri could not rest until he had taken retribution for the life of his best pal, his defenseless brother. Calls to New York turned up only a few shreds of information. It was reported that when Pucchini and Vittone's men went to Alegri's apartment, his clothes were cleared out and he was gone. Of course, Bruno knew that Alegri showed up unscathed in Sicily, but no more was known than that. No one he knew in New York could say for certain what happened, only that Pucchini called a meeting. Maybe Sal's name came up. John Vittone's whereabout was never known, whether he was in the city or not. Giacomo's men drifted back into their small section of Sardinia, and no one knew they were in Sicily in the first place. Giorgio Caruso was too much of a pro to ever speak of what he had done.

Vittone made only one mistake in this affair, and it would come back to haunt him and his daughter. The year before Alegri's death, Virginia had been stricken with pancreatic cancer, a virtual death sentence, as there is no known cure. Chemotherapy, surgery and radiation were helpless in the face of this disease, and she died in three short, pain-filled months. The morphine, fed to her intravenously, softened the pain, and John and Pia sat by her side every night during the last two weeks, when the pain would rip through her whole body. At her funeral, John was torn. He wanted to bury her with her engagement and wedding rings, so that they would be linked together for eternity, but he also wanted to have a part of her to remember for the rest of his life until he could rejoin her in heaven. John had a jeweler remove the two small baguettes that sat on either side of the two-karat diamond enmeshed in the platinum band of her wedding ring. Those two diamond strips had been soldered into his plain, gold wedding ring, and he wore the ring constantly, as a daily reminder for all the love they shared. It was an unusual piece for a man, and it sparkled when he wore it. He could not bring himself to take it off, even when he made the most dangerous mission of his life to Doprera.

Three weeks after the massacre of the Alegris, a worker at the vineyard went to move a supposedly empty barrel, to fill it with newly crushed grapes in the first stage of the winery process. He expected to turn the barrel on its edge in a circular fashion across the cement floor of the room, but when he put his gloved hands around the lid, the barrel was heavy, much heavier than it should have been. Upon opening it, he discovered the body of Sal Alegri, his whole body colored the purple of grapes. The alcohol preserved the body somewhat, as the flesh was still soft and supple, albeit hanging from the body by only a thread. The eyeballs and white vitreous inside the sockets had fallen out, and Sal's head was a hollowed out skull where the eyes had once resided. His lips had receded to lay bear his white teeth, and he looked like something akin to a Halloween costume.

Once again, Bruno Alegri appeared at the scene, and the police showed him the body of his nephew. Now he could be sure that Sal was the catalyst for the death of his brother. All he needed was to pin down the perpetrator, whom he was sure resided somewhere in New York, Sal's last place of residence before returning. Within hours of uncovering Sal's body, Bruno Alegri let it be known that whoever found the killer of his beloved brother and his son would be handsomely rewarded. As it turned out, Bruno did not have to look farther than a mile from his ancestral home.

Local men in Doprera gathered nightly at a local café called La Novo Contessa. The attraction to this bar, as opposed to 10 others, was the owner's daughter, a very quiet girl whose apron did not quite cover all her assets. Every man in the place thought that he had a chance with her, not knowing that she was waiting for her beau to graduate from the University in Rome.

One of the men seated at the bar, a couple of nights after the appearance of the corpse was an up and comer for Alegri's organization, and he listened as every word was uttered from the 22-year-old male seated two stools away.

"Yeah, I was working the day they found that New York guy. He was stuffed in a barrel," he told anybody who was listening.

"Who do you think did it?" his companion asked.

"Nobody knows. Nobody ever knows. Here, people like us, we die all the time. It'll never change. It's the Sicilian curse."

"No, this was different. Not Sicilian. There was no family feud here. He was nothing. He just got back here," the listener added.

"All I know is that a week before they found him, I saw four connected men walking around. One was really out of place. He looked like somebody in a magazine that ran a car company. He had a silk shirt and this crazy ring. I never saw a man with that kind of ring. It looked like a woman's ring. Diamonds and gold. I never saw them again, and all of a sudden, this Sal shows up dead." In Doprera, you lived a lot longer if you kept your mouth shut and said nothing. After he let his secret out, he could only hope that no one around was paying much attention to him.

Alegri's man was listening, though, and with both ears wide open. The next morning, Alegri had a description of the man he was hunting, and his associate had a $1,000 cash bonus. A transatlantic call was placed to a contact in Queens to learn the identity of the man with the ring. The reply was quick and to the point. John Vittone was the only wiseguy who had the balls to wear a ring like that. Gays on Queen's Boulevard were the only ones who wore such effeminate jewelry, but Vittone could wear whatever he wanted because everybody knew that he was a made man, and one of the most powerful.

"How do I get a picture, a photo of this Vittone?" Alegri questioned, wanting some more proof of the murders before he attacked.

"He's made a couple of mistakes, Bruno. Not many, but one or two. He tried to get fancy years ago, and had his picture taken at a ball with the mayor of New York City. I can arrange to get you a file copy from the newspaper."

"Do me a favor. Get me that picture. Send it by overnight express right to me. I'll take care of you on this."

"Bruno, you owe me nothing," the man responded, knowing that he could afford to be gracious because Bruno seemed so interested in this that he would not fail to send a gratuity.

When the photo arrived two mornings later, it was a good, clear shot. Vittone was a lot younger, but he was standing next to the mayor, smiling, with his wife next to him. The hair was full and combed straight back in the same style as now and it was as dark as ever. He was older now, naturally, but his face was still taut, with a crease on each side. The Roman nose was still aristocratic.

Alegri had his apprentice approach the grape picker from the bar with the photo.

"Have you ever seen this person before?" he questioned, holding the photo up in the men's room in the back of the same bar they both frequented a couple of nights before.

"Who wants to know?" was the suspicious reply.

"None of your business. But if you don't help me, the guy who's asking will make you his business. Besides, some Lira is in this for you. Seen him? Yes or no?"

"How much Lira?"

"A hundred thousand."

"Tonight?"

"Tonight."

This was a week's wage and too much to pass up. "He's the man I saw at the vineyard, but older. Same hair and face."

"Anything else you recognize about him?"

"He was wearing a ring, looked like a lady's engagement or wedding ring. Strange a man with eyes of steel and a girl's ring."

"Here's your money. Keep this to yourself. I don't want to hear one word about this. You've already done too much talking to people, and you know where that can lead."

"Believe me, I know. You must have overheard me the other night. Forget I told you anything about this."

Bruno made a second call to New York, and this time, he wanted to know more. "Who is this Vittone?"

"He is the breadwinner for the Pucchinis. The biggest narco guy in the United States. He took Tommy from being a two bit hustler into a zillionaire. He makes so much money, nobody, not even Tommy, gives him any guff. I guess he's got guys all around the world, real operators. Top guys who bring in huge hauls. He doesn't get caught, and nobody can finger him. You mess with him, and Tommy will come after you with everything he has. That would put a huge dent into the Pucchini family, because Tommy doesn't have the brains to do what Vittone does. No way! Tommy guards this guy with his life," Bruno's New York contact man emphasized, knowing the reputation of the Pucchini family and Vittone's reputation in it very well.

"If I can't go after him personally, how do I get him?"

"He's got a weak spot."

"What's that?"

"His daughter."

"What do you mean?"

"He never talks about her, but everybody knows about her. She's a top partner in one of the big Wall Street law firms. She only does those high profile international trials. If somebody gets caught selling secrets to the Commies for money, she steps in. The broad has it all—Ivy league, gorgeous, fancy clothes, you name it. Now that his wife died, she's his whole world."

There was a long pause after the New Yorker stopped talking. To Alegri, this was almost heresy. It was an unwritten rule of the mob, that you never went after anybody's kid. Wiseguy children were off limits, no matter what anybody did; the kids were safe, or they would all start killing off each other's offspring. They would turn into barbarians, and after all, they were civilized businessmen, just like any corporate executives, except they used physical force to run their companies. If Alegri went after Vittone's child, someone would be sure to come after Alegri's. Where would it all end?

But what were the choices? Alegri couldn't make a frontal assault on Vittone because the repercussions would be fatal. Just as he had known that somebody in New York had to be behind Sal's murder, Pucchini would know that any action against Vittone came from Sal's Sicilian relatives.

Vittone did the unthinkable in Bruno's mind though. Okay, so Sal had screwed up somehow he reasoned. The man on the other end of the line indicated that Sal did some double-dealing. Maybe Sal had to be taken out to set the record straight, but why the brother. The frail man was an innocent victim who would never hurt a fly. To Bruno, this was pure malice, done for no purpose other than to make Vittone feel big. Vittone went out of bounds by killing Bruno's brother, so now, Bruno was free to break the rules.

"How do I get to the daughter? No violence or anything like that; I only wanna teach him a lesson he won't forget."

"I don't know. Set her up. Get her disbarred. That'll hurt, real bad. To see his daughter broken would kill Vittone."

"How? How?" Bruno pleaded.

"Hmm, the usual stuff. Plant some stolen goods on her. Compromising photos with somebody bad. I don't know. A setup, a good setup."

"How about drugs. A few years in prison would drive this guy Vittone crazy."

"Too crazy. He wouldn't rest til he found out who did it."

Alegri was not intimidated. "Let him try. I'm 75. If he ever figures it out, I'll be dead. I'll take my chances. I loved my brother more than anybody in the world. He was kind, generous. He gave to the orphans, the nuns, the veterans. He loved everybody. He never bothered anybody. To avenge his death, I'll take my chances."

"What do you want us to do?" his willing accomplice asked.

"Get me somebody who can pull this off quietly. Quick, fast, it's over. Whoever does this gets paid and keeps quiet. They have no choice, because if they talk, Vittone will kill 'em. For enough money, they'll pull it off, and I can have some peace. I can't get my brother back, but I can get satisfaction; that's all I want. We won't be even, but it's enough. Get me the people quick. I don't want to have to think about this anymore."

∼ Chapter XXI ∼

NEW YORK, 1998

WHEN THE PLANE touched down in New York, John carried a secret: the identity of Alegri's two accomplices. He was not sure of what to do with them. The $20,000 he turned over to Tommy was split equally between them. That night in the den, John explained to Tommy, "It's over. Unfortunately, the father turned out to be tougher than the kid. But neither one will ever bother us again. Everybody will know the score has been settled, and they will go back as they were."

"John, if a man could ever pray for the perfect partner, you'd be the one. Nothing will stop our success, my friend," Tommy said.

"Only as long as we are careful, Tommy. We can never rest in this business." Then he broached the unspeakable. "You ever think about retiring?" This was the first time that Vittone ever dared to bring up the subject, but they were both getting older and the moment seemed right.

"Yeah … I do think about it. Everything has changed. The cops have too much technology, nobody's loyal. They're taking away the rackets. We're fighting with the blacks, Colombians, Mexicans, Russians. A new breed is coming in. My time is short in this business. I should get out, but the time never seems right. There's always a road block."

John was quick to respond. "One big score Tommy, and we can be gone. Enough to give everybody a little piece and fade away. That's the only way out. Leave people happy and go off where they won't think about us anymore. Not the cops, not our guys, no one. Open up a small legitimate business and stay out of the limelight. It can be done. Believe me, it can be done."

"You led me to wealth, John. Maybe you can lead me to the quiet life, too. We'll see."

Vittone left that night without disclosing the identity of Datale and Marucci. Their murders would stir up the press and the police and get everybody in the family thinking how it was every man for himself. Sal was the perfect target, a loner that nobody else cared about. Datale and Marucci were born and raised in Queens, and a lot of raw nerves would be exposed if anything happened to them. Besides, they wouldn't be doing any side deals for a long time after Alegri's demise. John was now more in control than ever. Punishing these two could only tip over the boat. Vittone decided to let them hang in the wind, to wonder if Alegri ratted on them. They would be looking over their shoulders everyday, and that was to be their penalty for now.

Letting Datale and Marucci live was a tactical blunder that would now be compounded. Alegri's contact man in New York put out some feelers as to who Alegri was friendly with in the Pucchini family. It was a short list—Datale, Marucci and one other soldier. Bruno Alegri's conspirator reasoned that a friend of Sal's would be more likely to want to avenge his death than a stranger, and besides, Pucchini was cheap and his street guys were low paid. The combination of greed and revenge was workable.

When approached, Datale was undaunted by the proposed mission. Bruno's man in America outlined the scheme to his attentive listener. "Here's my proposition. I'll land you two kilos of coke. You plant them inside apartment 12F of the Dorchester Co-op up on 53rd Street, and once the girl who lives there gets arrested, I'll give you $20,000. If you get caught, you've got big problems, and if you don't, nobody will be the wiser."

"You mean, all I got to do is get the drugs inside the apartment?"

"Rocco, if that was all I needed, I'd give a second-story man a grand. No, you've gotta tip off the cops and good enough so that they follow up, go to the apartment, find the stuff and put her in jail. This is $20,000, not $20. You gotta do the whole frame up."

"I can do that. No problem."

"We'll see, big guy. It's not that easy. The girl's name is Pia Vassar, and she's John Vittone's daughter. You fuck up, and you're a dead man. Still interested?"

Datale was unfazed by this revelation. He was doing the calculation in his head and when he added this $20,000 to the $20,000 that Sal Alegri had given him, he had a nice neat $40,000 which was like $4 million to a guy like him.

As long as he did it right and quiet, no one would be the wiser. He thought it was easy money, and sort of a back-hand way to get back at the bosses who paid him so little. "Count me in. I don't give a fuck about Vittone or anybody else. Just get me the stuff. I'll do the rest."

CHAPTER XXII

NEW YORK, DECEMBER, 1998

HIDDEN IN THE MIDDLE of 53rd Street, between Amsterdam Avenue and Riverside Drive, was the Dorchester, an unassuming, co-op building, 20 stories high, with 80 apartments. A plain brick facade masked the upper-class lifestyles that inhabited its interior. It was one of those buildings where young investment bankers and MIT engineers working for computer companies lived when they were not at the office, frantically working on the newest innovation that would reap millions.

John Vittone purchased a unit there for his daughter when she enrolled at Columbia Law. Very few students at the Ivy League school were in a two-bedroom apartment with 12-foot-high ceilings and a living room with a view of the Hudson River. This was a building with 24 hour doormen and a security staff. Vittone felt good that his daughter was safe at night inside its walls.

The mid-30s executives who retired there each night to sleep, often with a different bedroom partner, demanded that they be pampered, which is a job required of any superintendent. In the 1990s, superintendents no longer wore jeans and flannel shirts to work. They pulled into the garage underneath the building in BMWs and wore suits and white shirts. It was their job to make sure that every tenant was happy, and that all of their needs were attended to.

Art Johnson had been at the Dorchester three years, after working at a rental apartment building downtown that housed NYU professors and copy editors for magazines. The Dorchester was a mid-level promotion, a stepping stone to the top spot, general manager, in an upper east side building on 85th Street, where he could really start to make some money.

Datale planned well for his visit with Johnson. Pulling up to the front edge of the canopy that covered the sidewalk on the way to the inside lobby, Datale arrived in a rented green four-door Mercury. The electric window on the passenger side slid down, and Datale leaned over so the door man could see him while he held up a badge that he purchased the day before at the Army-Navy store. With his gray suit and striped tie and polished black shoes, he looked the part of a city Inspector.

"How ya doin?" Datale called out. The door man bent down and stuck his head in through the open window.

"Can I help you?"

"Yeah, I'm Roy Ivone, from the city building inspector's office. I need to see your manager, Mr. Johnson," Datale answered, holding up his badge long enough to show off the shiny metal before he shoved it back into his pocket.

"Does he know you're coming?"

"We don't announce when we're inspecting. Defeats the whole purpose, you know," Datale responded, with all the authority of his newfound position.

"Yeah, I guess so," answered the uninformed attendant. "Let me get somebody to park your car. I'll tell Mr. Johnson you're here."

"Thanks," Datale answered in his clipped New York accent as he shoved the gear into park and jumped out to go around the front of the car."

The doorman had already called the manager, telling him, "Mr. Johnson, there's a building inspector here to see you."

"A building inspector?" Johnson queried. Building inspectors didn't stop around unless there was an accident. There was nothing to inspect in the building other than the elevator, and another department handled that. "Okay, let him in," Johnson told his assistant, wanting to get this over with as soon as possible.

"Go down the hall to the left. Last door on the right," his greeter directed.

"Thanks," Datale acknowledged.

Rocco walked into a nicely carpeted office with two high-winged chairs and a beautiful French Provincial desk. This was where Johnson took the requests of his owners and barked out orders to his janitors.

"Hi, I'm Art Johnson. What can I do for you?"

"Mr. Johnson, I'm Roy Ivone, city building inspector."

"I've never seen an inspector out here. The building's in great shape. Who called you?" Johnson queried.

"I want to inspect apartment 12F."

"12F? Why 12F?"

"There may be water intrusion coming in from the windows."

"Who told you that?"

"Ms. Vassar, the owner, that's who."

"She called the city?" Johnson was perplexed. "Every owner calls me for any problems they have. This is crazy! The city won't fix a crater in the middle of West Side Highway, and a building inspector comes down because a tenant got water in her window. You gotta be kidding me. What are you up to? Who the hell are you?"

"I told you, I'm a city building inspector."

"How come I couldn't get an inspector down here if the building collapsed. Let's call the cops and see if they can vouch for you," Johnson told him, reaching for the phone.

"Art, forget the phone," Datale told him softly but sternly, putting his hand on top of Johnson's fingers that straddled the receiver.

"Who the fuck are you?" Johnson asked the man with the pock marked face and the barrel chest. His fingers were stubby with heavy hair, and Johnson knew that this was a tough guy.

"Art, stop it. Calm down. Listen to me. I need to get into 12F. You don't like the inspector routine. Okay. Your choice. I need to get in we can do this anyway you want."

Johnson stopped trying to dial. Datale sized him up. "Art, I did a little checking. You live up in the Bronx, off of Bronx River Drive, apartment 20. You got a nice little wife who works for the clerk's office at the Bronx County Courthouse. Kate. Right?"

"Yeah, you're right," Johnson said with his sweaty fingers still on the phone.

"Art, I didn't come over here to bother you. I even came to make your day." Datale opened his jacket to reveal a gun holder, with a snub nosed pistol. He reached into the inside pocket and pulled out a manilla envelope. He laid it on the desk. "There's 5,000 clams in there, Art. Not a bad pay day for no work. All hundreds. Go on, open it up. Count it."

"I'll take your word," Johnson said, expressionless.

"It's yours. I go in the apartment. Check the window. Five minutes. I'm out and on my way. You're $5,000 richer."

"I couldn't help you even if I wanted to. I've got the master key to one lock, but the owner has the only two keys to the top lock. That's the truth. No matter what you do, I can't get in. Only with the owner's consent."

"No problem, Art, no problem," replied Datale, who took a small plastic box out of the other pocket. The box was flat and when he opened it, pieces of metal that looked like blank keys at a locksmith's were lined up. Some had jagged edges. "Don't worry Art, I'll get in. Give me the bottom key. I'll worry about the top."

"And what if I don't?" Johnson asked.

"Art, you're gonna pick up five grand, and we don't need to worry about anything else, including your wife or …" He didn't finish anything more about Johnson's wife. There was no need.

Johnson loved his wife, and he loved money. He barely knew Pia Vassar. She left most mornings before he got there, and she was never home by the time he departed. He felt no allegiance to her.

"All right, here's the key, but you need to move fast. I've got security here and closed-circuit TV. I'll have to turn the camera over that door off somehow. You won't have a lot of time."

"I don't need a lot," Rocco told him, grabbing the key to the lower lock.

"I'll call my security guy on the walkie-talkie and tell him you're a building inspector just in case. But if anybody catches you, I don't know you. You're on your own."

"Art, you worry way too much."

Johnson gave the directions, "Take the elevator in the lobby. Step out at the 12th floor. Turn right, go to the end of the hall." Johnson took the envelope and stuffed it into his pocket.

One of Datale's prior jobs as a criminal apprentice was picking locks and burglarizing small businesses. The deadbolt was a piece of cake. Any amateur could turn the tumbler. A standard manufacturer made the lock, and Datale had a master that would fit almost any deadbolt in the country. He shoved the key in all the way and pulled it back, very slowly, until he could hear everything fall into place. The key turned smoothly to the left, and the lever barring the door moved out of its socket. The door opened, and he put the plastic case away and walked in.

He knew exactly where he wanted to plant the two packets that had the appearance of a package of sugar somebody would buy in the supermarket. He went to the freezer compartment and found boxes of ice cream. In between, he placed one bag far enough back so that the girl might not find it, but anyone else looking for it would be able to tell where it was if they knew it was there. The girl liked ice cream, he realized, and he left the first package right between the strawberry and chocolate chip mint. Another was placed in her closet. Both packages were hidden away, but easy enough for someone with some inside information to find. Once he was sure that everything looked just right, he left.

Chapter XXIII

MANHATTAN, DECEMBER, 1998

WHILE BRUNO ALEGRI was pulling the strings from more than an ocean away, he had no idea how lucky he was in his endeavors. At the same time that Datale was planting the drugs, a grand jury was being impaneled in the Federal Building in downtown Manhattan. Its target was the further breakup of the mob, and in particular, its stranglehold on the construction industry in the city and secondly, its drug trade, from which it cleared the huge profits to buy cement mixers and loan millions for building projects.

This grand jury, orchestrated by Jay Cavanaugh, was looking for any dent it could make into the structure of the last two intact Mafia families, which included Pucchini's. Through the arrogance and the sheer stupidity of the soldiers in the other New York City families, they achieved a high profile—most undesirable for the crime families—and were taken down. Pucchini's family, the second strongest among the five in the city, went to great lengths to ensure their own survival. Not once had Tommy's picture been taken by the press at a public gathering. He was meticulous in his silent activities. A modest lifestyle, coupled with a modest ego, kept him removed from the public's eye. Now he was almost the boss of bosses by default, and it was a job that he studiously tried to avoid, for with it came all the scrutiny of the local police and national law enforcement agencies.

Jay Cavanaugh now aimed his sights at Pucchini. The word was passed from the U.S. Attorney's Office for the southern district in New York to the state police, the city police and the sheriffs in New York's political subdivisions. A federal grand jury, with one purpose, now was in session. The feds told the local police officers and officeholders to put aside all of their conflicts and differences and finish off these criminal families while they seemed in total disarray. In return for their cooperation, city politicians were to be given priority in seeking vacancies on the federal district benches.

Datale, after going to Pia's apartment, had to move quickly, and placed a call to Lou Epstein, his best contact in the west side precinct. Since his early teens, Epstein wanted both power and money, which occupied his thoughts daily.

Datale paged Lou in the squad room, but to no avail. Datale needed to move fast, before the Vassar girl found the gifts he left in her apartment.

"Tell him this is big. He can reel in another Gotti," Datale fairly shouted at the operator.

"Sir, everything is big in New York. Sergeant Epstein's right in the middle of something really important. Give me your number, and he'll call you back."

Datale was frantic. Detectives got leads every 60 seconds from screwballs trying to play cops and robbers, and his message slips could lay around for days, if they were ever returned. The other problem was that if Pia ever discovered the drugs before the police found them, she would dump them and Alegri would be out a lot of money. Datale would then have two potential enemies: the Sicilians and Vittone.

Rocco decided this required drastic means. Izzy was a bag man known to Epstein. Izzy had strict orders to never contact Epstein at the station. If he needed something, he was to put the date and the place for a meeting on a piece of paper and slip it under Epstein's apartment door. When he got it, Epstein would drive by the meeting place and yell out the name of a bar where the two would rendezvous.

Datale now wheeled up his trump card and barked out to the operator, "Tell him it's Izzy. It's urgent."

The operator assumed this must be an informant, and she had standing orders to take seriously any message called in by these turncoats who were the mother's milk of the detective unit. Without snitches, all the wiretaps in the world couldn't link dons to the big crimes.

The intercom now blared out, "Sergeant Epstein, you're needed on the phone in reference to Izzy. Sergeant Epstein, call on line five."

Epstein stopped what he was doing. Either someone was really stupid, or something had gone awry. He had put the fear of God into Marucci, and it would take a major disaster to make him call the office.

"Take over," Epstein told his plain clothes, junior grade officer. "I'll be right back."

He grabbed the phone in his cubicle. "Yeah. This is Epstein."

It was better to keep up the ruse, Datale decided. He and Marucci were both Italian with thick New York accents, and they sounded alike, having spent years working together.

"Lou, it's Izzy."

Epstein was careful of what to say. If anyone was listening, he didn't want to tip off his rage. Normally, policemen were delighted to hear from these stool pigeons.

"Izzy. This is a surprise. A real surprise. What's up?"

"Lou, I've got a big one for you. This is going to make your career."

"What do you mean?"

"You ever heard of John Vittone?"

"Yeah, sure. I've heard of him. Why?"

"Well, he's hiding some stuff to be shipped out over at his daughter's apartment. She's a big shot lawyer in a huge firm downtown. She's almost as big as he is, Lou. I'm giving you two birds that can be brought down at the same time. There's coke in her refrigerator and in her closet. Get a warrant. You'll be a hero."

"What's in this for you?"

"Nothing, Lou. Nothing. You can owe me, but forget about that. You'll be a lieutenant, Lou. The address is 268 West 53rd Street. The Dorchester building. It's up to you Lou, but it's good, believe me."

"Okay, thanks," Epstein answered, hanging up.

What did all this mean? mulled Epstein, sitting down and forgetting about the interrogation of the two hoods down the hallway. Vittone was big. Everybody was always whispering his name. Nobody could get a take on him, and he was outside of the NYPD jurisdiction. Most of the time, he was holed up in Garden City, in

Nassau County, just over the city line. Epstein had never heard of the daughter, Yet, Marucci was always a straight shooter up until this point. With Marucci, Epstein made money, good money; now he could have the clout to go with it. Vittone was a Pucchini man and the United States Government would love this. If he could give this to a grand jury, he might bring down a lot of guys in the organization. The girl would turn on Pucchini to stay out of jail. Lawyers were weak when they got pushed. Epstein decided he would write an affidavit using the nickname of a street guy whom he successfully used before as the confidential informant, and give the feds the information. No one would be the wiser.

Epstein passed the information to the FBI with the caveat that they needed to move fast. The probable cause affidavit recited that the informant told Epstein that Vittone and his daughter were holding the drugs for a few hours until they could be moved out to the West Coast. The instructions to the FBI included the fact that John was a mob kingpin and if they could get the daughter, they could finally get their hands on him. The FBI agent who was reading the probable cause affidavit that was faxed over, and who was listening to Datale on the phone, took the bait.

"Come down here. I'll get the affidavit typed over in federal form while you're on your way. There's a judge sitting in a big automatic weapons case right now. I'll get him to sign the warrant to search the apartment when he comes in from lunch."

Judge Leonard Abrams was an autocrat in the courtroom. He limited the prosecution and defense to a certain amount of days for each side to present their case and limited lawyers to hours and even minutes to interrogate a witness. Everything was streamlined, and he tried his cases one after another.

Agent Graham was waiting for Abrams in his secretary's office when he reappeared from grabbing a sandwich that afternoon.

"Your Honor, Agent Graham, with the FBI. I have a warrant for you to review."

Abrams was moving quickly. "Listen. I'm going back on the bench right now. Leave it with my secretary, and I'll look it over at 4:30 p.m."

"Your Honor, I wouldn't bother you if it weren't important. This warrant may lead to a Mafia kingpin, as big as Gotti, and we need to move quickly."

The FBI man looked at the glare from the jurist's eyes and added, "Respectfully, your Honor."

Abrams hated the mob for selling drugs to school children and driving the honest businessman out of business through extortion and threats. He thought that these goons undermined American society and terrorized good, honest people.

"All right, you've got three minutes. You'd better have your ducks in a row."

"Yes sir, we do."

Epstein's statement detailed how, for years, he used a confidential informant and how the informant had always been reliable. The informant now knew that drugs lay in the Vassar apartment. He went on to say that the man had connections to organized crime and inferred that he could personally set out the entire organizational make up of the Pucchini family. He knew Pucchini personally and met John Vittone, whom the informant described as the biggest drug dealer in the city. Epstein made it sound like he knew the confidential informant's name and Abrams read the affidavit and statement quickly. The affidavit left out the fact that Pia Vassar was a lawyer.

"All right Graham. This is thin, but I think it's legally sufficient. If the kid's as bad as the father, she won't make a stink if you come up empty."

Graham knew that if the judge was told Pia was an attorney, he would be very reluctant to sign this document.

"Thank you, Judge. We'll keep you informed of what happens."

"Good luck, son. You fellas have done a good job over the past 10 years. We're all proud of you. We need to rid this disease from the city."

"Yes, sir."

Chapter XXIV

ELEVEN HOURS AFTER PIA'S ARREST

JOHN HAMPTON RECEIVED the bad news while he was reading a copy of the newspaper. He was on his first cup of coffee, and the only news item worth reading was the report about the Giants' teetering chances of making the playoffs.

He expected the telephone call to be from somebody down at the news desk, telling him that a politician somewhere was caught in bed with a gay lover or some other type of embarrassing situation. What he heard was a lot different.

"John," was the only word that came out of Pia's mouth. She intended to tell him the whole story, but that was all she could get out at the moment.

"Pia," he responded hesitantly, "What's the matter?"

When she didn't answer immediately, he asked her again, "What is it, baby, tell me? Settle down now and tell me everything," he said quietly, now hearing her sob into the phone.

"John, I can't believe it," she told him, finally able to stop crying long enough to talk. "I was arrested by the FBI last night, and I was in jail; I don't know what's going on. I'm so tired, you don't know. I want to see you. Don't tell me you've got to work or something."

"Pia, when did I ever tell you I had to work when you needed me?"

"I don't know. I'm just tired. I need you, sweetheart."

"I'm coming right over. Don't worry. We'll figure this thing out together."

"John, I'm scared. I'm really screwed, and I don't know what to do."

"Don't worry, we'll sort it out. Remember, I love you. We'll get through this together … okay?"

"Okay. Come over, quick. I want to be with you."

"Honey, I'm coming. I'll be there in 30 minutes."

Hampton sat on the green leather couch in Pia's living room, and she was lying down, with her head in his lap, looking up at him.

"I walked down the hall, put the key in the lock and it was like they appeared out of nowhere, three guys in dark suits. This lead guy, Graham, was professional. He showed me the warrant from the U.S. District Court, and then they went into my apartment, right to the refrigerator and my closet. It was almost like they knew where to go. They handcuffed me and took me to Riker's Island." With that, she stopped, and then continued. "John, prison, I couldn't do it, I'd kill myself. So help me God, I'd kill myself."

"Honey, you're not going to jail."

"Oh yeah, right. I'm dead in the water. All that coke, in these nice, neat little packages, was right in my apartment. And you don't know the worst," she said looking at him, seeing if he was ready for the bomb to fall. She paused, and waited to see if he wanted to hear the worst.

"What's the bad stuff?" he asked, with a feeling somewhere between his heart and his stomach telling him that he didn't want to know.

"Every time we made love, every time you took your clothes off in front of me, you really didn't know who I was. I wanted to tell you, but I didn't want to ruin everything. I didn't want to lose you."

"Who are you?" he asked hesitantly.

"My real name isn't Pia Vassar."

Hampton wanted to hear the rest. This was something like straight out of his column.

"My real name is Pia Vittone, and my father's in the Mafia."

"You're kidding? You're not kidding," Hampton added.

"No, I'm not kidding. It's true. My dad is John Vittone. He is part of the Pucchini family, at least that's what the papers report a few times a year, and John, if you're going to tell me that a blue blood can't love a Mafia girl, do me a favor, don't tell it to me now. I don't think I could take that right now."

"Pia. Stop acting crazy. I love you for the person you are, not your name or your father. Everybody's got a family, and they've all got a story to tell. My grandfather bootlegged whiskey and made a fortune during Prohibition. Did I ever tell you that? You still love me?"

The man always knew the right thing to say. If he had bolted, she was going to be on the next plane to Costa Rica where they had no extradition laws. With Hampton by her side, she had the strength to fight it out.

"My dad's getting me a lawyer this morning."

Hampton told her point blank, "You need to find out who framed you and why."

"John, that's the problem. I saw my father's eyes. He knows that somebody did this to me to get back at him. The deeper they dig, the more I'll implicate my father. That's why I'm dead. This is the perfect setup."

John Hampton had no answer for that. He could only hope that her father hired the best criminal lawyer in town or else Pia wouldn't be around for long.

CHAPTER XXV

MANHATTAN, EARLY JANUARY, 1999

THERE WAS ONLY ONE lawyer in the metropolis who John Vittone could trust for the defense of his beloved daughter, and that person was Leslie Gabrielson, known as the "shark" by prosecutors and judges alike. She prowled the hallways of the New York County and federal courthouses in lower Manhattan, looking for any loophole or police screw up that could free her clients. She was the most highly paid defense lawyer in New York, and Vittone was willing to pay any price to vindicate his child.

The tone of the initial meting in Gabrielson's office, after the grand jury indictment, surprised even the tough Sardinian. Sitting across from Leslie were Vittone, Pia and Mike McKenna, the private investigator for Leslie, who uncovered evidence and witnesses that won Gabrielson some of her biggest cases.

"Miss Vassar," Leslie started out, "You've got a tough case. Don't get me wrong, they're all tough, but this one is especially challenging. Let's see if I've got this all straight. You walked into your apartment building at night, went up to your door, and three FBI men were there to arrest you. They walked into your apartment and pretended to look around your living room and dining room, but within a few minutes, found a kilo of cocaine in your refrigerator and in your closet, almost as if they knew where they were looking. And you were the only person with a key to one of the deadbolts. To top it off, from what I remember reading about your father, when he appeared in front of the grand jury, he had some fairly huge baggage with his reputation for drugs, maybe giving you the motive and opportunity in the eyes of a jury."

The business about her father was putting it mildly. She didn't want to go any deeper into her father's involvement because it would divide the team now assembled in her office. "It's all a nice, neat package. I don't need to sugarcoat things. The United States Attorney has a prima facie case that he could probably get a conviction on tomorrow. We've got a lot of digging to do."

Pia already knew how bad it was, and when her own lawyer laid it out this way, it seemed hopeless. Vittone, more than anyone in the office, understood the gravity of the situation. He wanted a blunt, hard-charging barrister and he was now finding out just how tough she was.

"Leslie, unfortunately, you've described the situation quite accurately. How do I get out of this mess?" Pia calmly asked with a forced smile.

Leslie gave her a strong answer. "The good thing is, we know it's all bullshit, so if we dig deep enough, we can find out how they pulled this off. It's more than just crooks setting you up. The cops have to be in this somehow. The papers for the search warrant were a sham, and the cops moved so fast that they had to be up to something."

John and Pia kept quiet. They could sense that Gabrielson was leading up to a defense plan. Vittone was in the awkward position of knowing, almost with certainty, that Alegri's death was the catalyst for his daughter's downfall, but he certainly could not reveal that to Pia or her lawyer.

"Mike, I want you to go scout around Pia's building, the Dorchester, on the West Side. Talk to the building manager especially. Find out what he knows and what kind of guy he is. I'm going to look into this Sgt. Epstein and see how he came up with this story. Mr. Vittone, I don't know exactly what to do with you. Have you got any enemies who might be trying to hurt your daughter?" she queried, looking dead straight at him.

It took a lot to make Vittone sweat, but he could feel his face flush with embarrassment. "We've all got enemies, Ms. Gabrielson, perhaps even you," he replied defensively.

"Believe me, Mr. Vittone, I've got more than you, but right now I'm interested in yours. Think about it. If you come up with any thoughts, pass them along to Mike and me."

"I'll think about it," he said quietly.

Gabrielson turned her attention to Pia. "Listen, Pia. Just keep practicing law and leave everything to me. We'll win this one. Don't worry." With that, Leslie ended the first session.

Ten blocks south of Leslie's office in Manhattan, Cavanaugh was going over the case he thought would make his career and catapult him into the Republican nomination for governor of New York and into the governor's mansion in Albany. It was ironic at how his view of the case paralleled that of his opponent. As he explained it to his two associates who would be trying the case with him, "I think we've got her. The FBI, the most credible institution in the United States made the arrest, and they found a ton of drugs hidden in her apartment. The apartment security says the girl was the only one with access, and she's the only child of the biggest drug kingpin on the Eastern seaboard. She even changed her name to hide her links to her father. And folks, Gabrielson's team doesn't know it yet because they've only heard about his anonymous statement to the grand jury, but I've landed the biggest fish of them all, Vincent Noletti, a made Pucchini soldier. The guy turned, and I'm going to march him right into Judge Leonard Abram's courtroom and have him testify that John Vittone, Pia Vassar's father, is the number two man in the Pucchini organization and the drug brains behind the whole outfit. The morning after I convict the kid, we're going to charge Pucchini and Vittone with conspiracy and bring them all down. You two will be fighting to become the next United States Attorney after I leave the playing field."

His understudy, Linda Stauder, a Harvard graduate, asked, "Jay, doesn't this case bother you even a little bit? The confidential informant is unnamed, undisclosed, and the cops moved so fast, it's unbelievable. They get a call at 9:00 a.m., get the affidavit typed up in two hours, race to Abram's office, and the FBI nabs her at 7:00 p.m. that evening. And the drugs were very conveniently found, weren't they? Don't you think that she could have done a better job hiding the stuff? And she makes a fortune; why does she need to get involved in criminal activity? A favor to her father? I don't think so; she's too smart."

"Linda, I don't care. I'm looking at the big picture. Do you have any idea of how many people, kids, everybody that the Pucchinis get hooked on drugs and then once they got 'em, they keep them on a line, forcing them to rob just to maintain their habit." Cavanaugh really worked himself into a lather over this, and he was like a politician on the stump, giving a stem-winding speech. He was going to force himself to believe in this case. "The girl is just a small fish. If we get her, we bring down everybody and get these bastards off the streets and out of everybody's lives. This is like a holy crusade, and we're part of it."

His associates could only wonder in silence. Why would her father send her to law school, get her hooked up with a top firm so that she could be in the legitimate world, then turn around and get her mixed up with the mob and risk everything for something he tried so hard to avoid? Why would she jeopardize her life when there were millions of other hiding places in the city? It was useless to argue with their boss on this one; he was too far gone.

Laura Cavanaugh was the daughter of one of top executives for XEROX when it ruled the photocopy world with a virtual monopoly. She married Jay because he was tall and handsome and a guy with a future. But a great deal of money was one thing that she did not yet possess, and with three brothers and a sister, she got very little money from her parents. Hopefully, one day her father's estate would be rather substantial with his huge stock options and bonus arrangements, but that day was a long way off. After Jay's eight years with the government, she felt that he should have joined a big firm and gone over to the other side, defending criminals caught in multimillion dollar imbroglios and allowing him to earn a seven-figure salary.

Jay didn't want to work in a stuffy New York City firm with client quotas, daily meetings and long hours. He wanted to be in court, where the real action was. He promised his wife that he would get into politics immediately after he won his first case that threw some good publicity his way. The Vittone case was that case, and Laura Cavanaugh was already picking out furniture for her new address.

In bed that night, Cavanaugh came down from his high a few hours before in his office. He knew as well as his associates, that the Vassar case had some huge common sense glitches. Why the girl's father would want to get her mixed up in the drug trade did not make sense, and he was having a real hard time falling asleep. Counting sheep didn't help when the political stakes were this high for him.

"How's the case going?" Laura asked, hoping for a positive answer.

"The evidence is good. I've got a nice clean case, but it still bugs me. This Pia Vassar is bright, I mean brilliant, and is a top lawyer with one of the biggest firms in the city. She would not normally have done this kind of thing. It's stupid and would serve neither her nor her father any purpose. I can convict her, but everything tells me it was a setup. If I destroy her, and she's innocent, I wouldn't be real happy. I'd have to live with that forever."

"Jay, quit being so idealistic. You're doing society a favor. You can get rid of a whole Mafia organization with this one case. Everybody will be better off! You know that. There's no doubt that they kill, extort and they make it impossible for anyone to have an honest business. Jay, this is the right thing for the world and that includes us. She's not totally innocent, no matter what. She is her father's daughter. She had to be in on thousands of scams over the years, and you know it, baby," she said as she took off her nightie.

"I keep telling myself that, but I'm just not sure about this, sweetie."

"But, darlin', this is your one chance, your 15 minutes of fame. Don't blow it, Jay," she admonished him. "Jay, come here. Believe me, you're doing the right thing, honey."

⪼ CHAPTER XXVI ⪻

U.S. COURTHOUSE, NEW YORK, MAY, 1999

THE PUBLICITY FOR THE trial was immense. The local New York television stations, the flagships for the nationwide networks, had been allowed by the judge to set up inside the courtroom. Abrams wanted his moment of fame, too, and at the next federal judge's conference in Vegas, he would be the star of the show, lecturing on how to run a high profile case. The world was going to see how a no-nonsense judge operated.

The press was allowed 15 passes to enter the courtroom, and Hampton used all the power and prestige of his Pulitzer to get a front-row seat. Two tabloid fiction writers were in the courtroom, hoping to parlay the transcript of the proceedings into a million seller book. Cavanaugh appeared with his two legal beagles, prepared to give the judge written memos on any tricky issues that arose during the trial, and a jury consultant and three paralegals sat in the rest of the chairs that spread from the counsel table down to the far wall. The might and power of the U.S. Government was lined up against the forces of evil. Cavanaugh wanted the jurors to know that this was a monstrous case and this defendant had a lot of fire power of her own. She deserved this kind of attention for the kinds of crimes that she and her father committed.

Gabrielson, on the other hand, wanted to portray Pia as an innocent victim, a corporate attorney, alone in the world, with only her female lawyer by her side to protect her. She was no Mafia chieftain, but only a sacrificial lamb, the pitiful object of a contrived criminal setup. Her father might be a bad guy, but she did everything to rid herself of that kind of life. Behind them sat Alexandra Morariu, a picture of wholesomeness, and the three leading members of Pia's law firm, Chesney, Starcloth and Vining, putting a hold on their busy and lucrative practices to throw their full support to their innocent partner. No Mafia thugs were within 10 miles of the courthouse.

Abrams told all counsel and the defendant to meet him in his chambers before the jury was picked. There, he laid down the rules. No one was to make any lengthy objections, or any speeches, when rising to protest proposed testimony. They were limited to simply saying, "Objection, relevance" or "Objection, hearsay." Anything else was to be taken up at sidebar. No lawyer was to posture or attempt to inflame the jury. Court rulings were to be respected and not followed by any sighs or rolling of the eyes. "And you, Miss Vassar, you keep still, no matter what happens." The judge made it clear that no shenanigans were to be tolerated.

After the jury was chosen, Cavanaugh led off with his best witness, Special Agent Graham from the FBI.

"Agent Graham, please tell the jury what you did on the evening of December 8, 1998."

Graham swivelled in his chair so that he could look at Cavanaugh and the jury simply by changing the gaze of his eyes. I left the federal courthouse with a search warrant about 2:00 p.m., and went back to headquarters. I gathered two junior agents and ran a computer printout on Ms. Vassar and her father, John Vittone. We drove across town to the Dorchester co-op building and met with the manager and told him we wanted to search the apartment of one Pia Vassar. The manager explained that he did not have a key to the second lock, so we decided to wait for Ms. Vassar to return home that night. We wanted the suspect to be there when we made our investigation so that she could be confident that we had not planted anything there.

"We sat in the security manager's office, and around 6:00 p.m., he told us that the woman on the closed-circuit monitor entering through the front door of the building was Ms. Vassar. We took the stairs up to her apartment and when she opened the locks to her door, we came out of the staircase and presented her with our warrant."

"Did you proceed to execute that warrant?"

"Yes we did."

"And what happened when you conducted your search?"

"We found a bag of cocaine in her freezer and another in her closet."

"Are those the same bags that you found, sitting over on the evidence table?"

"Yes, Sir, they are."

"Madame clerk, please bring those up for the witness to examine," Cavanaugh asked politely.

"Agent Graham, how do you know that those bags are the same ones you found in Ms. Vassar's apartment?"

"My two agents and I put our initials on the bags along with the date and time, and we drove them directly to the lab where the contents were tested and have remained in a temperature controlled vault until we delivered them here this morning."

"What did you do with Ms. Vassar?"

"We read her the Miranda warning and rights."

"How did she respond?"

"She did not want to make a statement and wanted to see a lawyer."

"Where did you take her?"

"We handcuffed her and took her to Riker's Island where she was fingerprinted and had her photo taken. Her father appeared two hours later and made bail for her."

"How much bail did he post?"

"Objection, Your Honor," Gabrielson challenged. "Irrelevant, inflammatory and prejudicial."

"Sustained, that has nothing to do with the charges," Judge Abrams opined from the bench.

Since that was Cavanaugh's last question, he announced to the court that the witness was excused.

Gabrielson stood and told Abrams that she had nothing further on cross-examination, but that she also had subpoenaed Graham, and she was planning on calling him as a hostile witness. Abrams instructed Graham that he was temporarily excused from the trial, but that he might have to reappear.

Cavanaugh bellowed to the back of the room, "Mr. Marshall, please bring in Mr. Wong."

An Oriental man strode down the center aisle of the courtroom wearing a seersucker suit and a blue polka dot bow tie.

The clerk walked over to the witness stand and swore in the little, 60-year-old man. He placed a thick folder on the partition and told Cavanaugh the following story. On December 9, 1998, Agent Graham walked into his laboratory in the federal building at about 1:00 a.m., with two packages that looked like bags of sugar. Graham had laid them down on his counter, and he performed a routine acidity test on the contents of both containers. Before that, he tasted a speck of each. The tests confirmed conclusively his suspicions. Inside those bags was pure cocaine, with a street value estimated at $180,000. He, too, placed his initials on the bag, and the bags had never left his safe until Agent Graham had picked them up that very morning.

Again, Gabrielson had no questions.

Going over every detail of the search, the arrest and the laboratory testing took Cavanaugh deep into the afternoon session. It was 4:00 p.m., and Abrams wanted to beat the traffic home. "I want to thank both counsel for moving this case along," he told the jury. These accolades were really reserved for Cavanaugh, as Gabrielson said very little and nothing of importance. Abrams was trying to score some points for the prosecution. "We'll reconvene at 10:00 a.m." He banged his gavel and almost flew out the back door behind his bench.

When Leslie met with John, Pia and McKenna at 6:00 p.m. in her office she announced, "It's all gone just as we assumed. We'll let them dig themselves a grave. Tomorrow, we face the best witness they have. This Vincent Noletti that they've put on their witness list, has turned, we all know that. It's going to be a little uncomfortable, but do you think you can sit there perfectly still, Pia? He's probably going to detail the entire criminal careers of both Tommy Pucchini and your father."

Vittone's expression never changed. His daughter did the talking for them. "If our little plan works, I think I can take it."

"Good, just prepare yourself for some ugly testimony. And remember, the jury's gonna be glancing over at you constantly for your reaction. Remember this one good lesson: never change your expression no matter what the witness says."

At 9:45 the next morning Pia walked into court with a new member of her entourage. Gabrielson was, as usual, toting two heavy attache cases full of law books and notes. McKenna had boxes loaded on a wheel-in cart and Morariu, the faithful friend, tagged behind. Pia and a native Sardinian climbed the steps up to the entrance of the courthouse together. He wanted to test Vincent Noletti to see if he really had the guts to turn on John Vittone right in front of the man. Pucchini let it be known that Alegri died a violent death for his transgressions, and they could not believe that Noletti wanted to tempt the same fate. Both Sicilians and Sardinians had long memories.

Abrams gaveled the courtroom into silence and directed, "Call your next witness, Mr. Cavanaugh." Cavanaugh put on the two FBI men who accompanied Graham to Pia's apartment and they monotonously recited the same facts as Graham.

Then Cavanaugh called a motive witness—the witness who could hopefully establish the rationale for the crime.

"Ma'am, please state your name for the record."

"Madeline Hotchkiss."

"Ms. Hotchkiss, where do you work?"

"At the New York County Department of Vital Statistics."

"Have you brought with you here today some certified documents?"

"Yes, I have."

"Can you tell the jury what they reflect, please."

"These are official photocopies, showing that 12 years ago in this county, a Pia Vittone changed her name from Pia Vittone to Pia Vassar. Also, other records, including her law school transcripts from Columbia Law and her birth certificate, were changed to reflect her new name."

"Your Honor, the government moves for the introduction of these documents into evidence as government exhibit 36."

Gabrielson never got out of her seat, knowing that this tied Pia to her father and that Noletti would try to sink the both of them. "No objection," she called out.

"They will be received in evidence," Abrams directed.

A few minutes later, Arthur Johnson sat down on the witness stand for the prosecution. Cavanaugh took him through his testimony just like at the grand jury, which would hopefully show that only Pia Vassar had access to the co-op.

Amongst the answers to the questions, Johnson told Cavanaugh, "You've got to remember, I only keep one key to one lock for each apartment, and every unit has two locks. We have the bottom one, but not the top key. That way, a tenant can leave the top unlocked and if they want to let somebody in, the tenant can call me to open the door. It's impossible for anybody connected to management to get in without the tenant's permission."

Cavanaugh then moved to the next phase of his "entry to the apartment" evidence. "And, Mr. Johnson, did you keep a record of everyone who went in and out of the building on December 8, 1998?"

"Yes, sir, I did."

"Was there anyone who was unaccounted for?"

"No, sir, there were eight people, and they were all logged in to specific apartments as guests or workers. No one had anything to do with Ms. Vassar or unit 12F."

"Thank you for coming, Mr. Johnson," Cavanaugh concluded.

Gabrielson decided to make a soft attempt at cross-examination, so as not to tip her hand. "Of course, Mr. Johnson, somebody could have gained access to the building that you did not log in."

"That's highly unlikely. Almost impossible. We have great security and doormen and a locked building. It's 99.9 percent impossible."

"But there is always that one possibility?"

"Hardly," he responded with disdain etched in his face.

"That's all I have, Your Honor," Gabrielson announced.

Again, the jury was mystified at the notoriety that such a mediocre lawyer garnered over the years in the press.

The 33-year-old prosecutor saved his best witness for last. "Your Honor, now the U.S. Government calls Mr. Vincent Noletti to the stand." The elegant European sitting in the gallery and the defendant sat perfectly still. The jury scanned them and then turned their attention to the doorway the Marshall held open. A dozen FBI agents surrounded Noletti and escorted him to the stand. They stood next to him in the jury box and positioned themselves around the courtroom, as if expecting an assassin to rise up and shoot Noletti.

Pia knew late in the game of his testimony because he was listed on Cavanaugh's list of witnesses that he was required to file under court rules 10 days before. Noletti was well-coached and told to look at the far back wall and over the heads of the gallery, giving an impression that he was meeting Vittone's stare, when in fact he never saw him.

The testimony was as brutal as Gabrielson predicted. Noletti told of his 22 years as a soldier in the Pucchini family. He robbed at gunpoint, administered beatings, charged 50 percent a month on loans to hapless borrowers and terrorized them when they were a day late. He witnessed executions and dug graves. He took payoffs from legitimate contractors to his Capos. He was loyal, and whatever he had been called upon to do by the Pucchini family, he faithfully carried out.

Pia was waiting to see how far in his testimony Noletti would go, because she was 100 percent sure that her father never met Noletti. The Federal Rules of Criminal Procedure did not allow depositions to be taken, so neither Pia nor Gabrielson had any idea what the rat would attempt to pin on John Vittone.

Cavanaugh closed in for the kill. "Mr. Noletti, have you ever met John Vittone?"

"Yes sir, twice. One time out at the Garden City Hotel in Nassau County. I delivered some drugs to a guy on Staten Island, and I delivered the money he gave me to Mr. Vittone."

"Tell us about your conversation."

"I walked into the office, he came out and took the bag of money and said thanks."

"When was the other time?"

"I met him at Tommy's hangout, where he does business, at the Italian American Club in Ozone Park. We had a couple of beers. Everybody was celebrating a big score, a heroin deal, that Mr. Vittone pulled off. He was right there, dividing up the money and giving everybody their share. Everybody was talking about how Vittone was practically a don in his own right, running a worldwide drug network for Tommy, moving drugs around everyday and making millions. He was the brains and the moneymaker for the whole family. Vittone was the kingpin."

Cavanaugh could not wait for the coup de gras. The sight of Vittone did not intimidate Noletti one bit, and Cavanaugh could not believe his good fortune. Vittone came to court in all his arrogance, and now his daughter was going to prison for the rest of her life. The pretty girl in the pink silk suit and the ponytail with the pink bow would be wearing a prison smock and cleaning floors with a tooth brush.

"Mr. Noletti," Cavanaugh intoned with all his prosecutorial pomposity, "do you see Mr. John Vittone here today in this courtroom?"

"Yes, sir, I do. Sitting right behind his daughter, the defendant," Noletti answered, as he pointed straight at the dapper man.

Pia sat still, as did the man sitting behind her. They both met the stares of the jurors in a completely relaxed fashion.

After a few more questions, Cavanaugh sat down.

Every juror on the panel read about the famous Leslie Gabrielson, and now when she stood up, she grabbed their undivided attention. How was the greatest trial lawyer in the city going to pull this one out with the facts so weighted against her? She was a legal impresario, but they gave her no chance on this case.

Leslie decided to have a little fun before she bagged Noletti. "Now, you say sir, that you've met John Vittone and that you know his whole life story. Ever been to his house?"

"No, I don't think he'd be that stupid."

"Then you don't know where he lives?"

"No."

"Know what kind of car he drives?"

Noletti could not be sure of that, even though he thought it was a Mercedes. He decided to play it safe.

"No idea," he replied.

Gabrielson decided to get a little riskier. "How do you get out to Garden City? What exits do you take. On what street is Mr. Vittone's office, Mr. Noletti?"

"All I know is that you take the Expressway. The LIE. That's all I know. I only went once out there you know."

"What's Mr. Vittone's cell phone number?'

"Never called him."

"You're not real close to Mr. Vittone, are you Mr. Noletti?"

"Never said I was."

"But Mr. Noletti, you did say to this jury, under oath in front of Judge Abrams that you met Mr. John Vittone twice, didn't you? That you saw him and you knew what he looked like. Correct?" Gabrielson questioned as she walked over to the front row where the visitors sat and right next to John Hampton and the man Noletti had pointed at.

"Yes, I pointed him out."

"You pointed to this man right here; I have my hand on his shoulder. You pointed to him as the John Vittone you met in Garden City and in Ozone Park. You identified him as the drug kingpin on the Pucchini family."

"Yeah, I pointed out John Vittone right there." That was the man Cavanaugh had shown to Noletti in the picture with the mayor of New York taken 30 years before, and Cavanaugh had told him that morning, before taking the stand, that John Vittone had walked into court that day with his daughter and was sitting in the front row.

"Thank you, Mr. Noletti," Gabrielson answered. She continued, "That's all I have, Your Honor." The jury thought that this woman was vastly overrated.

"The government rests its case, Your Honor," Cavanaugh bid to the court.

"Your Honor, the defense moves for a judgment of acquittal," Gabrielson requested perfunctorily and without any forcefulness, knowing full well that the motion would never be granted, but wanting to maintain her rights on appeal.

"Denied," Abrams ruled.

"Your Honor, the defense calls Giuseppe Lombardo."

Abrams called out to Hank DeLong, his trusted Marshall. "Please check the hallway, Mr. DeLong."

Gabrielson shot back. "No need, Your Honor. Mr. Lombardo is

right here in the courtroom."

With that, the man Noletti identified as John Vittone stood up and walked into the well of the courtroom. Cavanaugh could not believe his eyes. "Objection, Your Honor, not disclosed on the witness list," Cavanaugh exclaimed.

The very circus that Abrams was trying to avoid was now beginning. "Counsel, approach the bench."

"Ms. Gabrielson, what's going on here?" Abrams almost yelled at her. He hated and despised Leslie Gabrielson for representing the vermin that she paraded into his courtroom every month.

"Your Honor, a friend of Ms. Vassar's came to court today as moral support. He had every right to do so. The U.S. Constitution guarantees an open courtroom," Gabrielson contended .

Abrams answered back, "I know what the U.S. Constitution says, Ms. Gabrielson. Why didn't you list this person as a witness?"

"I didn't know he was going to be a witness, Your Honor, until Mr. Cavanaugh made him into one. Surprise is a recognized defense to having to list a witness, Your Honor," she purred like a lion, for she hated Abrams, this conservative, law and order judge, just as much as he disliked her.

"I'm afraid she's right," Abrams said, betraying his prejudice toward Leslie and her client.

Gabrielson waited to trap Abrams for years. "We'll overlook any bias your last comment indicated, Your Honor," she practically snarled.

"Ms. Gabrielson, be real careful here. You're about one step from a contempt citation."

"I'll be careful, Your Honor."

"The witness may testify," Abrams conceded.

Gabrielson served up softballs. "What is your name, please?"

"Giuseppe Lombardo."

"Are you John Vittone?"

"No, I am not."

"Are you, or have you ever in any way, shape or form, been known as John Vittone?"

"Never."

"Have you ever called yourself by that name or held yourself out as John Vittone?"

"Absolutely not."

"Do you know the defendant, Pia Vassar?'

"Yes, I do. She's sitting right there."

"Are you her father, or in any way related to her?"

"No, I am not."

Leslie decided to let it go at that and not press her good luck. Lombardo grew up with Vittone in Carbonia, and it had been rumored around the small town for years that one man must have gotten tangled up in their two family trees. They looked very much alike, which was not that uncommon in towns where half the eligible husbands and fathers were shot down early in their youth, and the remaining ones were called upon to service more than one native girl.

Cavanaugh approached the witness. " Are you related to John Vittone?" he asked, trying to establish that Noletti made an honest mistake.

"No, sir, not that I know of."

"What do you mean, 'not that I know of'?"

"Nobody ever told us we were related. We didn't grow up related."

"Where are you from?"

"Sardinia."

"The same exact place as John Vittone, right?"

"Yes, sir."

"The same town?"

"Yes, sir, originally. And then he moved away."

"Didn't people mistake you for one another?"

"Not really, sir. Not the people who knew us. They could tell the difference."

Cavanaugh realized that Lombardo came up with the perfect answer. If Noletti really knew Vittone and met him, he should have known the difference. Lombardo was implying to the jury that Noletti was a liar.

"But you do look similar, you have to admit, don't you?"

"We both have black hair."

"And the same noses."

"I don't know about that. My nose is long. I don't compare it to other people," Lombardo laughed, and so did the jurors, to Cavanaugh's chagrin. Cavanaugh decided to sit down with whatever case he had left.

Gabrielson knew that she scored a lot of points, but the drugs were still in Pia's apartment, and that was a problem. Noletti still had detailed the Pucchini organization, and Cavanaugh would plead that he just made an honest mistake.

To show that Pia was not the only one who may have wanted to hide things in her apartment on December 8, the pugnacious female lawyer called the doorman at the Dorchester as her next witness. She also wanted to slow down the pace, after putting on Lombardo and putting serious doubt in the minds of the jurors.

"What is your name?" she questioned.

"Eddie Levine."

"And Mr. Levine, where do you work?"

"The Dorchester Co-op, on 53rd Street."

"How long have you been there?"

"It'll be five years in August."

"Did anybody out of the ordinary come into your building on December 8, 1998?" Leslie questioned, having prepared Levine for his testimony three times, and knowing what his answer would be.

"Yes, ma'am, they did."

"Who?"

"A New York City building inspector."

"How do you remember that?"

"Two reasons. He tipped me going in and going out, and nobody does both, especially a guy from the city. And I keep a little log of my own to protect my rear end."

"Why do you do that?"

"I don't want anybody to say I let somebody in that robbed the place or something."

"Does the manager know about your book?"

"I don't think so."

"Did you bring your log with you here today?"

"Yes."

"What's it show?"

"That an Inspector Ivone showed up and wanted to see the manager."

"Did he go in?"

"He did."

"About how long did he stay?"

"About 42 minutes, according to what I wrote down."

"Thank you, Mr. Levine."

Leslie turned to Cavanaugh and said, "Your witness."

Cavanaugh's cross with this witness did not go much better than the examination of Lombardo.

"You don't have any idea of what he did inside, do you?'

"No, sir, not at all."

"You don't know where he went, do you?"

"No, I don't."

"He could have been there for any reason, right?"

"That's true."

Jay turned to the judge. "Move to strike all the testimony of this witness as being irrelevant and immaterial."

"Miss Gabrielson, come up here," Abrams demanded.

Leslie got to the bench and Abrams focused on her. "Ms. Gabrielson, this testimony doesn't prove or disprove one fact in issue. People show up at buildings all day long, so what?"

"Your Honor, I'll link it up circumstantially, and we'll give an inference, at the very least, to the jury for our theory that somebody else went into the apartment."

Again, Abrams and Cavanaugh were at a loss for words. They both knew that the appellate courts allowed great latitude in developing alternative theories for the commission of a crime. As long as she represented she could tie this all up, they were stuck with it.

Cavanaugh pleaded, "This testimony doesn't prove anything."

"Overruled," the Judge ordered. Abrams was siding with Gabrielson much more than he had planned to when the trial began.

"Thank you, Your Honor," replied Gabrielson in her sweetest way.

Leslie had pulled off an upset with Noletti, and now she placed an outsider at the apartment house on the day of the crime. She needed to create more doubt in the minds of the jury, and the next witness called was the Dorchester's head of security.

When Gabrielson asked the security chief how the surveillance system worked, he told the 12 jury members that there were two cameras that scanned each side of the hallway on each floor of the building. The camera on each side would become fixed right before the elevator door was ready to open on that particular floor, and at that moment, the camera would shift its gaze back to the elevator and focus directly on whoever was getting on and off. That morning, at 7:50 the elevator stopped twice at the 12th floor, and there must have been a malfunction. Each time the camera moved its eye to see the occupant, no one was there.

Gabrielson acted incredulously. "Do you know how that could be?'

"Well, the elevator does malfunction from time to time. The elevator company has a maintenance contract, and they come out about every day for one thing or another. It could have been that."

"Or sir, someone who could have been pressing the floor buttons and sending the elevator up empty?"

"That's a possibility."

"Sir, tell the jury, have you ever seen that happen before?"

"Maybe once that I can think of; it's pretty rare."

"How much time would that leave the corridor unmonitored when that happened?"

"About three minutes each time, because you have to remember, the camera stays on the elevator until the door closes again and then on the lobby in front of the elevator for 30 seconds to focus on any person who might be getting out. Also, nobody realizes it, but the camera then scans every door all the way down the hall until it stops, and the whole corridor is in view."

"How long does that take?"

"I never counted. Two or three minutes."

"So, if the door opened and closed, then went down a floor or two to be sent back up to open and close again, the corridor would be uncovered for what, five, six minutes?"

"Sure, it's very possible."

"Now where is Miss Vassar's apartment located on the 12th floor?"

"At the far end of the corridor."

"Then we wouldn't know for a number of minutes what was going on in front of Ms. Vassar's apartment on the same day drugs were found there."

"That's right."

"Who besides you knows how the camera operates?"

"Only Mr. Johnson and myself."

Leslie turned a few degrees and looked squarely at the jury. "Only you and Mr. Arthur Johnson?" She wanted them to remember the building manager's name, and they got the point.

"Yes, Ma'am. Only me and Mr. Johnson."

"Thank you, Mr. Flynn," Gabrielson said quietly.

The damage was done. Everyone in the courtroom found it interesting that at the critical moment, the cameras were not surveilling Pia's apartment. Cavanaugh could only ask lame questions, like wasn't this ordinary procedure for the cameras to move if the elevator door opened, but he couldn't explain the gaping questions left by Gabrielson's examination. Now he was left with a surprise visitor, Noletti's misidentification, and a mysterious elevator.

In the office with Gabrielson that night, Pia was ecstatic. "You were terrific. You wowed them," Pia lauded her attorney.

"Pia, take it easy. First of all, you can't take the stand or Cavanaugh will kill you with questions about your father. You and I made that decision before the trial, and after the grand jury fiasco, it's still the way to go. But now, all the jurors are going to be wondering why you don't defend yourself. That looks bad, but you have no choice. Noletti still gave some powerful testimony about the Pucchinis and your father, and Cavanaugh will say Lombardo was all an honest mistake and a trick by us. Elevators malfunction all the time. Remember, they also show nobody getting on or off which, they will argue, means you were the only person going into your apartment that day. We've got a long way to go. Remember, only your fingerprints were on the refrig. Nobody else's." The FBI dusted the packages of cocaine, but Datale had been wearing gloves when planting his incriminating evidence. The only prints in the apartment belonged to Pia.

Pia sat back in the chair. She felt like all the wind went out of her sails. They had a long way to go, and later that night in bed, next to Hampton, she tossed and turned, woke him up, and started to talk about the case.

"She won't let me take the stand," she recounted to him as they went over the events in court.

"Baby, there's an old saying from Abraham Lincoln: 'A lawyer who tries to represent himself has a fool for a client.' You're a brilliant lawyer, but let Leslie handle the case. I hate to say it, but you didn't do yourself any favors in front of the grand jury."

"But John, it kills me. I take witnesses down in court all the time. I can hold my own in a courtroom better than anybody. Those guys at CSV didn't do me any favors. I got to the top on my own."

"Honey, let's face it, it's brutal, but you are your father's daughter, and you cannot take the stand."

She rolled over and thought about her life. He put his arm around her and neither one slept well that night. Both of them were worried and restless about the next day's events.

Sgt. Epstein vigorously fought his subpoena to testify at the trial through a motion hearing and an expedited appeal. He asserted that he had an obligation not to turn over the identity of his confidential informant, but the appellate court was quick to point out that Epstein's affidavit for the search warrant recited that he did not know the informant's name, only that he used him before and knew his street nickname. Epstein had very little to protect, and the chances of the informant being uncovered, and the mob seeking vengeance, were slim. The court of appeals entered a mandate compelling his appearance in court.

DeLong announced the next day's session, and Abrams walked in with his black robes flowing. "Are you ready to proceed, Ms. Gabrielson?"

"Yes. I'm putting on Sgt. Epstein."

Epstein listened to Leslie's introductory questions and relaxed a bit. He decided to stick to the affidavit. When asked about his informant, he explained, "Got a call from a guy we call "Shoeless" because he's always walking around in three pairs of socks and no shoes. He gave us tips before that worked out. He led us to a warehouse with stolen goods and a gun that was in a dumpster. He found a stolen car. Stuff like that. He was reliable." There was no way he was going to divulge Marucci's name, because that would practically guarantee a prison sentence for bribery as well as other charges.

"So, you have no idea what the name of this source is, officer?"

"Not his name, just his description, and I know his voice."

"And on one quick, nothing call, without meeting the guy or following up or investigating, you decided to file a probable cause affidavit, alert the FBI and get a search warrant."

"It was legally sufficient for Judge Abrams to sign it, and sure enough, drugs turned up in the apartment," he confidently told the jury as he smiled at them.

Abrams' face was frozen as he sat on the bench and wondered how he could ever have signed a warrant based on such thin evidence.

"You weren't doing this as a favor, or for somebody who wanted to frame Ms. Vassar, were you?"

"Objection, no basis, and no factual predicate for that question," Cavanaugh yelled out.

"I'll let it in." Abrams replied, assuming that Epstein could give a solid answer anyway.

"That's absolute hog wash, counsel, and you know it."

Epstein should never have thrown in the "you know it" because Leslie pounced immediately.

"Mr. DeLong, can you bring in the tape player; I want Mr. Epstein to hear something."

Hank DeLong rolled in a table with an audio cassette player and Leslie inserted the cartridge.

"Mr. Epstein, I want you to listen closely. This is a tape made of a call placed to the dispatch operator at your precinct on December 8, 1998, and her following page to you. The words, "Tell him it's Izzy. It's urgent," and the operator's message, "Sgt. Epstein, you're needed on the phone in reference to Izzy," played over the recorder loud and true for all the jurors to hear.

"Does that refresh your memory, officer?"

"When I got on the phone, all I remember that he said was that this was the shoeless guy. I don't remember any Izzy."

"You were getting a warrant executed to invade someone's privacy, trying to get them locked up, and you can't remember who called you?"

When Cavanaugh's objection to the comment was sustained, Abrams also cautioned Leslie. "That's your last speech, Ms. Gabrielson. Save it for closing. Do you understand me?"

"Yes, Sir," Leslie meekly replied, but she knew the jury was listening and that a ruling to strike the comment would not erase it from a juror's mind. Leslie dismissed Epstein as a witness, knowing that he left the stand looking like a liar or as a very evasive cop who was up to something.

Cavanaugh still thought he had a glimmer of hope, because no one came forward with any direct testimony that could prove that the drugs were placed in the apartment by anyone other than Pia. He met with the three FBI men numerous times before the trial to prepare their testimony, and each time, they regurgitated the same story of how they received the information from Epstein, met with this New York cop to get him to sign an affidavit, gone to Abram's chambers, and left from headquarters to travel to the Dorchester. There, they met the chief of security, waited for Pia to appear, and based on Epstein's tip, searched the apartment locating and impounding the illicit drugs. They made a thorough inspection of the inside of the apartment, and the only fingerprints in the area of the closet and the refrigerator belonged to Pia. They found no prints whatsoever on the drugs themselves, which had little meaning. If Pia or one of conspirators, presumably one of her father's henchmen, had made the plant, they would certainly have been careful not to leave any personal identification on the evidence. In his original glee at having such an airtight case, he never followed up on anything else that the FBI might have seen that night.

Gabrielson called to the stand as one of her final witnesses the man whom she hoped would put a nail into the coffin that contained the prosecution's case, "Your Honor, the defense would like to recall to the stand Agent Graham."

Graham strode in and walked down the aisle between the rows of benches stationed on either side of the room that were packed with onlookers.

The night of the arrest, Agent Graham was smitten by the style and modesty of this beautiful woman who spent an hour in his squad car on the ride over to Riker's. He told her at the jail that he hoped that he could find the truth in this matter.

A month before this trial started, Gabrielson walked the eight blocks from her office to the Manhattan offices of the FBI and strolled into the reception area outside Graham's personal office unannounced. Leslie was playing a hunch. Pia remarked on more than one occasion to her that Graham had been exceptionally nice that evening and had extended her every courtesy. Gabrielson was betting that Graham would break standard protocol and talk to this defense lawyer because of the impression that her client had made on him. Rarely, if ever, did the police talk to anyone for the defense without a subpoena.

Gabrielson's gamble turned out to be a winner. The receptionist announced that Graham would see her, and Leslie was ushered through a maze of hallways into Graham's room, where Graham rose and offered her a seat.

"Mr. Graham, we've met a few times in the courtroom at hearings, but never formally."

"And, Ms. Gabrielson, up until right this minute, I never thought we would."

"I doubt that it's because of any good feelings for me. Am I right?"

"This may shock you, but I don't have any bad feelings, either. In fact, I like the way that you put these prosecutors and judges on the defensive. They're all so arrogant and pompous, and when you confront them, it really makes me laugh sometimes. I don't laugh when you cross-examine me and try to make me look like an incompetent federal agent, but on the other hand, you're a challenge. I've won a few with you. We're probably about even. I don't take it personally, even when you get somebody off who's really guilty as sin. It's just part of the program. We just didn't prove our case well enough."

"A cop who doesn't take it personally. That's refreshing. But still, I'm sure you wanted to see me because I have a very nice client. True?"

"Bingo."

"Well, if you want to make sure that she gets a fair trial, then let me ask you something. I've read a thousand police reports, and you've read a lot more than that. It's impossible to get everything in the report. You were very detailed about everything that happened at the building and inside that apartment, but I need to know, is there anything else out there that might indicate her innocence?"

Graham studied Gabrielson intently. If he were dating her, he probably couldn't last an hour with her without having a shouting match. She was so intense, and her mind was so inquisitive, that she made him really edgy. This woman never relaxed, and she never let her guard down. There was always one more rock to look under, and she couldn't rest until she finished. Graham was a mover and shaker himself, but he wondered where she got that energy.

"Ms. Gabrielson, first let's talk off the record, OK?"

"That's fine with me."

"Yeah, you're right. I like your client. There's a lot to like. Beauty and brains is a very good combination these days. Number two, she was absolutely shocked when those drugs turned up in her apartment. I've arrested a lot of people, and she looked and acted very innocent to me. It all looked like a setup. I didn't like the smell of the case from the "get go," to be honest with you. But I would never admit that in open court. Never."

"That's all right. I didn't come here to make you look bad and embarrass you. I just came to find anything Cavanaugh may have overlooked."

"He's a good lawyer. I've done a lot of cases with him."

"I agree with you. I've been against him in court. He can hold his own. But Mr. Graham, none of us is perfect. We can't find every

204

single detail. I never had a case where I didn't look back and wish that I had done one more thing. I know you looked into this more than the usual case. Tell me something good. I can't believe you want to see some lesbian matron strip searching this girl every day for 25 years if she really didn't do it. You don't want to hurt her just because her father may not be on your list of favorite people."

"You're right." After a short pause, he told her the rest of the story. "When we initially got there, we do as we always do and looked for any sign of forced entry. We looked at the door, and it was un-damaged. Obviously, 12 stories up, they didn't come through the windows, but we looked anyway. Everything was in order and we left.

"I decided to go back the next morning by myself and look around. There was always the chance that somebody monkeyed with the locks. It's almost impossible to tell if a pro picked a lock, because even if he forced a generic key into the cylinder case, the metal on the pins of the mechanism would hold up and at best, only a micro-scopic shaving of the metal would occur, and there's no way to prove if that came from Ms. Vassar inserting a worn key into the casing. But I decided to look anyway, and I couldn't tell if any disruption in the lock occurred. I'd have needed to take out the whole assembly and bring it to the lab, and then they always tell me it's inconclusive."

Gabrielson was losing her patience, as she really didn't want to learn how a lock worked, but she figured that something good was coming, so she kept quiet.

Graham went on in his studied manner. "I decided to test the one lock that both the suspect and the building manager had a key to, so I went down to Mr. Johnson's office. He wasn't there, and I walked down the hall to the security office next to the lobby, and I found him in there with the security man, Flynn. They were watching the mon-itors, which kind of surprised me. I would think that the manager would have better things to do at the beginning of the day. I mean, how often do you really see something on one of those cameras? Once a week, once a month? I got the feeling they were watching me walk around the building, but I can't prove that.

"I said to Johnson, 'I'd like to see the key to the Vassar apartment for a minute, just to check the lock.' Johnson looked like I had just shot him. His eyes opened and he got stiff.

"I asked him again, 'Mr. Johnson, can I borrow the key for a minute to the Vassar apartment?'

"He said, 'Sure, come on back to the office.'

"As you know, the night before, he told us that he only had the key to the bottom, not to the top. We went down to his office and he opened the cabinet where he hung all the tenants' keys, and the one for Vassar was missing. 'I don't know, it's not here,' he told me. 'Sometimes, we give them to workmen and they don't bring them back. Or sometimes the tenant needs it and promises to return it but forgets about it.' I took him at his word, because it didn't seem to prove much one way or the other. He didn't have any reason to put drugs into her apartment, and he told me that no one went into the cabinet unless it was him.

"But sitting here today, maybe I should have put it into the report. It's our job just to make the arrest. We try to prove the positive, not the negative; that's your job, I guess."

Leslie knew that was always the problem with these cases. Once the cops put together the prima facie elements, they stopped hunting. All of their manpower and resources came to a grinding halt, and the accused had to go out and spend thousands investigating a case with private detectives who did not have the legal authority to enter buildings and apartments, and who could not force witnesses to cooperate. This was why when private lawyers and journalists donated their time after a conviction that didn't make sense was rendered, they found that the man on death row was innocent.

But the missing key didn't tend to show anything by itself. Johnson was just a shlump doing his job, and nobody could show who entered the apartment and made the deposit other than Pia.

But now, the trial had turned a little. The video cameras with the missing footage created some question in the jury's mind. Why had the door opened twice on the 12th floor and no one had gotten on or off? What was going on down at the end of the hallway while the camera was focused on the vacant 12th floor lobby? One of the only persons inside the building that day who was known to the jury was

Art Johnson. Gabrielson implicated him through the security chief's testimony.

Graham retook the witness chair and under questioning from Gabrielson recounted his conversation with Johnson. Cavanaugh, as he did with the other witnesses, tried to show that the missing key was nothing unusual. "Mr. Graham, isn't true that this was so meaningless, you didn't even bother to amend your report to include this conversation?"

"That's true."

"Apparently, what Mr. Johnson told you made sense because you didn't follow up on the conversation."

"I didn't think that it led anywhere in particular."

"You don't have one scintilla of evidence that anyone other than Pia Vassar entered that apartment in the weeks and days leading up to this crime do you?"

"No, I don't."

"You found no evidence of forced entry did you?"

"No. I didn't."

"That's all I have," Cavanaugh concluded.

Gabrielson created a little doubt here and there. All she needed was reasonable doubt about Pia Vittone being the only person with access to the apartment and she and her client would be winners. But at this point, it was very close. Noletti could have made an honest mistake, and the elevator could have malfunctioned. She was not going to parade into the courtroom Perry Mason-style, the surprise witness who would confess on the stand that, yes, he was the guilty one and not Pia. She was positive that whoever that person was, he was too closely aligned to the father, and his testimony was so poisonous to the Pucchinis, she would never find him. She would have to create that one last piece of reasonable doubt with Art Johnson.

Art Johnson was sitting in his office reading the paper, when Mike McKenna stormed in through the lobby and without knocking on the manager's door, practically jumped through the open doorway and dropped a subpoena on Johnson's desk. This was at 8:00 a.m.; Graham was scheduled to testify at 10:00 a.m. when the trial reconvened. Gabrielson decided to give him the least amount of time to collect his thoughts or create a cover-up. She was betting that while Johnson realized that his visitor never returned the key, he was too scared to have a locksmith come to the door of Pia's apartment and make a mold for a new key. If he were caught, it would raise too many questions. Besides, Johnson had to assume that the odds were in his favor after five months and that no one for the defense would ever guess that he no longer had the key. He already testified and in his own mind was off the hook now.

When the paper plopped down on the top of his desk, Johnson was startled and his head jolted upward to meet the look on McKenna's face. "What is this? Who are you?"

"Mr. Johnson, I'm Mike McKenna. I'm a private detective, licensed by the City of New York. Here's my card," McKenna announced, as he let the laminated plastic fall down to where the subpoena was laying. "Mr. Johnson, you need to pick that subpoena up and read it, because you're due in court in two hours. It's duces tecum, so you need to get busy."

"A subpoena for what?" the incredulous Johnson asked, fully believing that his involvement in the Vassar matter was over.

"A subpoena to appear in front of Judge Abrams at the federal courthouse at 10:00 a.m. in the case of United States versus Pia Vassar. You need to be there on time," answered the burly former Marine, who neglected to say that Graham would be leading off and that his testimony would take about an hour.

"I've already appeared. The only subpoena I got was from Mr. Cavanaugh. I'm finished."

"In law, you're never finished, Mr. Johnson. There's two sides to every case. The government goes first and then the defense. Both sides can subpoena you if they want to. The defense can put you on in their case."

"I can't get there that quickly," Johnson protested, now in a panic at the thought of having to face the gauntlet of questions all over again. "I've got too much work to do here, and this notice is way too short. Tell them I'm not coming. This is crazy."

"Mr. Johnson, I'm not telling Judge Abrams anything. All I know is that I'm certified to serve process, and I've served you according to the laws of the good old USA. Remember to bring with you the items asked for in the duces tecum part."

"Duces tecum. What the hell is that?" Johnson almost shouted.

"That's Latin for bring something with you into court. The sub-poena requires you to appear with an object. It should be easy. Read it," instructed McKenna, who was instructed by Gabrielson to pressure the manager as much as he could to see if he'd open the key locker Graham had looked at so that they would know whether or not he had the key before he took the stand and Leslie asked him the question.

Johnson picked up the two pages. The first commanded him to "Appear in the federal court in and for the Southern District of New York," at the time and place written on the face of the document, which was that very day at 10:00 a.m., just as McKenna had instructed him. He looked at the top and sure enough, the words "duces tecum" were typed in and the writ told him to bring with him everything listed on Exhibit A attached thereto.

When Johnson turned to the second page of the stapled doc-ument, to the page with the heading "Exhibit A," his worst fears were realized. There the words, "You are hereby required to bring with you to court all of the keys in your possession, both individually and as an agent, representative and/or manager of the Dorchester condo-minium, to that apartment and unit owned and or occupied by Pia Vassar, and generally described as Unit 12F."

At that moment, Johnson knew that he was in trouble. "Well, Mr. Johnson, just pull that key out of your cabinet there and bring it with you to court. That's not very hard."

But, the building manager was frozen in thought, and he had no intention of opening that metal locker in front of this aggressive investigator. "Listen, I'll get the stuff together. But tell them I need time to get there."

"Mr. Johnson, I'm just an officer of the court. The document I gave you says 10:00 a.m.; that's all I can tell you," McKenna responded, not wanting to push any further. He didn't want Johnson to complain to Abrams that he was unduly pressured. The man was not going to open the metal locker and Leslie would have to take her chances. "I'll tell Ms. Gabrielson that you've been served. We'll see you in court," McKenna added as he casually walked out of the small office.

Art knew that it was useless to try to duplicate the key. That would take hours, and thanks to Gabrielson's tactics, he was left only with minutes. He could take another key with him and claim that this was on the hook corresponding to Pia's apartment, but if they tested the key, it would just further implicate him. The best course seemed to be to plead ignorance. Someone had asked for the key and not returned it. He would keep it short and simple.

Johnson tried to rehearse his testimony on the taxi cab ride downtown to the courthouse, but playing dumb was the best that he could come up with. His hands were shaking, and his forehead was glistening with perspiration.

Graham testified exactly as he had previously in Leslie's office some four weeks ago when she had created the "missing key" issue. At the conclusion of Graham's testimony, the jury was left with a few more unanswered questions, but no direct testimony implicating anyone other than Pia as having the opportunity to bring drugs into the apartment. Cavanaugh could now argue that Leslie was simply grabbing at straws and blowing smoke out to the jury where no fire existed. The prosecutor could persuasively say that this "smoke" only showed how weak Leslie's defense really was.

Leslie Gabrielson did not have a reputation as the best because she lost cases. She was reasonably sure that Johnson never replaced the key that Graham found to be missing. If she could at least make him squirm in front of the jury, then she could circumstantially prove a conspiracy to frame her client. But it would take the best cross-examination of her career.

The cab pulled up in front of the courthouse with about three minutes to spare. Johnson sought out Hank DeLong who was standing in front of the double doors that led into the courtroom. "I'm Arthur Johnson, and I've been subpoenaed to be here at 10:00 a.m." DeLong gave him the suspicious look of a law enforcement officer and told him plainly, "There's another witness in front of you. Take a seat out here in the corridor, and I'll call you when they're ready." Johnson wondered who was inside testifying, but he asked nothing further and took a seat on the bench as he was told to.

A few minutes later, as Johnson watched FBI Agent Graham walk out of the courtroom, the thoughts of their meeting the day after the arrest flashed through his mind. Had Graham recounted the missing key to Gabrielson and the jury? Why was he following the FBI man to the stand? He had no time to guess because DeLong was beckoning him to come inside.

Johnson raised his right hand and the clerk read him the oath. He settled into the wooden chair, and he could feel the upright slats pressing against his back. Gabrielson approached like a graceful leopard stalking her prey.

"Good morning, Mr. Johnson."

"Good morning."

Leslie needed to break Johnson down on two issues: one was Inspector Ivone and the second was the missing key. If she accomplished that, then she could finish him off.

"Mr. Johnson, I subpoenaed your daily entry book for the Dorchester about two, three months ago in February or March 1999. Do you remember that?"

"Yes, I do."

"Did you turn that book over to my office?"

"Yes."

"In its complete, unaltered form?"

"Yes, it was exact."

"Here, let me refresh your memory," she said, handing him the entry book. "Look at December 8."

Johnson thumbed thorough the yearly log to the back entry. "I'm there."

"Good. Do you see a building inspector listed? Anybody named Ivone?"

"No, I don't."

She took him through eight names that were listed, and Johnson accounted for each one. Most were tradesmen who went to particular units, but the inspector was not listed. She also went over the fact with him that people come in and out all the time. The more people in the building, the greater the chances somebody planted the drugs.

"Do you write down everybody you meet with?"

"Yes, I do."

"But there's no reference to an inspector."

"I don't remember any inspector. But if he wasn't going in a unit, I might not jot it down. He could have been discussing a code or something. I don't know. I doubt any building inspector was there that day," Johnson explained, hemming and hawing. He had his eyes cast down at the floor and never looked at the jury.

Gabrielson wasn't going to let him off that easy. "What about this man, a Mr. Watts? He was trying to sell you furniture for the lobby, isn't that what you told us when you went down the list?"

"Yes."

"You listed him, but he didn't go into anybody's apartment."

"That's true. Sometimes I miss somebody, but I don't remember any inspectors."

"Did you know that your doorman, Mr. Levine, also keeps a log, and he did write down a building inspector that day who stayed 42 minutes?"

"No, I didn't know he had a log."

"This inspector just rings no bells?" Gabrielson queried, setting up her case for the finale.

"Miss Gabrielson, it doesn't matter, I only have one key, and it takes two to get into an apartment."

"Do you think in 42 minutes a locksmith or a professional thief could pick a lock?"

"I don't know, I never picked a lock."

"Do have security cameras?'

"Yes, we do."

"Did you look at the tapes of the Vassar corridor for the 8th of December?"

Johnson perked up and answered aggressively. "Yes, I did, and no one was in that corridor."

"Really, Mr. Johnson?"

"Really," he answered.

Gabrielson walked back to counsel's table and then spun around.

"Did you ever wonder why the camera was focused on the lobby and not the corridor?"

"That's what it does when the elevator opens."

"But Mr. Johnson, nobody got on or off, did they?"

"I don't remember."

"A lot of bad memories in this case."

Judge Abrams piped up, "Ms. Gabrielson, remember, no more speeches."

"Yes, sir," Gabrielson answered.

Leslie now launched her full and final assault. "Mr. Johnson, were you subpoenaed to appear here this morning?"

"Yes, I was."

"And were you asked to bring anything with you?"

"Yes."

"What was that?" Leslie asked, as she wanted to make this as suspenseful for the jury as possible.

"I was asked to bring the key to Ms. Vassar's apartment."

"The same key that you told us about when Mr. Cavanaugh questioned you."

"Yes, that one."

"The one bottom key that you always kept rather than the two to the top lock, that the tenant keeps."

"Yes."

"Didn't you tell us how it didn't make any difference if you had the bottom key, because you still didn't have the other top key?"

"I said that."

"Well, Mr. Johnson let's look at the other side of the coin for a second. Did you bring that key with you here this morning as the subpoena commanded?"

"No, I didn't."

Graham already told the jurors just minutes before at how the key to the Vassar apartment was missing hours after her arrest. Now, Johnson, the possible culprit, would reinforce that message to Leslie's assembled listeners. "And why didn't you bring it, Mr. Johnson?"

"Because I couldn't find it in the cabinet. It was missing. A workman must have used it and not returned it."

"Let's think about this a minute, Mr. Johnson. Would you agree with me that Agent Graham interviewed you the morning after the search of Ms. Vassar's apartment?"

"I remember talking to him."

"Do you remember him asking for the key at that time?"

"I do."

"And you couldn't produce it?"

"No."

"And you didn't have the key at that time, just as you don't have it now, right? Remember when you testified for Mr. Cavanaugh, how you boasted about how you kept a key, in case a tenant wanted you to let somebody in?"

"That's right."

"But you never told us when Mr. Cavanaugh questioned you that management's key was missing the next morning after December 8, did you?"

"No, I didn't."

"Why not?"

"Never thought about it."

"You made a big deal about the key, didn't you?"

"I guess so."

"But you didn't think the missing key was important?"

"Didn't dawn on me."

Leslie gave a "mmm" to the jury and nodded her head up and down.

"If Ms. Vassar wanted a workman to get in, she could simply leave her top lock open and have the workman come to you for the key to the bottom one?"

"That's true."

"Do you have any recollection whatsoever of any workman asking you for the key to her apartment or even coming around?"

"No, I don't."

"Then why would the key be missing? What reason in the world would you have had to take it off its place in your cabinet? Please tell the jury the answer to that question, Mr. Johnson," Gabrielson demanded as she turned on her heel and made eye contact with each member of the jury.

Leslie waited, but Johnson gave no answer. "Well, Mr. Johnson, what is the explanation for the mysterious missing key?"

"I'm thinking."

"Take your time."

"A cleaning person may have wanted it. I don't know. All I know is that it wasn't there."

"But you have no record whatsoever of any cleaning person coming in, do you?"

"No. I don't."

"And besides, Mr. Johnson, if she wanted someone in her apartment to clean, she'd just give them both keys or leave the top unlocked and have them see you for the bottom one. You would just open the door and keep the key. You wouldn't give it to the cleaning person, because after they left, you'd lock up. Isn't that right?'

"Speculative!" Cavanaugh yelled out, trying to stem the credibility hemorrhaging that this witness was undergoing.

"Overruled. It just calls for common sense, not what Ms. Vassar was thinking at a particular moment," Abrams ruled.

"You have no answer, do you Mr. Johnson."

"I don't; it wasn't there, and I don't know why."

Leslie was ready for checkmate, and the witness had led her into the perfect question.

"You really don't know Mr. Johnson?"

"No, how would I know. It was missing for some reason."

"Oh, I think you know, Mr. Johnson, and I think you know why the elevator went up empty."

Mike McKenna suffered Leslie's slings and arrows for years, including fits of rage, because she paid him promptly and better than any other private investigator in the city and he, in return, was the best at what he did.

In his initial interview at Johnson's office after Leslie saw Graham, McKenna spied a checkbook sitting on the edge of the super's desk. McKenna pretended to have an interest in Johnson's statute of a football player on his credenza, and came around the

other side of the desk for a closer look. It was a replica of the
Heisman trophy, and when Johnson left his seat for a second to get
the certificate that came with the bronze reproduction, McKenna
lifted the cover of the book long enough to read the words,
"Citibank."

Upon leaving the Dorchester, McKenna went to the Citibank
branch over on Governor's Island where he knew a teller. "Audrey,
do me a favor. Look up an Arthur Johnson for me. He lives up in the
Bronx. Look for anything unusual the week before and after December 8, 1998."

She punched the name into her computer and there it was; an
entry for 9:00 a.m. of December 9, 1998. Johnson was stupid enough
to deposit Datale's $5,000 into his checking account. Leslie did not
disclose the deposit slip on her pretrial exhibit list because she
wanted to surprise Cavanaugh and Johnson, and she didn't have to
place it into evidence; all she had to do was to get him to admit he'd
made it.

"Mr. Johnson, you do remember that you're under oath?"

"Yes, I do."

"You're subject to perjury if you don't tell the truth."

"Objection, argumentative, badgering," Cavanaugh roared.

"Sustained. Ms. Gabrielson, don't threaten the witness," Judge
Abrams pontificated.

"Yes, Your Honor. Mr. Johnson, did you or did you not make a
deposit into your checking account for $5,000 at Citibank on the
morning of December 9, 1998."

She didn't move to introduce the deposit slip because Cavanaugh
would surely complain that she had not listed it properly, but she
held it up at eye level, a few feet in front of Johnson so that he could
plainly see that it was a deposit slip, even though he could not read
the numbers on it.

"Yes, I did."

"And Mr. Johnson, wasn't that money from someone who bribed
you to let them onto Ms. Vassar's floor and into her apartment?"

"No, that's not true," came the quiet response.

"On December 8, at 7:00 p.m., Ms. Vassar is arrested, and 14 hours later, when the bank opens, you make a $5,000 deposit. Isn't that the most amazing coincidence in the world, Mr. Johnson?"

"It's just a coincidence."

"Well let's see. Tell the jury when was the last time you deposited more than $2,000 at any one time into that account before this."

"I don't know. I don't remember."

McKenna got the printout for the previous three years before he left the bank.

"Mr. Johnson, what if I told you that it was a few days after Christmas in 1997, when I assume you deposited all your Christmas tips."

"That's probably right," Johnson answered, his mind a complete blank, not knowing what to say.

"And of course, December 8 is well before Christmas and before you really start to get tips, right Mr. Johnson?"

"Right."

"That's all the questions the defense has of this witness, Your Honor."

The courtroom was deadly quiet as Cavanaugh approached the witness. The prosecutor had no earthly idea what reason Johnson would concoct for the deposit on such short notice, but Gabrielson destroyed him, and he had to at least make an attempt to reestablish his credibility.

"Mr. Johnson, sitting here five months after the fact, can you remember where that deposit money came from?"

There was no answer and Johnson did not attempt to give one. "I'd have to look at my records and talk to my wife. Maybe it was her money. I can't remember."

Cavanaugh hung his head and announced that he had no more questions, either. Johnson looked like a beaten dog on the stand, and to question him further would only be futile.

"Your Honor, the defense rests," Leslie announced full of confidence and the feel of victory. She looked every juror in the eye and could tell that there were just too many unanswered questions that were raised in this case. Pia sat back in her seat, knowing that Leslie created enough doubt about Johnson and an unauthorized entry into her apartment, that the jury would either have to unanimously acquit or end with a hung jury. There was no way that all 12 jurors were going to send her to prison with this many questions left open.

That night, with victory almost assured, John Vittone met with Tommy Pucchini. "Tommy I have never asked you for anything in 37 years. Tonight, I come to you with a request."

"Anything, John, anything."

"I never told you or anyone this. Before Alegri died, he confessed. Datale and Marucci were in that deal with him. They split the money up. One of them or both of them is behind the drugs being in my daughter's apartment. I now know this from the testimony of that cop, Epstein. I cannot breathe the air on this earth as long as they live."

"John, normally, it takes the full commission approval to hit a made man. But thanks to you, we have the power and the clout to weather any storm. Consider your problem solved. I'll talk to the commission for you. There'll be no problem when I explain the situation to the members."

"Thank you, Godfather," Vittone said, showing his appreciation by kissing the solid gold ring on Pucchini's right hand.

EPILOGUE

The jury's verdict of "not guilty" rang through the courtroom, but it had very little dramatic effect. Not a soul sitting in the courtroom, certainly not Jay Cavanaugh, was surprised by the result. But something in Cavanaugh's gut was strangely happy.

John F. Hampton forced his way through the railing, into the courtroom area, picked up Pia and carried her around the courtroom in his arms while she murmured, "Put me down. People will think we're crazy." He did not listen to her protests, and Judge Leonard Abrams decided not to admonish him.

Seated along the wall, in the back of the courtroom, was a man who looked a lot like Giuseppe Lombardo. John Vittone would let the rest of the world go to hell for this one morning. There was no way that he was not going to be there in his daughter's greatest moment of crisis. He watched Hampton gently move toward the back door of the courtroom, and he was glad that she finally met her man.

John Vittone, two months later, threw the biggest wedding of the year in New York City, where the seats of the chapel in St. Patrick's Cathedral were filled with all the mighty politicos and corporate chieftains that he had so wanted to emulate over the years. Hampton was nominated for another Pulitzer for his story of courtroom drama, and the marriage received international coverage.

As Vittone walked down the aisle that day, with his whole world on his arm, his uncle sat on the end of the front row, beaming. They had, indeed, come a long way from the hard-scrabble life of Carbonia. When John Vittone turned his daughter over to Hampton at the altar, after raising her veil and kissing her goodbye, he thought that no matter how brutal it had all been, that it was finally worth it.

Later that same year, the New York press carried banner headlines blaring that Tommy Pucchini was replaced by a former Colombian druglord and that his right-hand man, John Vittone, disappeared from the scene. It was implied that they were the victims of gangland violence, and that they would never be seen again.

The same day that the papers made this announcement, a small, 28 foot diesel powered fishing trawler left the harbor at Caprera. Aboard the vessel was an 87-year-old man and his nephew. When the boat reached the halfway mark between Corsica and Sardinia in the brilliant, purple waters, a little stand of bougainvillea that the older man placed in his fishing hat that morning fluttered in the wind and the two men dropped their lines into the sea.

About 3,800 miles to the west, the top female lawyer at Chesney, Starcloth and Vining whispered to Alexandra Morariu with a silly grin that she was going to take the rest of the day off to go home and get under the sheets with a guy she loved very much. Alexandra smiled and shook her head playfully in agreement with Pia's impromptu scheduling change.

She watched Pia close the door on the way out of her office and prayed that the sins of the father would never be cast upon this one good daughter, woman, and wife.